Thomas Hood

Up the Rhine

Thomas Hood

Up the Rhine

ISBN/EAN: 9783337365899

Printed in Europe, USA, Canada, Australia, Japan

Cover: Foto ©Andreas Hilbeck / pixelio.de

More available books at **www.hansebooks.com**

BY

THOMAS HOOD.

A NEW EDITION.

WITH A PREFACE BY HIS DAUGHTER.

The German Muse.

LONDON:
E. MOXON, SON, & CO., 44 DOVER STREET.
1869.

PREFACE.

MANY of the general readers of Thomas Hood's Works
are, I believe, unacquainted with the present volume,
which, from a combination of unfortunate circumstances, did not attain the large circulation it so
eminently deserved, as a characteristic specimen of
its Author's lighter style. "Up the Rhine" first
appeared in 1840, and met with such general appre-
ciation from the public, that the first edition was
sold out in a fortnight, and the second launched.
But, from adverse circumstances over which my
father had no control,* the work was then virtually
swamped, and, since then, only rare chance copies
were to be met with until its re-issue in the Library
Edition of the Complete Works. It was on its first

* See "Memorials of Thomas Hood."

publication, (to its Author's mischievous amusement,) reprinted piratically in Germany, where, in spite of its tolerably hard rubs at the manners and customs of the Rhinelanders, it had a ready sale.

It has now been considered advisable to re-publish it, nearly in its original form; and it is hoped that its acquaintance will be made by many new readers, and that it may also be equally welcome to old friends. The present edition contains the quaint original illustrations, drawn on the wood by my father, which were necessarily excluded from the Library Edition of his Complete Works.

FRANCES FREELING BRODERIP.

CONTENTS.

[At the beginning of this year (1840) appeared "Up the Rhine," the result of my father's residence in Germany. It was so eagerly sought after, that in a fortnight the first edition was gone. Of late years it has been very difficult to obtain a copy of the original publication, though a German re-print is sold on the Rhine pretty generally.— T. Hood, jun.]

UP THE RHINE.

PREFACE TO THE FIRST EDITION.

To forestal such Critics as are fond of climbing up a Mât de Cocagne for a Mare's Nest at the top, the following work was constructed, partly on the ground-plan of Humphrey Clinker, but with very inferior materials, and on a much humbler scale. I admire the old mansion too much, to think that any workmanship of mine could erect a house fit to stand in the same row.

Many persons will doubtless differ with me as to the inferences I have drawn from things seen and heard abroad. But we are all liable to mistakes : and I may have been as wrong in my speculations as was another Traveller in Germany, who, seeing a basketful of purple Easter Eggs, exclaimed, " Good heaven ! what colour can their hens be ? "

Should the members of the present family party be found agreeable or amusing, by the great family circle of the Public, I may be induced, next year, to publish their sub-

sequent Tour in Belgium.   In the meantime, my dear Public,
to adopt the words of another Traveller :

> "Where'er I roam, whatever realms to see,
> My heart, untravell'd, fondly turns to thee."

1st *December*, 1839.   THOMAS HOOD.

PREFACE TO THE SECOND EDITION.

THE reader of Robinson Crusoe will doubtless remember
the flutter of delight and gratitude the Ex-Solitary was
thrown into, after his return to England, by receiving from
his Factor such very favourable accounts of the prosperity
of his Brazilian plantations. " In a word," says he, " I turned
pale and grew sick ; and had not the old man run and
fetched me a cordial, I believe the sudden surprise of joy
had overset nature, and I had died on the spot."

Something of this joyful surprise it was my own pleasant
lot to feel, on learning from my Publisher, that in one short
fortnight, the whole impression of the present work had
been taken off his hands, " and left the world no copy."—
A fact the more gratifying from occurring at a season afford-
ing topics of such engrossing interest, as Prince Albert—the
Queen's marriage—the Chartist outbreaks—and the new
Penny Post,—a measure which, by imposing one uniform
rate on Peer and Peasant, has established a real Republic of
Letters.   So flattering a reception quite overpowered me
with joy and gratitude ; and, like Robinson, my feelings were
not properly composed till I had quaffed off a flask of Hoch-
heimer to the health of all the friends, known and unknown,
who had relished my Rhenish outpourings.

To be candid and confidential, the work was not offered to the public without some misgivings.

A plain Manufacturer of Roman Cement, in the Greenwich road, was once turned by a cramped showboard into a "MANUFACTURER OF ROMANCEMENT;" and a Tour up the Rhine has generally been expected to convert an author into a dealer in the same commodity. There was some danger, therefore, that readers might be disappointed or dissatisfied at not meeting with the usual allowance of real or affected raptures, sentimental lays, romantic legends, enthusimoosy and the foodle ages. In fact, one of my critics (it is the fashion now for the reviewed to retaliate on their reviewers, as Roderick Random flogged his schoolmaster) plainly snubs my book, for not being like others on the same subject, and roundly blames the author for not treading more exactly, like an Indian disguising his trail, in the footprints of his predecessors. According to this gentleman (he is not Miss Martineau), I engaged in a somewhat heretical enterprise, which no man of ordinary sensibility would have embarked in. I took my apparatus of caricature up the Rhine, quizzed Cologne Cathedral and the façade of the English National Gallery, and turned the storied scenery, the fine traditions, and the poetic atmosphere of the abounding river into a succession of drolleries.

In reply to these serious charges, I can only say that heretical enterprises—witness Luther's—are sometimes no bad things. That the animals most inclined to pursue the follow-my-leader system are geese. That a man of ordinary sensibility ought to be shy of exhibiting it where such extraordinary sensibilities had been paraded beforehand. That I have never even seen the National Gallery; and instead of quizzing the Dom Kirche of Cologne, have admired and lauded it in the highest terms. That I expressly declined to touch on the scenery, because it had been so often painted, not to say daubed, already; that I left the fine legends precisely as I found them; and that the poetic atmosphere remained as intact, for me, as the atmosphere of the moon. Since Byron and the Dampschiff, there has been quite enough of vapouring, in more senses than one, on the blue and castled river, and the echoing nymph of the Lurley must be quite weary of repeating such *bouts rimés* as—the Rhine and land of the vine—the Rhine and vastly fine—the Rhine and very divine. As for the romantic, the Age of Chivalry is Burked by Time, and as difficult of revival in Germany as in Scotland. A modern steamboat associates as awkwardly with a feudal ruin, as a mob of umbrellas with an Eglintoun "plump of spears."

With these explanations and apologies I take my leave; fortunately possessing the unquestioned privilege of printing, publishing, and selling my proceedings, without committing myself, the Sheriffs and the Judges; or setting the Speaker, the Chief Justice and Mr. Commissioner Reynolds by the ears; I gratefully present my Second Edition, with my warmest acknowledgments, to an indulgent public, without any fear of that presently awful personage the Serjeant at Mace.

T. H.

23rd January, 1840.

TO GERARD BROOKE, ESQ., LEMINGTON, HANTS.

MY DEAR BROOKE,
Your reproach is just. My epistolary taciturnity
has certainly been of unusual duration ; but instead of
filling up a sheet with mere excuses, I beg to refer you at
once to "Barclay's Apology for Quakerism," which I presume
includes an apology for silence.

The truth is, I have had nothing to write of, and in such
cases I philosophically begrudge postage, as a contradiction
to the old axiom *ex nihilo nihil fit*, inasmuch as the revenue
through such empty epistles gets something out of nothing.
Now, however, I have news to break, and I trust you are not
so good a man as "unconcerned to hear the mighty crack."
WE ARE GOING UP THE RHINE!!!

You, who have been long aware of my yearning to the
abounding river, like the supposed mystical bending of the
hazel twig towards the unseen waters, will be equally pleased
and surprised at such an announcement. In point of fact,
but for the preparations that are hourly going on before my
eyes, I should have, as Irish Buller used to say, some considerable doubts of my own veracity. There seemed plenty of
lions in the path of such a Pilgrim's Progress ; and yet, here
we are, resolved on the attempt, in the hope that, as Christian dropped his burthen by the way, a little travelling will
jolt off the load that encumbers the broad shoulders of a
dear, hearty, ailing, dead-alive, hypochondriacal old bachelor
uncle. If my memory serves me truly, you once met with
the personage in question at one of our coursing meetings :
if not, you will be glad to have what Willis the *Penman*
calls a *Pencilling*, but which ought rather to be denominated

an *Inkling*. Imagine, then, a handsome, stout, well-built
specimen of the species, somewhat the worse for wear, but
still sound in wind and limb, and in possession of all his
faculties—a little stiff in the anatomical hinges—but still
able to find a hare and not bad at a halloo—in short, the
beau ideal of a fine old country gentleman, for such he is.
But here comes the mystery. To all appearance a picture of
Health, painted in the full florid style by Rubens himself, or
one of his pupils, my hale uncle is a martyr to hypochondriasis, not the moping melancholy sort anatomised by old
Burton—not the chronic kind—but the acute. Perhaps he
has some latent affection of the heart or obstructions of the
liver, causing sudden derangements of the circulation, and
consequent physical depressions,—I am not physician enough
to determine,—but I have known instances of the same
malady in other individuals, though never so intense. As
jovial a man, between his paroxysms, as you shall find in a
chimney corner, the next moment he sees a coffin, as the
superstitious call it, fly out of the fire, and fancies his
Death-Fetch standing on the domestic hearth. But as
Shakspeare says, "a coward dies many times before his
death," and my uncle is certainly no exception to the canon.
On an average he has three or four attacks a week,—so that
at the end of the year his "dying moments" would probably
amount to a calendar month, and his "last words" to an
octavo volume.

As you may suppose, it is sometimes difficult to preserve
one's gravity during such solemn leave-takings at Death's
door, at which you know he is only giving a runaway knock.
Like the boy in the fable, he has cried "Wolf!" too often
for those about him seriously to believe that the Destroyer
is at hand ;—though at the same time, being thoroughly
in earnest himself, and long habit and frequent rehearsals

having made him quite at home in the part, he performs it so admirably and naturally, that even his familiars are staggered and look on and listen, with a smile and a tear. As yet I have never seen the stranger who was not horrified, by what appeared so sudden a visitation, as well as edified by the manly fortitude, good sense, and Christian spirit with which the victim invariably prepares for his departure. He has made his will, of course ; and I verily believe every member of the family has his instructions for his funeral by heart. Amongst other memorials, there is an old family watch,—nicknamed *entre nous*, the Death watch,—which he has solemnly presented to me, his unworthy nephew, a hundred times over. On such occasions, I always seriously accept the gift, but take care to leave it about on some shelf or table in the way of the owner, who, when the qualm is over, quietly fobs the time-piece, without any remark on either side, and Nunky, Nevy, and Watch go on as usual till another warning. I once ventured to hint that he died very hard ; but the joke was not well taken ; and he often throws my incredulity in my teeth. " Well, God bless you, my boy," he said the other day, in his *gravest* manner, though I was only to be a week absent, " Well, God bless you, Frank,—for you've seen me for the last time. You know my last wishes. Yes, you may grin,—only don't be shocked at your return if you find the shutters closed, or the hearse at the door !"

Such is my worthy hypochondriacal uncle, with his serio-comic infirmity,—and I assure you there is not a particle of exaggeration in the account. For the last five years he has paid a neighbouring practitioner 200l. per annum to look after his health,—and really the post is no sinecure, for besides the daily visit of routine, the Esculapius is generally sent for, in haste, some twice or thrice a week, extra, how-

beit the attack not unfrequently goes off in a hit at backgammon.   A whimsical instance just occurs to me.   My
uncle, who is both a lover, and a capital judge, of horses, and
always drives a remarkably clever nag, chose one morning to
have a warning in his gig,—influenced, doubtless, by the
sight of his medical adviser, who happened to be some
hundred yards in advance.   The doctor, be it said, is a
respectable gigman, who also likes a fast horse, and having
really some urgent new case on his hands, or being unwilling
to listen to the old one, he no sooner recognised the traveller
in his rear, than he applied a stimulant to his steed, that
improved its pace into twelve miles an hour.   My uncle did
the like, and as pretty a chariot race ensued as any since the
Olympic Games.   For a mile or two the doctor took the lead
and kept it; but his patient was too fast for him, and by
degrees got within hail, bellowing lustily, "Hang it, man,
pull up! I'm dying, doctor, I'm dying."—"Egad," cried the
doctor, looking over his shoulder, "I think you are! And I
never saw any one *going so fast.*"

It is with the sanction—indeed by the advice—of the me-
dicus just mentioned (an original of the Abernethy school),
that we are bound on an experimental trip up the Rhine,
to try what change of scene and travelling will do for such
an extraordinary disease.   The prescription, however, was
anything but palatable to the patient, who demurred most
obstinately, and finally asked his counsellor, rather crustily,
if he could name a single instance of a man who had lived
the longer for wandering over the world?   "To be sure I
can," answered the doctor, "the wandering Jew."   This
timely hit decided the battle : my uncle, who is no hand at
repartee, gave in ; and at this present writing, his passport
is made out for Rotterdam.   In common with most invalids,
he likes to have womankind about him ; so he has invited

his sister, a widow, to be of the party, and she, in turn, has stipulated for the attendance of her favourite maid. Your humble servant will make the fourth hand in this Rhenish rubber ; and for your sake, I intend to score with pen and pencil all the points of the game.

My kindest regards to Emily — and something more ; remember, should I ever get beyond prosing, all verses belong to her from,

Dear Brooke, yours ever very truly,

FRANK SOMERVILLE.

TO PETER BAGSTER, ESQ., SOLICITOR, CANTERBURY.

MY DEAR OLD FRIEND,

Being about to leave England, and most likely for good, it's my wish to give you a parting shake of the hand, as far as can be done by letter before I go, time and circumstances forbidding my personally taking a last farewell. At present our destination is only Germany; but inward feelings tell me I am booked for a much longer journey, and from which no traveller returns. As such I have informed all parties concerned, that my will is lodged in your hands ; and, regarding the rest of my worldly affairs, you had full instructions in my leave-taking letter of a month back. I had another terrible warning on Wednesday week, which, I am convinced, would have proved fatal, but providentially Dr. Truby was in the house at the time. What is remarkable, up to my seizure I had been in an uncommon flow of spirits, for Morgan and Dowley, and a few more of the old set, had come over, and we rubbed up our old stories and old songs, and I was even able myself to comply with the honour

of a call for the Maid of the Valley. But the moment the
company was gone I had an attack ;—which is convincing
to my mind of the correctness of the old saying about a
lightening before death. Such repeated shocks must break
down the constitution of a horse ; and, mark my words, *the
next will be my whoo-oop !*

In course, you will be as much surprised as I am myself,
at a man with my dispensation undertaking a visit to foreign
parts. But, between one and another, I was fairly mobbed
into it, and have been in twenty minds to call back my
consent. But a man's word is his word ; and, besides, I
wish my nephew to see a little of the world. Poor Kate will
go along with us, in hopes the jaunting about a bit will make
her forget the loss of her husband, or as she calls him, "Poor
George." I did want the Doctor to join, and made him a
handsome offer to that effect, over and above his expenses ;
but he declined, on the plea of not leaving his other patients,
which, considering the terms we have been on for so many
years, I cannot help thinking is a little ungrateful, as well as
hard-hearted, for he knows I ought not to go ten miles
without medical help at my elbow. But I suppose the
constant sight of death makes all physicians callous, or they
could not feel the pulse of a dying man, much less of an old
friend, with a broad grin on their faces. Talking of departing,
I trust to you to regularly pay up the premium on my life
assurance in the Pelican. I did hope the policy would be
voided by going abroad, which would have put a spoke in
our tour ; but, unluckily, it gives me latitude to travel all
over Europe. But whether on an English road or a foreign
one, for it will never be in my bed, is all one. So every
place being alike, I have left the choice to my nephew, and
he has fixed on the river Rhine. In course, he undertakes
the lingo, for I can neither parley vous nor jabber High

Dutch ; and though it's not too soon, mayhap, to look out for a new set of teeth, it's too late in life for me to get a fresh set of tongues. Besides, all foreign languages are given to flattering; and, as a plain Englishman, I should never find complimentary ideas enough to match with the words. There is the French inventory of my person in the passport, which I made Frank translate to me. You know what an invalid I am ; but what with high complexion, and robust figure, and so forth, Mounscur has painted me up like one of the healthiest and handsomest young fellows in the county of Kent !

So you see I am down in the way-bill ; and, provided I get to the end of the first stage, you will perhaps hear from me again. If not, you will know what has happened, and act accordingly. If I last out to Holland, it will be the utmost. I have betted old Truby two dozen of hock wine, against port and sherry, I shall never get to Cologne. Well, God bless you, my old friend, and all that belongs to you, from, dear Peter,

Your very faithful humble servant,

RICHARD ORCHARD.

P.S.—If I forward a few gallons of real Hollands to your London agents, Drinkwater and Maxwell, do you think they will send it down to Canterbury ?

TO GERARD BROOKE, ESQ., LEMINGTON, HANTS.

DEAR GERARD,

You will stare at receiving another letter dated London ; but we have been delayed a week beyond our time by my uncle, and a mysterious complaint in his luggage,

which, for several days, would not pack up for want of a
family medicine chest that had been ordered of the celebrated
Butler and Co. of Cheapside. Moreover, it appeared that
the invalid had applied for more last words of medical advice
from Dr. Truby; but instead of a letter, who should walk in
yesterday evening but the Doctor himself! The fact is, he
has a real regard for his Malade Imaginaire, though he sets
his face against the fancy, and had made this sacrifice to
friendship. My uncle's eyes glistened at sight of the familiar
figure. "Ay, ay," said he, with sundry significant nods,
"you are come to prevent my going." "Quite the reverse,"
answered the other; "I suspected you would hang on hand,
and have come thirty miles to help in giving you a shove
off." Our Hyp looked a little disconcerted at this rebuff.
"At least, doctor, you have something of importance to my
health to remind me of?" "Not a syllable." "Mayhap,
then, you have brought me some portable sort of medicine
for travellers in a small compass?" suggested my uncle,
expecting a welcome supplement to Butler's repository.
"I have brought you," said the doctor, speaking leisurely,
as he vainly tried to extract some refractory article from his
coat-pocket, "something more to the purpose,—very useful
to travellers too,—an invention of a professional friend; you
did not know the late Dr. Kitchiner?—it's a most invaluable
defence against sudden attacks." "Mayhap," cried uncle,
now eagerly assisting in the extricating of the parcel, "it's a
self-acting blood-letter." "It's more likely to prevent blood-
letting," answered the doctor, at last producing the imple-
ment, "a sort of night-bolt, for securing your bed-room door
at a strange inn." — "Good God," exclaimed my uncle,
reddening like one of his own turkey-cocks, "is it possible
you could so forget the nature of my sudden attacks! I am
not likely to die in my bed; but if I do, it will be from

nobody coming near me; and here you are for keeping every soul from the room!" "Nevertheless," said the doctor, " I still recommend the night-bolt. As a lady never faints without water and smelling salts, and help at need, I am convinced, by analogy, that a locked door, and nobody at hand, must be the best preventives of *some sorts* of apoplexy that can be devised." The wry face with which this illustration was received you may imagine, now that you have a key to the character. The doctor is not only a shrewd practitioner, but a humourist, and doubtless intended his night-bolt as a piece of practical irony on his patient's monomania; if so, our Abernethys and such medical eccentrics have more common sense in their oddities than some regular practitioners in their common-places. However, my uncle having been worsted in the encounter, his sister, who is sufficiently anxious on the subject of health, but with reference to everybody's constitution except her own, then took up the argument, and anxiously inquired, "What her poor dear brother ought to do in case of any travelling accidents—for example, wet feet?" "In that case, madam," replied the doctor, with a low bow and a marked emphasis, " *don't* let him change his shoes, *don't* get him dry stockings; and *don't* let him bathe his feet in warm water. That has been his practice during the first fifty years of his life, and it has agreed so well with him, that I do not feel justified in making any alteration." "To be sure," said. my aunt thoughtfully, "he used to ride through brooks, and rivers, and never shifted himself, and yet never had anything on his lungs. And I do remember once when he spent a fortnight in London on a visit, he took ill, and after thinking of everything that could have caused it, he could not account for it in any way except through missing his damp feet. But then as to his diet, doctor;—what ought he to eat?" "Whatever he can get, madam," said the doctor, taking another grave pinch of snuff; "but as he values his life, let him avoid—anything else, for depend upon it, madam,—*it never can do him any good.*" This oracular response defeated my poor aunt, who, by way of covering her retreat, then pulled him aside, and with a glance at your humble servant, inquired if the air we were going to was favourable to my constitution, for I was delicate, like "Poor George." Of course, I pricked up my ears, and had an appropriate reward. "Madam," said he, "a young Englishman, on going abroad for the first time, generally gives himself so many airs, that the one he is going-to is of the least possible consequence."

I subsequently contrived to ask the doctor confidentially, whether his patient would require any particular treatment whilst abroad. "Medically," said he, "none at all. Your worthy uncle's complaint is a very common one, in kind, if not in degree. With old women who have been active in their youth, it takes the form vulgarly called the fidgets— with country gentlemen, in their decline, it becomes hypochondriasis. They cannot live as hard as they used to do, and so they think they are dying as fast as they can. Your fox-hunters and so forth are particularly liable to the disease. They are used to a kicking, bumping, jumping, thumping, jolting, bolting, scrubbing, scrambling, roll-and-tumble sort of existence, and the nerves and muscles will not subside kindly into quieter habits. To make the matter worse, a pedestrian, when he can no longer walk, will ride ; but your equestrian, when he is past riding, will not condescend to walk. When he is unequal to horseback, instead of taking to coach-back, or boat-back, he takes to a high-backed chair, and backgammon. What your uncle really wants is a mill to grind him young again. There is no such mill on earth, but the next best thing is to go in search of it. Take

my word for it, the secret of your uncle's dying is, that he
has more life in him, or steam, than the old machine knows
how to get rid of." "Yes, yes," muttered my uncle, who had
been musing, but caught the last sentence, "I always knew
I should go off like a burst boiler!" "The Lord forbid!"
ejaculated my aunt, who had been absorbed in her own
steamboat speculations — and having thus, in sporting
language, changed our hare, we had a burst with high
pressure that lasted for twenty minutes. At the conclusion
my aunt asked the doctor if he knew of any remedy against
sea-sickness. "Only one, madam, the same that was adopted
by Jack the giant-killer against the Welsh ogre." "And
what was his remedy?" inquired my aunt, very innocently.
"A false stomach, ma'am; put all you feel inclined to eat or
drink into *that*; and I will stake my professional character
against it coming up again!" Just at this juncture his
lynx eyes happened to alight on the medicine-chest, "I
do hope that box is insured!" "Good heavens!" exclaimed
my aunt, "is there any danger? We have not insured
anything!" "Because," exclaimed the doctor, "if your
nephew is any better than a George Barnwell in disguise, he
will take the first opportunity for pitching that trash overboard." My uncle's back was up in a moment. "By your
leave," he said, "I did once have occasion to call in Doctor
Carbuncle in your absence, and he prescribed for me more
trash, as you call it, in ten days, than you have done in as
many years." "No doubt he did," answered the imper-
turbable Truby. "He would send it in by the dozen, like
Scotch ale or Dublin porter, or any other article on which
he gets a commission. Fat bacon, for instance, was once in
vogue amongst the faculty for weak digestions, and he would
favour you with that or any other gammon, at a trifle above
the market price." "Well, I always thought," exclaimed

my aunt, "that Doctor Carbuncle was considered a very
skilful man!" "As to his other medical acquirements,
madam, there may be some doubts, but you have only to
look in his face to see that he is well *red* in *nose*ology."

This palpable hit, for Carbuncle happens to have a very
fiery proboscis, quite restored my uncle's good-humour. He
laughed till the tears ran down his face, and even cracked a
joke of his own, on the advantage of always hunting with a
burning scent. The doctor, like a good general, seized this
favourable moment for his departure, and took his patient
by the hand—"Well, *bon voyage*, and fine weather on the
Rhine." "I shall never see it," cried my uncle, fast relapsing
into a fit of hypochondriacism. "Pooh! pooh!—good-bye,
and a fair wind to Rotterdam." "I shall die at sea,"
returned my uncle; "at least if I reach the Nore. But
mayhap I shall never get aboard. It is my belief I shan't
live through the night," he bellowed after the doctor, who,
foreseeing the point the argument must arrive at, had bolted
out of the room and closed the door. "A clever man," said
my uncle, when he was gone; "and no doubt understands
my case, but as close as a fox. I only wish he would agree
to my going suddenly—I should not die a bit the sooner for
his giving me over."

Once more, farewell, with love to Emily from, dear Gerard,
yours, &c.,

FRANK SOMERVILLE.

TO GERARD BROOKE, ESQ., LEMINGTON, HANTS.

MY DEAR BROOKE,

Your prophecy was a plausible one, but as the
servant girl said, after looking out of a window in Piccadilly,
for the Lord Mayor's show, "it did not come to pass."
Instead of returning to Kent, we actually sailed from
London on Wednesday morning, by the Lord Melville ; and
here follows a log of our memorable voyage.   It will prove a
long one I foresee, but so was our passage.

To believe our tourists and travellers, our Heads and our
Trollopes, it is impossible to take a trip in a hoy, smack, or
steamer, without encountering what are technically called
characters.   My first care, therefore, on getting aboard, was
to look out for originals ; but after the strictest scrutiny
among the passengers, there appeared none of any mark or
likelihood.   However, at Gravesend, a wherry brought us
two individuals of some promise.   The first was a tall, very
thin man, evidently in bad health, or, as one of the sailors
remarked, performing quarantine, his face being of the same
colour as the yellow flag which indicates that sanitary
excommunication ; the other was a punchy, florid, red-
wattled human cock-bird, who, according to the poultry
wife's practice, had seemingly had two pepper-corns thrust
down his gullet on first leaving the shell, and had ever since
felt their fiery influence in his gizzard.   In default of their
proper names, I immediately christened them, after Dandie
Dinmont's two celebrated dogs, Pepper and Mustard.   I had,
however, but a short glimpse of their quality, for the yellow-
face went forward amongst the seamen, whilst the red-visage
dived downwards towards the steward's pantry.   In the

B

meantime we progressed merrily ; and had soon passed that
remarkably fine specimen of sea-urchin, the buoy at the
Nore. But here the breeze died off, an occurrence, before
the invention of steamers, of some moment ; indeed, in the
old shoy-hoy times I was once at sea three days and two
nights between London and Ramsgate, now a certain passage
of a few hours. But now calms are annihilated, and so long
as the movement party are inclined to dance, the steam-
engine will find them in music ; in fact, I could not help
associating its regular tramp, tramp, tramp, with the tune of
a galop I had recently performed.

But these musings were suddenly diverted by the appearance of one of the most startling and singular phe-
nomena that ever came under my notice. Imagine on one
side the sea gently ruffled by a dying wind into waves of a
fine emerald green, playfully sparkling in the noon-tide sun ;
on the other hand, a terrific pitch-black mass rising abruptly
from sea to sky, as if visibly dividing "the warm precincts of
a cheerful day" from "the dark realms of Chaos and Old
Night." But I am growing poetical. Suppose, then, if you
have ever been under the white Flamborough Head, a black
ditto, quite as bluff and as solid, and which you might have
mistaken for some such stupendous headland but for the
colour, and that on looking upwards you could find no
summit. So strong was the impression on my own fancy,
that when my aunt inquired where we were, I could not
help answering, in allusion to the hue and build of the
phenomenon, that we were off Blackwall. "You are right,
sir," said a strange voice—"I have observed the same black
and wall-like appearance in the West Indies, and it was the
forerunner of a hurricane." I looked for this prophet of ill-
omen, and saw the yellow-faced man at my elbow. "It
would be a charity," exclaimed my aunt, "to give the captain

warning." "*He* knows it well enough," said the stranger,
"and so does the steward ; yonder he runs to the caboose,
to tell the cook to gallop his potatoes and scorch his roasts,
that he may lay his cloth before the gale comes." "A gale,
eh !" mumbled the red-face, who had just climbed from
below, with his mouth still full of victuals—"why don't the
captain put back ?" "We have gone about once," said the
yellow-face, "to run into Margate ; but the master thinks,
perhaps, that he can edge off, and so escape the storm, or
only catch a flap with its skirts. There it comes !" and he
pointed towards the black mass now rapidly diffusing itself
over the surface of the sea, which became first black, and
then white, beneath its shadow ; whilst a few faint forks of
lightning darted about between the base of the cloud and
the water. The waves immediately round us had gradually
subsided into a dead calm, and there was no perceptible
motion but the vibration from the engine : when suddenly,
with a brief.but violent rush of wind, the vessel gave a deep
lurch, and thenceforward indulged in a succession of rolls
and heavings which took speedy effect on the very stoutest
of our passengers. "Renounce me ! " said he, " if I like the
look of it !" " Or the feel of it, either," said a voice in an
under-tone. The red-faced man turned still redder—fixed
an angry eye on the speaker's complexion, and was evidently
meditating some very personal retort; but whatever it might
be, he was abruptly compelled to give it, with other matters,
to the winds. If there be such a thing as love at first sight,
there certainly are antipathies got up at quite as short a
notice ; and the man with the red face had thus conceived
an instinctive aversion to the man with the yellow one, at
whom he could not even look without visible symptoms of
dislike. "And how do *you* feel, sir ?" inquired the sufferer
as I passed near him, just after one of his paroxysms.

"Perfectly well as yet." "The better for you, sir," said the peppery man, rather sharply. "As for me, I'm as sick as a dog! I should not mind *that*, if it was in regular course; but there's that yellow fellow—just look at him, sir—there's a liver for you—there's disordered bile! a perfect walking Jaundice! *He's* the man to be sick, and yet he's quite well and comfortable—and I'm the man to be well—and here I can't keep anything! I assure you, sir, I have naturally a strong stomach, like a horse, sir—never had an indigestion—never! and as for appetite, I've been eating and drinking ever since I came on board! And yet you see how I am! And there's that saffron-coloured fellow, I do believe it was his sickly face that first turned me—I do, upon my honour —there's that yellow-fevered rascal—renounce me! if he isn't going down to dinner!"

As had been predicted, we dined early, and, *par conséquent*, on half-dressed vegetables, a piece of red beef, superficially done brown, and a very hasty pudding. The coarse inferior nature of the fare did not escape my uncle's notice : "but I suppose," said he, "a keen salt water appetite is not particular as to feeding on prime qualities." The words were scarcely uttered when he suddenly turned pale, and laid down his knife and fork. Never having been at sea before, and aware of some unusual sensations within, he instantly attributed them to the old source, and whispered to me to forbid my stirring. "I am a dead man—but don't alarm your aunt." Guessing how the matter stood, I let him scramble by himself to the deck, from which in a few minutes he returned, filled a glass of wine, drank it off, and then gave me a significant nod. "Another reprieve, Frank. It's very unpleasant, but I'm convinced what has just happened was the saving of my life. The circulation was all but gone, when a sort of convulsion of the stomach set it a-going again, and gave me time to rally." "Accidents that will happen at sea," remarked our skipper. "And on shore, too," replied my uncle very solemnly. "Captain, I have been dying suddenly these ten years." The captain screwed up his lips for a whistle, but it was not audible. "And for my part, sir," said our Daffodil, "I envy you your apoplexy. *I* am going, going, going, going by inches."

At this announcement the cabin-boy hastily pulled out an assortment of basins, selected a large blue and white one, and placed it conveniently at the feet of the speaker. From the first glimpse of the sickly-looking passenger, our steward's-mate had pitched upon him for a pet-patient,—he had watched him, listened to him, and whenever "Boy" was summoned in a strange voice, he invariably tried first at the yellow-man. To his surprise, however, the latter only gave the utensil a slight touch with his foot, saying, "It will do very well at a pinch, and boy—(yes, sir)—another time when you bring me such a thing as this—(yes, sir)—let me have the kettle along with it,—(yes, sir)—the sugar, a few lemons, and a bottle of rum." The boy, in sea phrase, was taken all aback. "Renounce me," whispered the Red-face, who happened to sit next me, "renounce me, if he don't mean punch: I can't stand him!—I can't upon my soul!" and off he rushed again upon deck.

By this time the motion of the vessel had considerably increased, and between fear and curiosity, and certain more physical motives, the whole of the company successively went above to enjoy what proved to be a very bad look out. The whole sky had now gone into sables, and like Hamlet seemed contending with "a sea of troubles." On the lee side, swaying by the backstay, stood the man with the red face, turned by recent exertion almost into purple. Instead of the languor and depression usually ascribed to the sea

malady, it seemed to put him up instead of down, and his
temper rose with his stomach. "I am worse than ever!" he
said to me, almost choking between his affliction and his
passion, "and there's that yellow wretch, quite composed,
with a d——d cigar in his mouth! I can't understand it,
sir—it's against nature. As for me—I shall die of it! I
know I shall!—I shall burst a vessel, sir. I thought I had
just now—but it was only the pint of port!"

As he spoke the vessel shipped a heavy sea, and heeled
over almost on her beam-ends. "I suppose," said my uncle,
"that's what they call a water-spout." "It's a squall!"
said the Yellow-face. "It's a female scream," cried my
aunt, wringing her hands, and in reality we heard a shrill
cry of distress that drew us in a body towards the fore-part
of the vessel. "It's the lady o' title," said the mate, "she
was above 'sociating with the passengers, and preferred
sitting in her own carriage—lucky she didn't go overboard
coach and all." My worthy uncle indignantly declared the
thing to be impossible. "Do you pretend to say there's a
human being shut up in that carriage, because she won't
even condescend to be drowned along with her fellow-
creatures?" By way of answer, the mate and assistants
contrived to drag the human being out of the vehicle, and
certainly, between fright and a good ducking, she was a very
forlorn-looking specimen of her order. "Well," muttered
my uncle, "this is dignity with a vengeance! I should
have thought even a lady of title might prefer a comfortable
cabin to sitting in such a bathing-machine, even with coronets
on the top." "Poor thing," interposed my aunt, "it's the
nature of her bringing up." "No doubt of it!" retorted
Nunkle, "but to my mind it's an unchristian bringing up
that prepares one so badly for going down." This shot
silenced my poor aunt, but it did not prevent her from

paying all possible attention to the Woman of Quality, on her way to the ladies' cabin, where she was deposited, at her own request, in a high berth. And so ended for the present the little episode of Lady D—— and her own carriage.

And now, my dear Gerard, imagine us all to creep like the exclusive lady into our own narrow dormitories, not that we were sleepy, but the violent pitching of the ship made it difficult, if not impossible, for any mere landsman to sit or stand. Indeed it would not have been easy to sleep, in spite of the concert that prevailed. First, a beam in one corner seemed taken in labour, then another began groaning,—plank after plank chimed in with its peculiar creak,—every bulkhead seemed to fret with an ache in it—sometimes the floor complained of a strain—next the ceiling cried out with a pain in its joints—and then came a general squeezing sound as if the whole vessel was in the last stage of collapse. Add to these the wild howling of the wind through the rigging, till the demon of the storm seemed to be playing coronachs over us on an Æolian harp,—the clatter of hail, the constant rushes of water around and overhead—and at every uncommon pitch, a chorus of female shrieks from the next cabin. To describe my own feelings, the night seemed spent between dozing and delirium. When I closed my eyes I had dreams of nightmares, not squatting ones merely, but vicious jades, that kicked, plunged, reared with and rolled over me : when I opened them, I beheld stools, trunks, bags, endowed with supernatural life, violently dancing—change sides, down the middle, back again, all round, and then, *sauve qui peut*, in a sudden panic making a general rush at the cabin stairs. In the midst of this tumult struggled a solitary human figure, sometimes sitting, sometimes kneeling, sometimes rolling, or desperately clinging to the table,—till the table itself burst its bonds, threw a preliminary summerset, and taking a

loose sofa between its legs, prepared for a waltz. It was a
countryman of Van Tromp who had thus resolved not to be
drowned in his bed ; and as even fright becomes comical by
its extravagance, I could not help laughing, in spite of my
own miseries, to see the poor Dutchman at any extraordinary
plunge clapping his hands as ecstatically as if it had been
meant for applause.   To tell the truth, the vessel occasionally
gave such an awful lurch, that I seriously thought we should
be left in it.   At last towards morning our terrors were brought
to a climax by a tremendous crash overhead, followed by a
prodigious rush of water, under which the Lord Melville
seemed to reel and stagger as if it had been wine, whilst part
of the briny deluge rushed down into the cabin and flooded
the lower beds.   Our *claqueur*, poor Mynheer, clapped his
hands long and loudly, taking it of course for the catastrophe
of the piece.   The vessel had been pooped, as it is called, by
a monstrous wave which had torn four men from the helm,
where they were steering with a long iron tiller, and had
thrown them luckily almost to the funnel instead of over the
quarter, when they must inevitably have perished.   On such
angles, in this world, depend our destinies !

On going on deck I found the captain and the pilot
anxiously looking out for the buoys which mark the entrance
into the Maas.   " I congratulate you, sir," said the yellow-
face,—"steam has saved us,—mere canvas has not been so
fortunate," and he pointed to the hull of a large ship with
only her lower masts standing ; she had gone down in shoal
water, her stern resting on the bottom, whilst her bows still
lifted with the waves.   " And the crew ? "   The yellow man
significantly shook his head—" No boat could live in such a
sea."   For the first time, Gerard, I felt sick—sick at heart.
I have seen many completer wrecks, with their naval anatomy
laid quite bare, but from that very circumstance, their wooden

ribs and vertebræ being thus exposed, they looked more like
the skeletons of stranded marine monsters ; whereas, in the
present instance, the vessel still preserved its habitable shape,
and fancy persisted in peopling it with human creatures,
moving, struggling, running to and fro, and at length in
desperation clinging to the rigging of those now bare spars.
I had even painted, Campbell-like, that wretched character, a
Last Man, perched in dreary survivorship in the main-top,
when, in startling unison with the thought, a voice muttered
in my ear, " Yes ! there he is !—he's been up there all night
—and every soul but himself down below ! " The speaker
was the red-faced man. " A pretty considerable bad night,
sir," said his Antipathy, by way of a morning salutation.
" An awful one, indeed," said the red-face,—" of course you've
been sick at last ? " " Not a notion of it." " Egad, then,"
cried my uncle, who had just emerged from the companion,
" you must have some secret for it worth knowing ! " " I
guess I have," answered the other, very quietly. " Renounce
me, if I didn't think so ! " exclaimed the red-face in a tone of
triumph—" it can't be done fairly without some secret or
other, and I'd give a guinea, that's to say a sovereign, to
know what it is." " It's a bargain " said the yellow-face,
coolly holding out his hand for the money, which was as
readily deposited in his palm, and thence transferred to a rather
slenderly furnished squirrel-skin purse. " Now then," said
the Carnation. " Why, then," said the Yellow Flower of the
Forest, with a peculiar drawl through the nose, " you must jist
go to sea, as I have done, for the best thirty years of your life."
The indignation with which this recipe was received was
smothered in a general burst of laughter from all within
hearing. Luckily we were now summoned to breakfast, where
we found my aunt, who expatiated eloquently on the horrors
of the past night. " I really thought," she said, " that I was

going to poor George." "Amongst sailors, ma'am," said our
rough captain, very innocently, "we call him Old Davy."

In consequence of the sea running so high, we were unable
to proceed to Rotterdam by the usual channel ; and were
occupied during a great part of the second day in going at
half-speed through the canals.   Tedious as was this course, it
afforded us a sight of some of the characteristic scenery of
that very remarkable country called Holland.   We had
abundant leisure to observe the picturesque craft, with their
high cabins, and cabin windows well furnished with flower-pots
and frows,—in fact, floating houses ;—while the real houses
scarcely above the water level, looked like so many family
arks that had gone only ashore, and would be got off next
tide.   These dwellings of either kind looked scrupulously
clean, and particularly gay ; the houses, indeed, with their
bright pea-green doors and shutters, shining, bran new, as if
by common consent, or some clause in their leases, they had
all been freshly painted within the last week.   But probably
they must thus be continually done in oil to keep out the
water,—the very Dryads, to keep them dry, being favoured
with a coat, or rather pantaloons, of sky-blue or red, or some
smart colour, on their trunks and lower limbs.   At times,
however, nothing could be seen but the banks, till perchance
you detected a steeple and a few chimneys, as if a village had
been sowed there, and was beginning to come up.   The
vagaries of the perspective, originating in such an arrangement, were rather amusing.   For instance, I saw a ruminating
cow apparently chewing the top of a tree, a Quixotic donkey
attacking a windmill, and a wonderful horse, quietly reposing
and dozing with a weathercock growing out of his back.
Indeed it is not extravagant to suppose that a frog, without
hopping, often enjoys a bird's eye view of a neighbouring town.
So little was seen of the country, that my aunt, in the

simplicity of her heart, inquired seriously, "Where's Holland?" "It ought to be hereabouts, madam," said the yellow-face, "if it wasn't swamped in the night." "Swamped, indeed!" said the red-face ; "it's sinful to mistrust Providence, but renounce me, if I could live in such a place without an ever-lasting rainbow overhead to remind me of the Promise." "They'd be drowned to-morrow, sir," said the captain, "if they wasn't continually driving piles, and building dams, like so many beavers on two legs." "They have all the ways of beavers, sure enough," chimed in my uncle, "and, egad!" pointing to a round-sterned fellow at work on the bank, "they have the same breadth of tail."

Amongst other characteristic features of the landscape, if it had land enough to deserve the name, we frequently saw a solitary crane or heron at the water's edge, watching patiently for food, or resting on one leg in conscious security. I pointed them out to my uncle, who, sportsman-like, was taking aim at a stork with his forefinger, when a hand was suddenly interposed before what represented the muzzle of the gun. It was the act of Mynheer the *claqueur*. My uncle reddened, but said nothing, though he afterwards favoured me with his opinion. "The Dutchman was right. I have been thinking it over ; and I have a misgiving we are too wasteful of animal lives. In England, now, those birds would not live a week without being peppered by the first fellow with a gun." "Because," said I, "we can sleep in England in spite of Philomel ; but the Dutch nightingales are more noisy, besides being as numerous as their frogs, and they are glad to preserve any birds that will thin them out." "No, no, Frank," replied my uncle, gravely shaking his head; "it's beyond a joke. I didn't say so before the Dutchman, because I don't choose to let down my native land : there's plenty of travellers to do that with a pretended liberality; but I don't set up for a cosmo-polite, which, to my mind, signifies being polite to every country except your own." "I have never heard the English accused," suggested your humble servant, "of wilful cruelty." "Not as to humankind, Frank: not as to humankind; but haven't we exterminated the bastards—I mean to say bustards; and haven't we got rid of the black cock of the walk—I should say the woods? As for the storks, they're the most filial and affectionate birds to old parents in all nature, and I take shame to myself for only aiming at them with a finger. God knows, I ought to have more fellow-feeling for sudden death!"

It was night ere we arrived at Rotterdam, safe and well, with the exception of my uncle's umbrella and great-coat, supposed to have been washed overboard by the same sea that endangered the lady and her carriage. Whilst the rest of the family comfortably established themselves at the Hôtel des Pays Bas, I took a hasty ramble by moonlight through the city, and have thrown my first impressions into verse, which, according to agreement, please to present with my dear love to your sister.* In plainer but not less sincere prose, accept the hearty regard of,

My dear Gerard, yours ever truly,

FRANK SOMERVILLE.

TO ——

COMPOSED AT ROTTERDAM.

I GAZE upon a city,—
A city new and strange,—
Down many a watery vista
My fancy takes a range;

From side to side I saunter,
And wonder where I am ;
And can *you* be in England,
And *I* at Rotterdam !

Before me lie dark waters
In broad canals and deep,·
Whereon the silver moonbeams
Sleep, restless in their sleep ;
A sort of vulgar Venice
Reminds me where I am ;
Yes, yes, you are in England,
And I'm at Rotterdam.

Tall houses with quaint gables,
Where frequent windows shine,
And quays that lead to bridges,
And trees in formal line,
And masts of spicy vessels
From western Surinam,
All tell me you're in England,
But I'm in Rotterdam.

Those sailors, how outlandish
The face and form of each !
They deal in foreign gestures,
And use a foreign speech ;
A tongue not learn'd near Isis,
Or studied by the Cam,
Declares that you're in England,
And I'm at Rotterdam.

And now across a market
My doubtful way I trace,
Where stands a solemn statue,
The Genius of the place;
And to the great Erasmus
I offer my salaam;
Who tells me you're in England,
But I'm at Rotterdam.

The coffee-room is open—
I mingle in its crowd,—
The dominoes are noisy—
The hookahs raise a cloud;
The flavour, none of Fearon's,
That mingles with my dram,
Reminds me you're in England,
And I'm at Rotterdam.

Then here it goes, a bumper—
The toast it shall be mine,
In schiedam, or in sherry,
Tokay, or hock of Rhine;
It well deserves the brightest,
Where sunbeam ever swam—
"The Girl I love in England"
I drink at Rotterdam!

TO MISS WILMOT, AT WOODLANDS, NEAR BECKENHAM,
KENT.

MY DEAR MARGARET,

As I predicted, our travels began in trouble, and
from the course of events, will end, I expect, in the same
way. What could be more unfortunate than to come to the
Continent in a storm so awful that I cannot bear to think of
it, much less to describe it, beyond saying, that between
raging winds and waves, and thunder and lightning, nature
itself seemed on the point of being wrecked! But I must
not repine; for though I have been frightened to death, and
shaken to pieces, and worn down by sea-sickness, and subjected to all sorts of discomforts and disagreeables, and
within an inch of being drowned at sea myself, it was all to
wean me from my losses and restore my peace of mind. As
such, it is my duty to reflect on nothing but my brother's
affection, however distressing in its effects on my own weak
nerves. It took us two whole days to reach Rotterdam,
though it was but a remove from one danger to another, for
the country of Holland lies so low in the water, that they
say it would be as fatal to spring a leak as in a ship. Indeed,
as my own eyes assured me, we were often swimming higher
than the tops of the houses; a dreadful consideration, when
you think that a water-rat, by boring a hole in the banks,
would do more havoc amongst the inhabitants than a loose
tiger. As it is, the poor people are compelled to employ a
whole army of windmills,--though how the water is to be
ground dry into dry ground is beyond my chemical knowledge. I do not quite know what he means, but my nephew
says the natives live like a party in a parlour and all damned.

Still it was a change for the better, after all the dreadful
sights and motions, and noises and smells, of a ship, to come
to a quiet room and a comfortable meal. Above all, it was
a real luxury to repose in a steady bed, with snow-white
sheets, though, my spirits being overtired, I did nothing but
cry all night long. But it is my dispensation to travel for
the rest of my days through a vale of tears. Mentioning
snow-white sheets, if cleanliness can ever be carried to excess,
it is in Holland :—indeed, I fear I shall hardly be able to
put up with English neatness when I return. The very
servants have such caps and kerchiefs, and aprons, and lace,
and so beautifully got up, I can compare it to nothing but a
laundress on a pleasure party taking a day's wear of her
mistress's best things. It is quite delightful to see,—though
not unmixed with painful recollections, for you know how
precise your dear late brother was about his linen. He was
quite Dutch in that. Of course, they have a wash every
week-day, besides the grand one on Saturdays, when they
really wash up everything in the place except the water.
As an instance of their particularity, at almost every house
there is a sort of double looking-glass outside the window,
as if for seeing up and down the street ; but Frank says it
is, that the Dutch ladies may watch, before being at home to
a friend, whether he has dirty boots or shoes.

We have seen the principal sights of Rotterdam, the
statue of Erasmus, the Arsenal, the Cathedral, with its
monuments of Dutch Admirals, and its great organ, which
plays almost too powerfully for mortal ears. But what
most took my fancy was the curious pleasure-grounds round
the town, with their outlandish summer-houses and little
temples. They are all what you and I should call Old
Bachelor's Gardens, laid out in fantastic figures and formal
walks, but full of the finest plants. I never saw such superb

flowers of their kind, or smelt so delicious a perfume. How
the Dutch gentlemen can reconcile themselves to smoking
tobacco in the midst of such a paradise of sweets, I cannot
imagine, unless it is to kill the caterpillars; but their noses
are surely insensible to good or bad smells, or they would
never allow so many stagnant ditches and ponds covered
with duckweed, that towards evening give out a stench fit to
breed a plague. But such is life, sweet in the morning, but
oh, how different in savour at the close! Knowing your
partiality for flowers, I intended to send you a few of the
fine sorts, particularly tulips and hyacinths, and was lucky
enough, as I thought, to find out a shop, with roots and
plants in the window, and a clerk who spoke a little English,
and politely helped me in selecting the choicest kinds.
Indeed, they had all such fine names they were sure to be
good. The young man himself very civilly carried the parcel
home to the hotel : but judge of my feelings when I came
to look at the bill. I can only say I screamed! What do
you think, Margaret, of seventy odd pounds for a few bulbs!
But that's where I miss your dear brother,—for, as you know,
I used to leave all bargaining and accounts, and money
matters, and in short everything, to poor George. The consequence was, we had quite a scene, which I need not say
was extremely distressing in a strange hotel. To add to my
agitation, my nephew was absent, and when I wanted to
consult my brother, he was in his own room in one of his old
fits, and nothing could be got from him except that he had
done with this world. In the mean time the foreign clerk
grew impatient, and at last worked himself into such a
passion that he could not speak English, and Heaven knows
what violence he threatened or would have done, if my
brother, hearing the noise, had not rushed in, and scuffled
him down the stairs. In the end, Frank had to go to the

C

shop and arrange the matter, but as he declines saying on what terms, I am convinced it cost no trifle to get the Dutchman to take back his bulbs. It was as much as I could do, when all was over, to keep from hysterics, especially as my brother chose to be extremely harsh with me, and said it was very hard he could not go out of the world without a parcel of trumpery flowers distracting his latter end. But I was born to troubles, and as the proverb says, they never come single. The roots might be an error in judgment, but there could be none about the Dutch linen ; which, of course, must be cheaper in Holland than anywhere else. Accordingly I laid in a good stock of shirting and sheeting, and napkins and towelling, for home use ; but although the quality was excellent, and the bill quite reasonable, this good bargain cost me as much vexation as the bad one. My brother, indeed, did not scold, but though both he and my nephew wished me joy of my purchase, I saw by their faces that they meant quite the reverse. Such an untoward beginning quite scares me, and fills me with misgivings that in going farther I shall only fare worse. It grieves me to think, too, how *you* would delight in this tripping up the Rhine, instead of taking my place at Woodlands, whilst I am only fit for domestic duties and the quiet of home. A heavy heart, weak nerves, and broken spirits, are bad travelling companions, and at every step, alas ! I am reminded, by some dilemma or other, what a stay and guide a woman loses in a husband like poor George.

Providentially we have not suffered as yet in our health, but I shall not be easy on that score till we leave Holland, as there is a low fever, they say, peculiar to the country, and very apt to attack the English, unless they smoke and drink drams all day long. Our next stage is by steamboat to Nimeguen, which is in a state of war against the Belgians for being Roman Catholics. Frank says the best plan would be to convert the Belgians to the Church of England, and then they would take the Thirty-nine Articles instead of fighting about Twenty-four. And for the sake of peace, and to save bloodshed, I devoutly hope it may be settled in some such way. But fatigue compels me to close. Pray distribute my kindest regards amongst all friends, and accept my love from, dear Margaret,

Your affectionate sister,

CATHERINE WILMOT.

P.S.—Martha begs me to forward the enclosed. She has had her own troubles, but has become more reconciled; though not without flying occasionally to her old trick of giving warning. But her warnings are like my poor brother's, and I really believe she would be heart-broken if I took her at her word. Like her mistress she has been buying bargains —though more as foreign curiosities than for use, except a beautiful brass milkpail, which I have taken off her hands for the dairy at Woodlands.

TO REBECCA PAGE, AT THE WOODLANDS, NEAR BECKENHAM, KENT.

DEAR BECKY,

Littel did I think I shud ever ever ever rite you again! We have all bean on eternitty's brinx. Such a terrifickle storm! Tho' we are on Shure, I cant get it out of my Hed. Every room keeps spinnin with me like a roundy-bout at Grinnage Fair. Every chare I set on begins rockin like a nussin chare and the stares pitch and toss so I cant go up them xcept on all fores. They do say elevin

other vessels floundered off the Hooks of Holland in the
same tempest with all their cruise. It began in the arternoon, and prevaled all nite,—sich a nite O Grashus! Sich
tossin and tumblin it was moraly unpossible to stand on
. wons legs and to compleat these discomfortables nothin wood
sit easy. I might as well have et and drunk Hippokickany
and Antinomial wine. O Becky the Tea-totlers only give up
fomentid lickers, but the Sea Totlers give up everything.
To add to my frite down flumps the stewardis on her nees
and begins skreeking we shall be pitcht all over! we shall
be pitcht all over! Think I if *she* give up we may prepair
for our wartery graves. At sich crisisus theres nothin like
religun and if I repeted my Catkism wunce I said it a
hundered times over and never wonce rite. You may gudge
by that of my orrifide state, besides ringing my hands till
the nails was of a blew black. Havin nose wat else I sed
for in my last agny I confest every partical I had ever dun,
—about John Fútman and all. Luckly Missus was too
much decomposed to atend to it but it will be a Warnin for
the rest of my days. O Becky its awful wurk when it cums
to sich a full unbuzzuming and you stand before your own
eyes stript nakid to the verry botom of your sole. Wat
seemed the innocentest things turn as black as coles. Even
Luvvers look armless but they aint wen all their kisses cum
to fly in your face. Makin free with triffles is the same.
Littel did I think wen I give away an odd lofe it would lay
so heavy. Then to be shure a little of Missus's tea and
sugger seams no grate matter, partickly if youve agreed to
find yure own, but as I no by experence evry ownce will turn
to a pound of lead in repentin. That wickid caddy Key give
me menny a turn, and I made a pint as soon as the storm
abatid to chuck it into the bottomless otion. I do trust
Becky you will foller my xampel and give up watever goes

agin yure conshins. If I namo tho linnin I trust youl
excusc. Charrity kivers a multitud of sins, and to be shuro
its a charrity to give a-way a raggid shurt of Masters pro-
vidid its not torn a purpus which I fear is sum times the
case. Pray say tho like from me to Mister Butler up at tho
Hall, he will tako a Miss I no,—partickly as I hav drunk
unbeknown wino along with him, but when yure at yur last
pint what is Port in a storm! Won minit yuro a living
cretur, and tho next you may bo liko wickid Jonas in tho
belly of Wales.

The ouly comfort I had besides Cristianity was to givo
Missus warnin witch I did over and over between her attax.
No wagis on earth could reckonsilo me to a sea-goin place.
Dress is dress and its hard on a servent to find too nasty
grato broke loose Trunks between them has battered my
poro ban box into a pan cake. To make bad wus, as the
otion they say levels all distinkshuns, and make won Wom-
man as good as a nother I thought propper to go to sea in
my best, and in course my waterd ribbins is no better for
being washt with serges, or my bewtiful shot silk for gitting
different shades of smoak blacks,—besides spiling my nice
kid gluves with laying hold on tarry ropes, not to name bein
drensht from top to toe with rottin salt water, and tho personable risk of being drownded arter all. But I mito as
well havo tould tho ship to soot itself as my Missus. I
verrily belcavo from her wild starin at mo sho did not no
wether I talked English or Frentch. At last Martha says
sho we aro going to a wurld where there is no sitivations.
What an idear! But our superiers aro always shy of our
society, as if even hevin abuv was too good for servents.
Talking of superiers there was a Tittled Lady in Bed in tho
Cabbin that sent every five minits for the capting, till at long
and at last he got Crusty. Capting says sho I insist on yuro

gitting the ship more out of the wind. I wish I could says
he. Dont you no who I am, says she very dignifide. Yes
my Ladyship says the capting, but its blowin grate guns,
and if so be you was a princess I couldn't make it blow littel
pistles. Wat next but she must send for the Mate to ask
him if he can swim. Yes my lady says he like a Duck. In
that case says she I must condysend to lay hold on yure
harm all nite. Axin pardin my ladyship says he its too grate
honners for the like of me. No matter says she very proud-
like, I insist on it. Then I'm verry sorry says the Mate
makin a run off, but I'm terrible wanted up abuv to help in
layin the ship on her beam ends. Thats what I call good
authority, so you may supose wat danger we was in.

Howsumever here we are thenk providens on dry land if
so be it can be cauld dry that is half ditchis and cannals, at
a forin city, by name Rotter D—m. The King lives at the
Ha-gue and I'll be bound it's haguish enuf for Holland is a
cold marshy flatulint country and lies so low they're only
saved by being dammed. The wimmin go very tidy but the
men wear very large close for smallclose and old fashionable
hats. But I shouldn't prefer to settle in Holland for Dutch
plaices must be very hard. Oh Becky such moppin and
sloppin such chuckin up water at the winders and squirtin
at the walls with littel fire ingins, but I supose with their
moist climit the houses wouldn't be holesum if they warn't
continually washing off the damp. Then the furnitur is
kept like span new without speck or spot, it must be sum-
boddy's wurk to kill all the flies. To my mind the pepel are
over clean—as John Futman said when his master objectid to
his thum mark on the hedge of the plate, a littel dirt does
set off clenliness thats certin. Then as to nus mades they
ought to have eyes all round their heds like spiders to watch
the childrin by the cannals, thenk God I ant a Dutch parent,

I should be misrable for fear of my yung wons gittin to the keys. Lawk, an English muther in Holland wood be like a Hen with Ducklins!

We have seen many fine sites, and bildings, and partickly the Butcher's Hall, which is all of red Brix, pick't out with wite, jest as if it was bilt of beefstake. Likewise the statute of Erasmis who inventid pickle herrins,—they do say in any orange bovine revolushuns it jumps into the cannal, and then cums out agin when the trubbles is over—but in course that's only a popish mirakle. Then there's the House of Fears,—fears enough I warrant for every other hole and corner in the town was ravaged and ransackt by the French, —and the pore soles every minit expecten naber's fare. But that cant hapin agin, as in the case of beseiging they open all their slowces, and the Dutch being amphibbyus, all the enemy is drowndid xcept themselves. As respects vittles, we do verry well, only I am shi of the maid dishes, being sich a mashy forren country, for fear of eatin Frogs. Talkin of cookin, wat do you think Becky of sittin with a lited charcole stow under yure pettecots? Its the only way they have for airin their linnin,—tho' it looks more like a new cookery receat for How to smoak your Hams. But I hear Missus bell, so with kind luve to all, includin John Futman, I remane in haste, my dear Becky Yure luving friend,

MARTHA PENNY.

TO GERARD BROOKE, ESQ.

MY DEAR GERARD,

At last we have turned our backs on the good city of Rotterdam, and made our first advance up the Waal branch of the fashionable river. As you are aware, the banks of the Lower Rhine are of a very uninteresting character : to sing their beauties one needs only, with Desdemona, to "sing all a green willow, sing willow, willow, willow." In such a case there is but one alternative. In the absence of good scenery and decorations, the traveller must turn for entertainment to the strolling company on board, and such *pièces de circonstance* as they may happen to present.

It is one of the discomforts of striving against the stream on the Rhine, that you must start extravagantly early, in order to accomplish the next stage before night. To aggravate this nuisance, the garçon appointed to rouse us crowed, like the "bonnie gray cock," a full hour too soon ; and then, by way of amends, called us as much too late ; so that we had to save our passage and passage-money (paid beforehand) by a race to the quay. Short as the course was, it led to a great deal of what the turf-men call *tailing*, Your humble servant was first on board, my Uncle made a bad second, my Aunt a worse third, her maid Martha barely saved her distance, and the baggage was nowhere at all. In fact, the steamer was already on the move before our Dutch porters made their appearance, so that the greater part of the luggage was literally pitched on board, with a clangor and clatter that excited a peal of merriment from ship and shore. "In the name of heaven, what is all this ?" inquired my Uncle, who noticed a considerable addition to our sundries. "Oh, it's the beautiful brass pail," moaned my Aunt, writhing in pantomimical distress ; "and look how it's all battered and bruised !" whilst her maid indignantly collected a shower of wooden shoes, intended to be presented as foreign curiosities to her fellow-servants at Woodlands. My Uncle shrugged up his shoulders and made a wry face at the prospect. "Zounds, Frank !" he said to me in an aside, "if we gather at this rate in our progress, we shall come to a stickfast in

the end, like the great snow-ball in Sanford and Merton.
To my mind, your poor Aunt is making a toil of a pleasure ;
however, the more little trouble she gets into, the more likely
to forget her great one. Though, to be sure, it sounds odd,"
he continued, observing me smile, "for a widow to be wiping
away her tears with a brass-pail."

I had now time to look round, and, on taking a survey of
the company, was not sorry to recognise our old acquaintance
the red-faced man, looking as ruddy as a Dutch apple, but
like an apple that had been bruised. From whatever cause,
there was a discoloration round his right eye, which hinted
plainly with Lord Byron, that

"Sometimes we must box without the muffles,"

especially when we are blessed with a temper as hot and hasty
as a pepper-castor with a loose top. He eagerly pounced
upon me as one with whom he could pour out his bottled-up
grievances, and thus they began their audible effervescence :
—" Glad to see you, sir ; here's a pretty eye for the beauties
of the Rhine—black as my hat, sir ;—well it wasn't knocked
out !" I sympathised of course, and inquired how it
happened. "How, sir ? it could only happen in one way.
I've heard of black devils, and blue devils, and renounce me
if I don't think there are yellow ones."—" You do not surely
mean our old shipmate the American ?"—" Yes, but I do,
though. You remember how unpleasant he made himself
to every person on board—wouldn't be sick or anything. As
for me, it was natural instinct or something, but I hated him
from the first time I set eyes on him. It gave me a turn to
look at him. I felt as if I was turning bilious myself ; I did
indeed ! If I don't cut him, thought I, the moment we get
on shore, my name's not Bowker—John Bowker. So I

asked him at Rotterdam to recommend a good inn, and he
named the Skipper House. That was enough for me, and
off I took myself to the Bath Hotel. Well, sir, what next?
After supper, and making myself comfortable, up I went to
bed, and what do you think I saw?" Here Mr. John Bowker
made a solemn pause, and looked me full in the face; his
visage grew redder, except the black circle, which seemed to
darken; he knocked his hat down over the damaged eye,
fiercely rammed his doubled fists into his pockets, drew in a
long breath, and then resumed in a voice quite guttural from
the broil within : "Renounce me, sir, if I didn't see his
infernal jaundice face on the clean pillow!"—"Very unpleasant indeed."—"Yes, sir; there it was, all yellow in the
middle of the white—just like a poached egg. By the bye, I
don't think I shall ever eat one again—he has quite poisoned
the idea, sir, he has, upon my life !" There was an expression
of loathing about the red face as he said this that would
have delighted Dr. Johnson, who has recorded his opinion
of a "good hater." However, I affected concern, and inquired
how the ontoward event had originated. "Originated !—
phoo, phoo—no such thing. It was done on purpose, sir,
sheer *malice prepense.* I told him quite civilly, I was afraid
of a little mistake. 'I'm afraid there is,' said he : 'what's
your number?' 'My name,' said I, 'is Bowker—John
Bowker—and I'm number seventeen.' 'Ah,' said he, 'that's
just where it is—my name is Take-care-of-yourself, and I
reckon I'm number one.' Cool, sir, wasn't it? and I tried to
be cool too, but I couldn't—blood will boil : it's human
nature, sir—and mine began singing in my ears like a kettle.
Thought I, this must be vented somehow, or I shall burst a
vessel ; it's a dread of mine, sir, that some day I shall burst
a vessel, if my passion isn't worked off—and between that and
his grinning at me, I couldn't help making a punch at the

fellow's head : I couldn't, upon my soul. That led to a scuffle, and the noise brought up the master and the garsoons —however, the end was, I got my bed and this beautiful black eye into the bargain—for the landlord soon proved my right to number seventeen."—"And what excuse," I asked, "did the usurper offer for his intrusion?"—"None in the world, sir. Not a syllable! except that the Skipper House happened to be full, and my bed happened to be empty. Confound his yellow face!—I thought it was jaundice, or the American fever—but it's brass, sir,—brass lacker. But that's not the end. 'In course,' said he, 'you'll allow a half-naked individual about twenty minutes or so to make himself decent and collect his traps?' Well, sir, having vented my warmth, I was quite agreeable, and how do you think he spent the time?" Here another pause for the speaker to muster all his indignation. "Why, sir, when it came to fresh making the bed, he had wound and rolled up both the sheets into balls, hard balls, sir, as big as your head!"—"An old trick," I remarked, "amongst nautical men, and called reefing."—"Nothing more likely, sir," said the red face; "he'd been thirty years at sea, you know, as he told me when he swindled me out of my sovereign. However, there were the two sheets—the only pair not in use—and the devil himself couldn't pick an end out of them, landlord, garsoons, and all. Renounce me if I don't believe they're in statu quo at this very moment—I do, upon my life!" The fervor with which he made this declaration quite upset my gravity : and he joined at first in my mirth, but stopped short as abruptly as if he had been seized by a spasm. "No, no, sir," he said, with a serious shake of his head—"the thing's beyond a laugh. It's my remark, sir, that I never took a strong dislike to a person at first sight without his giving me good reason for it in the end. Mark my words, sir,—that

turmeric-faced Yankee is my evil genius. He'll haunt me
and spoil my pleasure wherever I go. He has poisoned the
German ocean for me already, and now, sir, he'll poison the
river Rhine—he will, sir, as sure as my name's Bowker
—John Bowker—he'll poison the Rhine, and the Baths,
and the Hock wine, and everything—as certain as I stand
here!"

Absurd as this picture will seem to you, my dear Gerard,
it is nevertheless sketched from nature. And, after all, how
many of us there are who, in the pilgrimage of life, thus
conjure up black, blue, or yellow-faced bugbears to poison
our river Rhines! But, not to moralise, suppose me now
driven by a smart shower into a rather noisy, very odoriferous,
and piping-hot cabin, the rule against smoking having been
reversed, by turning the prohibitory placards with their
faces to the wall. Here I found my Uncle good-humoredly
playing, or rather trying to play, at dominoes with a German,
the only difficulties being that the German and English
games are as different as the two languages. Still they
persevered with laudable patience, each after his own fashion,
till they had finished two glasses a-piece of curaçoa. "It
is very extraordinary," remarked my Uncle, as he rose up,
neither winner nor loser, "that in spite of the thousands
and thousands of English who have passed up and down
the Rhine, the natives have never yet learned to play at
dominoes!"

A complaint from a countrywoman at the next table was
quite in keeping. For some minutes past she had been
calling out "Hoof! hoof! hoof!" to our squat little Dutchman of a garçon, who in return only grinned and shook his
head. "It's really provoking," exclaimed the lady, "to have
such a stupid waiter. He doesn't even know the French for
an egg!"

Our first stoppage was at Dordrecht, or Dort, a quaint, characteristic town, that looked like an old acquaintance, its features being such as are common on the pictorial Dutch tiles. Here, amongst other additions to our living freight, we obtained a private soldier, of whom his wife or sweetheart took a most affectionate leave—as of a house lamb about to be butchered by "les braves Belges." Again, and again, and again, she called him back for more last words, and imprinted fresh editions, with additions, of her farewell, upon his lips, but the warning bell of the steamer rang, fatal as curfew to the light of love—the weeping female gave her warrior one more desperate hug, that almost lifted him off his feet; he tore himself from the arms that dropped listless, as if she had no further use for them in this world—the paddles revolved—and there on the quay, so long as Dordrecht remained in sight, we beheld the forlorn frow, gazing, as motionless and inanimate as one of the staring painted wooden dolls indigenous to her country. "Poor souls," murmured my Aunt, who had been looking on with glistening eyes; "what a horrid cruel thing is war, when it comes home to us!" My Uncle, too, gave utterance to a thought which sounded like an echo of my own: "Egad, Frank, there wasn't much Dutch phlegm in that!"

I was too much interested by this episode to notice the advent of another passenger, till he was announced in an angry whisper. "There he is again!—Curse his yellow face! —I thought he was a day a-head of me!" and lo! the American stood bodily before us, having halted at Dordrecht to inspect the saw-mills, and the ponds for containing the huge rafts of timber that float thither down the Rhine, from Switzerland and the Black Forest. His old opponent glared at him fiercely with his sound eye, and very soon found fuel for the flame. The deck of a steamer is supposed to be

divided amid-ships by an imaginary line, aft of which the
steerage passengers are expected not to intrude. In the
Rhenish vessels this trespass is forbidden, by sundry polyglott
inscriptions, under penalty of paying the higher rate of
passage; and the arrangement affords a curious test of
character. · A modest or timid individual, a lover of law and
order, scrupulously refrains from passing across the boundary;
another, of a careless easy disposition, paces indifferently
within or beyond the invisible fence, whilst a third fellow
(ten to one he wears his hat all aslant) ostentatiously
swaggers to the very stern, as if glorying that there is a
privilege to usurp, and a rule to be broken. It was soon
apparent to which of these classes our American belonged.
"Look at him, sir," growled Mr. John Bowker, giving me a
smart nudge with his elbow, "*do* look at him! He's a
steerage passenger, and see where he is, *con*found his im-
pudence! sitting on the skylight of the best cabin. Pray
come here, sir;" and seizing me by the arm, he dragged me
to the paddle-box, and pointed to the deck regulations,
conspicuously painted up in three different languages.
"There, sir, read that;" but he kindly saved me the trouble,
by reading aloud the English version of the rules—"There's
the law distinctly laid down, and yet that yellow scoundrel—"
He broke off abruptly, for the yellow scoundrel, himself,
attracted by our movements, came to see what we were
looking at; deliberately read over the inscriptions in French,
Dutch, and English, and then quietly resumed his seat on
the skylight. "Cool, isn't it?" asked the chafing Bowker,
"he can't say *now* he has had no warning. Renounce me if
I don't name it to the captain, I will, upon my life! What's
to become of society, if we can't draw a line! Subversion of
all order—levelling all ranks; democracy let loose; anarchy,
sir, anarchy, anarchy, anarchy!" Here his vehemence

inciting him to physical action, he began to walk the deck, with something of the mien of a rampant red lion; but still serving up to me the concoctions of his wrath hot and hot. "I suppose he calls that American independence! (*A walk.*) Sir, if I abominate anything in the world, it's a Yankee, let alone his yellow face. (*Walk.*) It's hereditary, sir. My worthy father, John Bowker, senior, could never abide them—never! (*Walk.*) Sir, one day he met a ship captain, in the city, that wanted to know his way to the Minories. Says my father, 'I've an idea you're an American.' 'I guess I am,' said the captain. 'And pray, sir,' said my worthy parent, 'what do you see in my face to make you think I'd tell a Yankee his way to the Minories, or anywhere else?' Yes, sir, he did, upon my life. He was quite consistent in that! (*Another walk and then a full stop.*) I suspect, sir, you think I am warm?" I could not help smiling an assent. "Well, sir, I know it. I *am* warm. It's my nature, and it's my principle to give nature her head. I've strong feelings, very; and I make a point never to balk them. For instance, if there's a colour I detest, it's yellow. I hate it, sir, as a buffalo hates scarlet—and there's that Yankee with a yellow face, yellow eyes, yellow teeth, and a yellow waistcoat—renounce me, if I don't think he's yellow all through, ugh!" and with a grimace to match the grunt, he hurried off to the bows, as if to place the whole length of the vessel between himself and the object of his aversion. Still, with the true perversity of a self-tormentor, who will neither like things nor let them alone, he continued to watch every movement of his enemy, and was not slow in extracting fresh matter of offence. "I must go below," he muttered as he again approached me, "it's an infernal bore, but I *must!* There's no standing him! I can't walk the same deck! It's forbidden to talk to the helm, and there he is drawling

away to the steersman! Renounce me, if he isn't telling
him the story of the rolled-up sheets—I know it by his
grinning! Sir, if I stay above, I shall have a fever,—he'll
change my whole mass of blood—he will, as sure as fate;"
and with a furious glance at the yellow face, down scrambled
the peppery-tempered gentleman to cool his heat—like
Bowker, senior, "he was quite consistent in that"—with a
stiff glass of hot brandy and water.

As you know, Gerard, I am not professedly a sentimental
traveller, like Sterne, yet I could not help moralising on
what had passed. Mr. John Bowker seemed to me but a
type of our partisans and bigots, political and religious, who
take advantage of any *colourable* pretext on the *palate* of
their prejudices, to shut their hearts against a fellow-
creature, who may wear green to their orange, or pink to
their true blue. In short, Heaven knows how far I might
have carried my reflections on the iniquity of hating a man
for his yellow face, if I had not suddenly recollected that, ere
now, many a human being has been stolen, enslaved, bought
and sold, scourged, branded, and even murdered, merely
because he happened to have a black one. Should you still
require an apology for these extra ruminations, I must refer
for my excuse to the sight of the fortress of Gorcum, where
nineteen Catholic priests suffered death for the faith that
was in them; and to a glimpse of the castle of Lowenstein,
in which Grotius was imprisoned for his opinions, and
reduced to compose his renowned treatise "De Jure Belli et
Pacis," where he could neither be comfortably at peace nor
conveniently make war.

I have said that steaming up the lower Rhine is sufficiently tedious; and it was eight o'clock P.M. ere we arrived
at Nimeguen, a frontier town, chiefly remarkable as the
place where the triple treaty was signed in 1678, between

France, Holland and Spain. It will interest you more to
remember that Sir Walter Scott spent a night here on his
last memorable journey towards Abbotsford and his long
home. There is a story current that the innkeepers eagerly
sent their carriages to await the arrival of the steamer which
conveyed so illustrious a personage, and that Sir Walter
unconsciously availed himself of the vehicle belonging to one
hotel to convey him to a rival establishment, of course to
the great chagrin of the coach-proprietor. For our humble
selves, we have set up our rest with Doctor, or Dokter,—a
name which doubtless had a charm for my hypochondriac
Uncle, quite independent of the recommendation of the
German with whom he had played at dominoes, and who
was probably a genteel "toûter" in disguise. However, the
house is clean, quiet and comfortable, with a small garden in
the rear, and a painted wooden figure of a Dutchman at
the end of the main walk ; to which figure, by the way, I
caught my Uncle bowing, hat in hand, mistaking it, no
doubt, for our Doctor himself. This wooden statuary is,
timberly speaking, quite a branch of the Dutch fine arts, and
surely art must be in its second childhood when it returns
to playing with dolls. On which theme, my dear Gerard, I
could write an essay, but my paper being filled up, as well as
my leisure, I must conclude with kind regards to yourself,
and love to Emily,

Yours, &c.,

FRANK SOMERVILLE.

TO PETER BAGSTER, ESQ., SOLICITOR, CANTERBURY.

MY DEAR PETER,

I take shame to myself for not writing you before, as you could only come to one conclusion. But you have been long prepared for such an event, and consequently the less shock to your feelings; still, an old friend is an old friend, and I heartily beg your pardon for the sorrow I am sure you would display at my loss. As for black clothes, being professional wear, you would be at no cost, I trust, on that score, but I do hope you have not added to trouble by acting on my last will. But you were never hasty in law matters. No doubt it was my bounden duty to let you hear from Rotterdam, and my mind misgives there was some sort of promise to that effect, provided I lived over the voyage. At all events, I owe you an apology, and it is a melancholy excuse to make, but from day to day I expected there would be news to break by another hand, that would fully account for my silence. I had two very smart warnings, one in a storm on board ship, and the other ashore, but both so nigh fatal that the next *must* be the finish. Though I am not sensibly weaker or worse, reason dictates that I am sapping in my vital parts; and at last, even my constitution seems to have given in. If I only felt any bodily pain I should be a deal easier, but I am more comfortable than I have been for years, which I take to be about the worst symptom I could enjoy. Mayhap a mortification has set in, and my inward feelings are dead and gone beforehand, and in that case I shall go off in a moment, like a hair trigger. So much for the good to be done my health by the river Rhine ! The present is writ at Nimeguen, and it will take two days more to get to Cologne, so that I am as sure cf the port and sherry that Truby bet me as if it was in my own cellar. Well, God's will be done ! Nimeguen is as nigh to Heaven as Beckenham in Kent ; and a thousand miles north or south, east or west, make no odds in our journey to a world that has neither latitude nor longitude.

Now I am here, I am not sorry to have had a peep at such a country as Holland ; but being described by so many better hands in books of travels, besides pictures, I need not enlarge. If you only fancy the very worst country for hunting in the whole world, except for otter dogs, you will have it exactly. Every highway is a canal ; and as for lanes and bridle-roads, they are nothing but ditches. By consequence, the lives of the natives are spent between keeping out water and letting in liquor, such as schiedam, aniseed, curaçoa, and the like ; for, except for the *damming* they would be drowned like so many rats, and without the *dramming* they would be martyrs to ague and rheumatics, and the marsh fever. Frank says, the Hollanders are such a cold-blooded people, that nothing but their ardent spirits keep them from breeding back into fishes ; be that as it may, I have certainly seen a Dutch youngster, no bigger than your own little Peter, junior, toss off his glass of *schnapps*, as they call it, as if it was to save him from turning into a sprat. It is only fair to mention that Dutch water seems meant by Providence for scouring, or scrubbing, or washing, or sailing upon, or any other use in nature, except to drink neat. It costs poor Martha a score of wry faces only to hear it named, for she took one dose of it for want of warning, and it gave her a rattling fit of what she calls the Colliery Morbus.

As regards foreign parts, I was most taken with Rotterdam. It is a fine outlandish business-like city, with a real

Dutch medley of quays, and canals, and bridges, and steeples, and chimneys, and masts of ships, all in one point of view. The same forming, altogether, a picture that, to my mind, might be studied with advantage by certain folks at home. Not to name party spirit, which poisons every public measure in England, there is far too much of separating matters that ought never to be considered apart. By way of example, we hear the landed interest, and the funded interest, and the shipping interest, and so forth, talked of night after night in Parliament as if they were all private interests, instead of public ones; or what is worse, in opposition, instead of being partners in one great national firm—namely, Agriculture, Commerce, Manufactures and Company. As such, it is neither just nor wise for one branch to be protected or encouraged at the expense of the rest; and besides, I have made up my mind that the welfare of any member, in the long-run, must be looked for in the prosperity of the whole. If we wish, then, to thrive as a nation, instead of splitting our bundle of sticks, we must bind them all up together, and consider our commerce, and agriculture, and manufactures, in one cluster, like the chimneys, the fine elm-trees, and the ships' masts on the Boomjes, as it is called, at Rotterdam. Those are my sentiments, though it is not speaking, mayhap, like a landowner with well-nigh a thousand acres in his own hand. But I am not going to favour you with a batch of politics, and besides I am called to meals, where I have promised myself the pleasure of drinking your health, old friend, in a bumper of Madeira, that has made a voyage to Java, in the East Indies.

DEAR PETER,

Since the above, you will be concerned to hear I have had another very serious attack. It took place in

Dokter's garden, having gone into the same after dinner to
enjoy a little fresh air, when all at once I went off quite
insensible, and nobody being by, except a painted wooden
image of a Dutchman, it is unknown how long I remained in
that state, and certainly should never have recovered, but
for a providential cold shower of rain that brought me to by
its shock to the system. My nephew will have it, that
indulging in a glass of wine beyond the common, I only
went to sleep in the bower; but relations are always
sanguine, and particularly the youthful, and his affection,
poor fellow, makes him hope the best. In my own mind,
I am quite convinced it was suspended animation, and
especially by being so terrible cold in my extremities.
Truby makes light of these runaway knocks, as he calls
them, but my own sense tells me, Peter, they are warnings
that Death intends to soon call upon me in earnest. As
such, you may suppose I am not best pleased to be pestered
with matters, disagreeable at any time to freeborn principles,
but particularly to a man under my serious circumstances.
I allude to the passport system, whereby an Englishman
abroad is treated like so much liquor, or wine, or soap, at
home, that can't be moved without a permit. Here was a
fellow just now wanting me to show myself up at the police-
office to be vizeed, and so forth; but for an individual going
to another world to be passported out of Holland into
Prussia seemed such an idle piece of business, not to say
presumption, that I declined stirring in it. Master Frank,
however, thought otherwise, and not being in my solemn
frame of mind, was so obstinate on the subject that we
almost came to words. So the end is, I have been vizeed,
and identified behind my back, and made passable in
Germany, forsooth, for six months to come!

Sister Kate rubs on in her usual way, in tolerable health,

but taking on about poor George   She has got already into
two or three travelling troubles, and by way of companion
has encumbered herself with a bale of Dutch linen as big as
a baby.   And now, God bless you, and likewise all of the
name.   Something tells me it is a last farewell, from

Dear Peter, your sincere and dying friend,

RICHARD ORCHARD.

P.S.—I had the pleasure of forwarding a few gallons of
real Dutch Hollands, which by this time should be on their
road to Canterbury.   It is called Schiedam, and makes a
capital mixture, provided you don't brew it like a Mounseur
in the house here, who makes his spirits and water without
the spirits.   That reminds me of your old joke against Bob
Rugby, the classical schoolmaster, about mixing the Utile
and Dulce.   "Utile and Dulce be hanged ! " says you, "the
French drink it, and it's nothing but sugar and water."

———————

TO GERARD BROOKE, ESQ.

MY DEAR GERARD,

You will be glad to hear that we have escaped un-
drowned from that water-logged country called Holland,—a
country, which, between its carillons and its canals, might be
described by a punster as "wringing wet."

We left Nimeguen with something of the ill-will with
which we are apt, unjustly, to remember a place where we
have suffered pain or experienced disappointment.   And
truly, to be cheated of great nature's second course, to be
balked unnaturally of one of the most important non-natu-
rals, is enough to upset one's moral as well as local affections.

My Uncle says little, considering himself continually as on the brink of a sleep eternal ; but my Aunt complains that she has never had a regular night's rest since she left London ; whilst her maid declares, with a yawn, that foreign travelling is very racketty work, and has more than once hinted to her mistress that going abroad formed no part of her engagement. As for myself, I join with Dr. Watts' sluggard in wishing, tautologically, for "a little more sleep, and a little more slumber,"—but seem far more like a door *off* the hinges than *on* them, according to the serious poet's absurd simile. And all this gaping, and eye-watering, and drowsihed and discontent to be the work of a ridiculous Cockney, whom our evil fortune, personified in a Dutch *touter*, had conducted to the same hotel. He had been a unit of our sum total of passengers from Rotterdam, but had escaped any particular observation by his insignificance. Boxcoated, bandana'd, and shawled, a compound of the coachman, the coxcomb, and the clerk, there was no difficulty in classifying the animal at a glance—still in spite of a slang air, a knowing look, and the use of certain significant phrases, that are most current in London, there was such a cold-muttonish expression in his round unmeaning face as assured you that the creature had no harm in him—that he was little likely to murder sleep or anything else. However, about midnight, when number one was dozing, number two dreaming, number three snoring, and number four, perhaps, panting under the nightmare of a heavy hot supper, the populous establishment was suddenly startled broad awake by two violent explosions that frightened the whole neighbourhood from its propriety. In the first confusion of the senses, I really fancied, for the moment, that the Belgians were attempting to carry the city by a *coup-de-main*. In fact, Nimeguen being in a state of war, the alarm turned out the guard, and by the time I had donned my nether garments, some dozen soldiers were battering and clamouring for admittance at the door. On sallying from my room, I found the stairs and passages thronged with figures, male and female, in various degrees of nudity, amongst whom, our maid Martha was eminently conspicuous, having, for reasons of her own, exchanged her plain *bonnet-de-nuit* for her day-cap, with flaming geranium ribbons, the only article of full-dress on her person, or indeed amongst the whole party. As her mouth was wide open, she was probably either screaming or scolding, but her individual noise was lost and smothered in the confusion of tongues, that turned the lately quiet hotel into a second Babel. Some shouted "Fire !" others cried "Murder !" and one shrill feminine voice kept screaming, "The French ! the French !" In the mean time, the patrol gained admittance, and with little ceremony forced their way up stairs towards the chamber to which we had traced the two reports. The door was locked and bolted, but was speedily burst open with the butt-end of a musket, the company entered, *en masse*, and lo ! there was our Cockney, in a bright coloured silk handkerchief for a turban, sitting bolt upright in his bed, and wondering with all his might at our intrusion, and that he could not quietly and comfortably let off his fire-arms at Nimeguen, as he had done ever since Marr's murder, out of his own little back window at Paddington or Dalston. It was not an easy matter to explain to him the nature of his misdemeanor, or to convince him afterwards that there was any harm in it. The landlady scolded in Dutch, the garçon jabbered in French, the serjeant of the guard threatened and swore in all the languages he could muster, whilst the Cockney bounced and blustered in bad English, that he was a free-born Briton, and so forth, and had a right to let off pistols all over the world. The squabble ran so high, that our countryman stood a fair chance, I was told, of a night's lodging in the guard-house, but at length the matter was adjusted by his being mulcted, ostensibly in default of having a license to carry arms, in a sum, which, of course, was spent in schnapps at the canteen. Moreover, he had an intimation that the damaged door would certainly appear amongst the items of his bill, and in Holland travellers' bills are anything but "easy beakers."* Finally, he had to endure from his fellow-tourists all the maledictions and reproaches to be expected from persons subjected to that severest of trials of temper, the being waked out of a first sleep, especially when having to start by an early steamer allows no time for a second one. As thunder turns small beer, the untimely explosions had soured the whole mass of the milk of human kindness—every word that fell was like an acidulated drop, and having literally clothed the devoted Cockney with curses, as with a garment, the mob of nightcaps retired to their pillows, and

   " "We left him alone in his glory."

I was rather curious to observe what sort of countenance the author of the disturbance would wear the next morning; but when he made his appearance amongst us on board the steamer, instead of looking chop-fallen or abashed, there was such an appearance of complacent self-satisfaction in his face, as convinced me, that on his return to London he would brag of his noisy exploit at Nimeguen, to his comrades of Walbrook or Lothbury, as "a famous rumpus." I am afraid such exhibitions are but too common with Cockney travellers, who persist in perverting the end of the old adage, "When

---

* In the "Orbis Pictus," a Dutch-built polyglott school-book, birds of the *soft-billed* kind are rendered into English as "*easy beakers*."

you are at Rome," &c., into "Do as you do at home." But
remember I am far from intending to apply the term Cockney
exclusively to the native of our own metropolis, who, if the
whole horizon were canvas, would turn it into a panorama of
London. Perhaps there are no more finished *badauds* extant
than your French ones, of whatever rank, who fancy that
the whole world is in France, and that all France is in Paris.

On reviewing the motley company on board, I was sorry
to note the absence of the red and yellow faced men, the
Mustard and Pepper that had hitherto served me for condi-
ments. But, for the present, the amusement was to be
furnished by a member of our own party. My aunt, as you
ought to know, is a simple, gentle creature, timid and helpless even for a woman, but as strong in her affections as weak
in her nerves. In a word she resembles Chaucer's Prioress,
who was "all conscience and tender heart." To this character
she owes most of her travelling adventures, one of which I
must now describe,—but under the seal of secrecy, for it is
as sore a subject, with her, as the victorious *phoca* to Hector
M'Intyre in the "Antiquary." Next to her standing regret
for "poor George," it is one of her stock troubles that she is
not a mother, and like some hens in the same predicament,
she is sure to cluck and cover the first chick that comes in
her way. To her great delight, therefore, she discovered
amongst the company a smart, dapper, brisk, well-favoured
little fellow, with long flaxen ringlets, curling down his back,
—a boy apparently about eight years old,—a great deal too
young, in her opinion, to be sent travelling, and especially
by water, under nobody's care but his own. Such a shameful
neglect, as she called it, appealed directly to her pity, and
made her resolve to be quite a parent to the forlorn little
foreigner. Accordingly, she lavished on him a thousand
motherly attentions, which at first seemed to amuse and

gratify her *protégé*, though he afterwards received them with
an ill grace enough. Still she persevered, womanlike, in
bestowing her tenderness on its object, however ungrateful
the return—indulging, from time to time, in strictures on
Dutch fathers and mothers, and their management of children,
in a language which, fortunately, was not the current one
of the place. At last, to raise her indignation to the climax,
she saw her adopted urchin betake himself to practices which
she scarcely tolerated in children of a larger growth. "It
was quite folly enough," she said, "to have dressed up a boy
like a man, without teaching him or at least allowing him to
imitate grown-up habits :—for instance, smoking tobacco—
and, as I live," she almost screamed, "the little wretch is
going to drink a glass of Dutch gin !" Such a sight upset
all her patience—

> "To be precocious
> *In schnapps* she reckoned was a sin atrocious."

But as a temperance exhortation in an unknown tongue
could be of no possible use, she appealed at once, like some
of our Chartists, to physical force, and made a determined
snatch at the devoted dram. This was a mortal affront to
the long-haired manikin, who resisted with all his might and
mane, and being wonderfully strong for his age, there ensued
a protracted struggle, that afforded infinite amusement to
the company on deck. My aunt tugged, and hauled, and
scolded in hissing English—the little fellow scuffled and
kicked, and spluttered abundance of guttural German,
proving, amongst his other accomplishments, that he was not
at all backward in his swearing. Temperance, however,
gained her point, by spilling the obnoxious liquor; and in
revenge, the manikin vented his spleen by throwing the
empty glass into the Rhine. So far all was well. My aunt

had fought triumphantly for what she considered her duty, and a great principle ; but her satisfaction was doomed to be short-lived. My uncle, who had watched the fray with unequivocal signs and sounds of amazement, could not help congratulating the victorious party on such an unusual exertion of spirit, and its signal success, for the defeated urchin had rushed off to digest his discomfiture in the fore-cabin. "Not," said my uncle, "that I'm one of your wishy-washy tea-totallers ; but a colt's a colt, and what is fit drink for a strong man may be a bad draught for a boy." "I ax pardon, sare," interposed our conducteur, who had been one of the heartiest laughers, at the skirmish, "bot de leetle gentleman is not von boy—he is ein zwerg—vat you call von kleines mannchen."—"I suppose," cried my uncle, "you mean a dwarf?"—"Ja! ja! von dwarf," answered the con-ducteur, "he have nine-und-zwanzig jahrs of old." Imagine, dear Gerard, the effect of such an announcement on a shrinking delicate female, with sensitive feelings, nearly akin to prudishness, like my poor aunt! I confess I felt some anxiety as to the direction of her first impulse. Providen-tially, however, instead of urging her to jump overboard, it only impelled her to rush down below, where we found her in the pavilion, struggling, by Martha's help, with the hysterics, and fervently wishing, between her sobs, that she had never—never—never left Woodlands. She had not only let herself down, she considered, but all her sex ; and espe-cially her own countrywomen. "What could the foreigners think," she asked, "of an English lady, and above all, a widow, scuffling like a great masculine romp or hoyden with a strange man, no matter for his littleness—what can they say of me—oh! what *can* they say ?"—"Why, as for that matter, Kate," answered my uncle, playing the comforter, "whatever they say of you will be said in a foreign lingo, so

you are sure to hear nothing disagreeable." "But it's what
they will think," persisted the afflicted fair one. "Phoo !
phoo !" said my uncle, "they will only think that you fought
very like a woman, or you would have chosen a fairer match."
But the mourner was not to be soothed with words ; nor,
indeed, by any thing short of engaging the pavilion for her,
as a *locus penitentiœ,* where she could bewail her error, and
her shame, under lock and key. "I'll tell you what it is,
Frank," said my uncle, after we had enjoyed a hearty laugh
together, out of my aunt's hearing, "it must never be named
to poor Kate,—but from this time forward I shall think that
little Gulliver and his nurse Glumdalstitch was not such an
out-of-the-way story after all ! "

I subsequently learned, that the little manikin in the
steamer was a great man at Elberfield, in the cotton line ;
and our conducteur forewarned me, that I should probably
meet with several copies of this pocket edition of the human
species in the Rhenish provinces, and particularly two
brothers, born at Coblenz. It is singular that the empire
has been equally prolific in natural and supernatural dwarfs.
To Germany our show caravans and Lilliputian exhibitions
have been indebted for many of their most remarkable
pigmies ; whilst imps, elfins, little gray men, "and such
small deer," literally swarm in its romantic mythology ;—a
coincidence I humbly submit to the speculations of our
philosophers.

At Lobith we reached the frontier, and passed from the
guardianship of the Triton, or John Dory, or Stock-fish, or
whatever else is the Dutch tutelary Emblem, under the
protecting wings of the Black Eagle, which we soon saw
displayed, in the attitude of a bird of prey on a barn-door.
Our passports were consequently in requisition at Emmerich,
the first Prussian town, and led to a scene on the part of

our Hypochondriac, which he had already rehearsed at
Nimeguen. Accordingly, to the request for the document,
he quietly answered that there was no need. "But, sare,
you shall go to Cologne," said the conducteur. "Sir, I
shall do no such thing," retorted my uncle with some
asperity, as if arguing the point with old Truby himself.
"Sare, as you please," returned the conducteur, with the
national shrug and grimace; "but you must not go by de
Preussich frontière wizzout de visé." "My good fellow,"
said my uncle, smiling gravely, "I am going beyond the
great frontier of all, and where your King of Prussia can't
stop me, with all his police, and his army to boot." "Teufel!
vere is dat?" exclaimed the German, astounded by this
apparent denial of the power of an absolute monarch. "It's
another and a better world," said my uncle, solemnly, and
with a shake of the head that, like Lord Burleigh's, was a
homily in itself: "and mark my words, sir, I shall be there
before night." It was now time to interfere; and, by dint
of expostulation, I obtained the paper. "Well, Frank,
there it is,—but, mind, it's a dead letter. Do what you
like with it, only don't let me be troubled with any such
worldly formalities again."

Apropos de bottes—our conducteur, a shrewd fellow, with a
taste for humour, told me he had seen a passport the day
before, wherein the bearer described himself as a "man of
property," and, by way of giving weight to the document, it
was indorsed by the Right Honourable the Lord Mayor of
London, and one or two of the Aldermen. What a characteristic trait of a moneyed Cit on his travels!

Whilst our papers were under the inspection of the police,
the familiars of another inquisition boarded the vessel, and
commenced their function. They conducted themselves very
civilly; but it would be bad policy indeed, at the threshold

of a grand and profitable exhibition—and such is the Rhine
—to allow vistors to be disgusted by any official rudeness at
the threshold. The search, therefore, was politely strict, but
nothing objectionable was discovered, except a certain bale of
Dutch linen, at which the officers made a dead set. I was
about to interpose on behalf of the owner, when her maid
resolutely undertook the defence. The holland, she said,
was honestly come by and paid for, and belonged to her
mistress. " Bot it is goods for a tax," said the officer. " It's
no such thing," said Martha, positively, and becoming unconsciously an advocate for free trade ; " the Dutch charged
no taxes on it, and it stands to reason it can't be taxed in
Germany." " You shall see de boke," said the officer,—" you
know vat is a tariff ?" " It's a fiddlestick," retorted Martha,
waxing angry. " It is de Yarman Commercial Leg," said the
douanier. " Leg or no leg," replied the championess, " it's
not going to walk off with my missis's property." " Why for,
den, you not declare it ?" asked the officer ; whereupon the
maid declared she knew nothing about declarations. " If you
seize the linen, you shall seize me," said she, and suiting the
action to the word, she seated herself on the bale with the
dignity of a Lord Chancellor, the fountain of all equity, on
nis woolsack. The officers looked puzzled and undecided how
to act, when they were fortunately relieved from the dilemma
by a personage who had hitherto taken no more notice of the
matter than if he had literally done with the things of this
world. "Martha, ask my sister to step here." Up jumped
the unconscious maid to perform this errand ; but her back
was no sooner turned, than, pointing to the linen, my uncle
addressed the douaniers ; " Take it, gentlemen, and welcome.
It is heartily at your service, to make into shirts or towelling,
or whatever you or your wives think proper." The officers
stared and seemed to doubt the purport of this speech, till I

translated it into the best German I could muster. Then
they stared still more, as if thinking, not without reason, that
Englishmen are very droll people ; but suddenly recollecting
themselves, they made a low bow, first to my uncle, then
another to me, and then, without a word, handed the bale
over the side, and took their departure. "I'll tell you what
it is, Frank," said my uncle, "many persons in such a case
would have stood out, but in the first place we have got rid
of a great incumbrance, and in the second place, before it got
to Woodlands, the Dutch linen would have cost more than
double its worth. Above all, its being seized will be a
comfort to your aunt. Yes, you may laugh, but there's
nothing in life so good for a fretful person as a real vexation.
That's my remark ; and take my word for it, for a week to
come, Kate will be far more angry with the King of Prussia,
than troubled about poor George."

But, however right in his theory, my uncle found himself
mistaken as to the conductor that was to carry off the shock.
The moment Martha returned, and discovered that she had .
been robbed, like a hen off her eggs, she set up a clamour
that could only be silenced by her master's acknowledgment
of his own share in the transaction. Big with this fact, she
ran back to her mistress, and when we afterwards dined in
the pavilion, for my aunt declined appearing at the *table-
d'hôte*, she did not fail to bring her Dutch cloth on the table.
"It was hard enough," she said, "to be disappointed, in what
she did for the best, without the pain of owing it to her
own brother's cruel connivance." Her own brother looked a
little foolish at this remark, and had she been content with
her advantage, would have probably been worsted, but when
she went on to charge him with ingratitude, seeing that the
beautiful Dutch linen was intended for a new set of shirts
for himself, his constitutional infirmity supplied him with a

defence. "Well, well, Kate, let bygones be bygones. What is done is done, and it's no use taking it to heart. And besides, Kate," he added, quite seriously, "you have one comfort, and that is, if the Dutch linen was to be made into shirts for me, I should never, you know, have lived to wear 'em."

To borrow a phrase that fell from the Cockney, "the steam-boat passes a night on board" between Nimeguen and Cologne, and in the interim the passengers sleep as they may or can, without any accommodation for the purpose. In default of a berth, a *corner* is the best resting-place; but to obtain such a nook I had to dispossess a score of German pipes. Here I dozed, sitting, till towards morning, when methought a bell began to ring, the paddles stopped, and the vessel brought up with a jolt against something hard. Some dozen of outlandish figures, in fancy caps, immediately roused up, and, each selecting a pipe, groped their way out of the dingy atmosphere of the cabin, where as many other shapes, some still more foreign, and every one armed with a meerschaum, as speedily filled their places. The bell rang a second time, the paddles revolved, the vibration recommenced, my eyes closed again, and when they opened to the daylight I was told that we had stopped and exchanged some of our live stock at Düsseldorf.

A few of the bipeds we had obtained by this transaction were, as to costume, extremely grotesque. One of them, a short, squat, vulgar-looking personage, particularly attracted my uncle's notice. "In the name of wonder, Frank, what can that long-haired fellow be?—the one yonder in the black velvet cap, with a notch cut out of the brim, like a barber's basin." "I suspect," said I, "he is a painter, or would-be painter, from Düsseldorf; that cap is an imitation of Raphael's, and the great hat near it is a copy of Rubens's."

E

My uncle received this intelligence with a "Humph." All kinds of foppery are his especial aversion, and he did not conceal his disgust. "Painters, indeed! Take my word for it, Frank, they are rank daubers. It's my notion that people who are so full of themselves are always empty of everything else. As for their Raffaele and Rubens hats, I'd back a common London house-painter agin them in his paper cap. No, no, Frank; a man that makes such an exhibition of himself will never cut a figure at Somerset House."

In the meantime, these young masters strutted about as complacently as if they had really rivalled the old ones by an "Assumption" and a "Transfiguration." The Raffael-esque hero, in particular, had arranged his *chevelure* so elaborately after that of Sanzio, as to prove that, if not other-wise skilful, he could handle a hair-brush. But the thing was a profanation; and I could not help favouring the brace of Burschen with a mental apostrophe.—"Gentlemen, instead of dressing after Rubens and Raffaele, you ought to have gone naked long before them—in the savage ages, gentlemen, when you might at once have exercised your art, and gratified your personal vanity, by painting your own bodies."

That vented me; and now, Gerard, for fear of mistakes, please to turn to the noble work on Modern German Art, by the Count Athanasius Raczynski, and there you will find that Düsseldorf can turn out painters, and good ones too, as well as lay figures.

Now, then, methinks you cry, for Cologne;—but my hand is tired, and my pen is worn out, and I must reserve that ancient city (it smells high, but it will keep) for another letter. All love to Emily, from, dear Gerard, yours very truly,

FRANK SOMERVILLE.

P.S.—You remember Grundy, not the celebrated old lady of that name, but our school-fellow at Harrow. He has just put up at our hotel on his way homewards, full of grumbling and grievances, and anathematising the Rhinelanders for having "extorted" him. Right or wrong, his indignation has turned his complaint into verse, and here follows a copy of what Mr. Grundy says of the natives :—

YE Tourists and Travellers, bound to the Rhine,
Provided with passport, that requisite docket,
First listen to one little whisper of mine—
Take care of your pocket !—take care of your pocket !

Don't wash or be shaved—go like hairy wild men,
Play dominoes, smoke, wear a cap, and smock-frock it,
But if you speak English, or look it, why then—
Take care of your pocket !—take care of your pocket !

You'll sleep at great inns, in the smallest of beds,
Find charges as apt to mount up as a rocket,
With thirty per cent. as a tax on your heads,—
Take care of your pocket !—take care of your pocket !

You'll see old Cologne,—not the sweetest of towns,—
Wherever you follow your nose you will shock it ;
And you'll pay your three dollars to look at three crowns,—
Take care of your pocket !—take care of your pocket !

You'll count seven Mountains, and see Roland's Eck,
Hear legends veracious as any by Crockett ;
But oh ! to the tone of romance what a check,—
Take care of your pocket !—take care of your pocket !

Old Castles you'll see on the vine-covered hill,—
Fine ruins to rivet the eye in its socket—
Once haunts of Baronial Banditti, and still—
Take care of your pocket!—take care of your pocket!

You'll stop at Coblenz, with its beautiful views,
But make no long stay with your money to stock it,
Where Jews are all Germans, and Germans all Jews,—
Take care of your pocket!—take care of your pocket?

A Fortress you'll see, which, as people report,
Can never be captured, save famine should block it—
Ascend Ehrenbreitstein—but that's not their *forte*,—
Take care of your pocket!—take care of your pocket!

You'll see an old man who'll let off an old gun,
And Lurley, with her hurly-burly, will mock it;
But think that the words of the echo thus run,—
Take care of your pocket!—take care of your pocket!

You'll gaze on the Rheingau, the soil of the Vine!
Of course you will freely Moselle it and Hock it—
P'raps purchase some pieces of Humbugheim wine—
Take care of your pocket!—take care of your pocket!

Perchance you will take a frisk off to the Baths—
Where some to their heads hold a pistol and cock it;
But still mind the warning, wherever your paths—
Take care of your pocket!—take care of your pocket!

And Friendships you'll swear, most eternal of pacts,
Change rings, and give hair to be put in a locket;
But still, in the most sentimental of acts—
Take care of your pocket!—take care of your pocket!

In short, if you visit that stream or its shore,
Still keep at your elbow one caution to knock it,
And where Schinderhannes was Robber of yore,—
Take care of your pocket!—take care of your pocket!

TO REBECCA PAGE, AT THE WOODLANDS, NEAR BECKENHAM, KENT.

DEAR BECKY,

  This is to say we ar all safe and well, tho' it's a wunder, for forrin traveling is like a deceatful luvver, witch don't improve on acquaintance. Wat haven't I gone thro since my last faver! Fust morbust by bad Dutch warter, and then frited to deth at Nim Again with a false alarm of the Frentch, besides a dredful could, ketched by leaving my warm bed, and no time to clap on a varsal thing, xcept my best cap. Well, I've give three warnins, and the next, as master says, will be for good, even if I have to advertize for a plaice, but ketch me sayin no objexshuns to go abroad. Not but Missis have had her own trials, but that's between our two selves, for she wouldn't like it to git about that she have had a pitcht battel with a dwarft for a glass of gin. Then there's the batterd brass pale, and the Holland—only think, Becky, of the bewtiful Dutch linnin being confisticated by the Custom-house Cæsars! It was took up for dutis at the Garman outskirts. But, as I tould the officers, the King of Garmany ortn't to think only of the dutis dew to himself, but of his dutis towards his nabers. The Prushian customs is very bad customs, that's certin. Everything that's xported into the country must pay by wait, witch naterally falls most heviest on the litest pusses. There's dress. Rich fokes can go in spidder nets and gossumers, and fine gorses, but pore

peple must ware thick stuffs and gingums, and all sorts of
corse and doreable texters, and so the hard workin class cum
to be more taxt than the upper orders, with their flimsy
habbits.   The same with other yuseful artikels.   Wat's a
silvur tooth-pick in wait compared with a kitching poker, or
a filligre goold watch to an 8 day clock.   Howsumever, the
Dutch linnin was confisticated in spite of my teeth, for
Master chose to giv up the pint, and he desarves to go
without a Shurt for his panes.

Amung other discomfits, there's no beds in the vessles up
the Rind.   So, for too hole days, we have been damp shifted
as they call it, without taking off our close, and, as you may
supose, I am tired of steeming.   Our present stop is at
Colon.   They say its a verry old citty, and bilt by the
Romans, and sure enuff Roman noses didn't easily turn up.
The natives must have verry strong oilfactories, that's certin.
O, Becky, sich sniffs and guffs, in spite of my stuft hed!
This mornin it raind cats and dogs, but the heviest showrs
cant pourify the place.   It's enuff to fumigate a pleg.   Won
thing is the bad smells obleege strangers to buy the O de
Colon, and praps the stenchis is encouraged on that account.
The wust is, wen you want a bottel of the rite sort, theres so
menny Farinacious impostors, and Johns and Marias, you
don't know witch is him or her.

Colon is full of Sites.   The principle is the Cathedrul, and
by rites theres a Crane pearcht on the tiptop, like the Storks
in Holland; but I was out of luck, or he was off a feeding, for
he wasnt there.   So we went into the Interium witch was
performing Hi Mass, that's to say, me and one of the hottel
waiters, who is playing the civel, and I can onely say its enuff
to turn one's hed.   Wat with the lofty pillers, and the picters
and the gelding and the calving, I felt perfeckly dizzy, but
wen the sushin came rainbowin thro the panted glass winders,

Four-in-hand.

and the organ played up, and the Quire of singers with their
hevinly v'iccs, and the Priest was insensed with the perfumery,
down I went, willy nilly, on both nees, and was amost con-
troverted into a Cathlick afore I knowed were I was! Luckly,
I rekollected Transmigration, witch I cant nor wont believe
in, and that jumpt me up agin on my legs. Next, we see
a prodigus chest, all of sollid Goold, and when you look
through a little grating, you see the empty skulls of the wise
kings. They're as brown as mogany, with crowns on, and
their christian names ritten in rubbies, if so be it ant red
glass. For they do say, wen the Munks run away from the
Frentch they took the goold chest, and the three wunderful
wise heds, along with them, and sackreligiously pickt out the
best part of the volubles and jowls. As another piece of
profannity, the hart of Mary de Medicine is left under a
grave stone, in the church pavement—but where the rest of
her boddy have been boddy snatcht to noboddy nose.

The next site was certinly an uncommon one—a church
chock full of the relicks of morality. I over heard Mr.
Frank say, its praps the chastist stile of arkitecter in the
world. Howsomver, its full of the Skellitons of Saint Ursulus
and Elevin Thowsend Old Maids. Their bones are stuck in
the scaling, and into the walls, and under the flore, and into
glass cases, — its nuthin but bones, bones, bones. But no
wunder there was so menny spinsters afore time, considering
that now-a-days they're tied down to won chance, namely, a
Cathlick sweat-hart. Wat do you think, Becky, of three
hundred yung wimmin, onely the tother day, binding their
selves, by a solum act and deed, in black and wite, never to
marry any yung man as is Reformed? Theres a pretty way
to cause everlastin seperations, instead of mattermony,
between the male and female sects! And as for the marrid
alreddy, theyre to take an affidavid that every Babby they

have shall be brought up a Pappist ! Wat can cum of such
a derangement but unlegitimit constructions and domestic
squabblings.   If anny thing can interdeuce discomfiture
betwixt man and wife, its religus biggamy—I shuld have
said Biggotry, but they boath sound the same.   For my own .
parts, insted of objectin to a Cathlic, I should feel my
Christian deuty to embrace him, as praps the happy Instrument under Grace of making him a convict.   But enuff of
Saints Ursulus and her Elevin Thowsend Old Maids.   Onely
among other curosities, there was the identicle stone jarr as
held the warter as was turned into wine at the marridge
in Galilee—an odd thing, thinks I, to show up a Weddin
Relict along with so menny marters to Single blessidness.
But arter all, the real mirakle, praps, is to see so menny
single peple in a mob.

Next to fine sites, Colon swarms with raggid misrable
objects, but I'm sorry I can't stop to shock you with them,
being wanted to pack up.   You know what that is with a
figitty Missis, who is never happy xcept she's corded up over
night, and on a porter's back in the morning.   To-morrow
youl find us on the map of Coblense.   I did hope we had
dun with steeming, and were to go Dilligently by land ; but
after seeing the Male cum in, Master declined.   Sure enuff,
the coatch is divided into three cages, and catch me tra-
velin, says he, in a wild Beast carrivan.   Besides, says
he, if the leaders chuse to be misleaders, we are shure
to be over a precipus, for its a deal esier, says he, for the
horsis to pull us down, then for the Postylion to pull 'em up,
But sich is forrin traveling—as regards sarvants—if you an't
drownded, yure broken neckt, without any advantage to
yureself.   But I've fully maid up my mind, that the fust
axident shall be a thurow split and a rupter, and a break off
of evry thing between me and Missis.   Lord nose I'm willin

Tom Pipes.

I do beseech you play upon this pipe.

to live and die for her, but not to have a put out sholder or a fractious leg.

Give my love to Cook, and to Peggy, and to John Futman, not forgettin Mister Butler up at the Hall—and tell them my Hart is in its old place, in spite of a change of sitivation. With the same sentimint towards yureself, I remane, dear Becky, yure luving Frend,

MARTHA PENNY.

Poscrip.—Don't go to supose any think partickler betwixt me and the Vally de Sham de place. To be shure, he did try to talk luve nonsinse in broken English, and asked me how I shud like a Germin man. Man means husband in their languidge. But as I tould him there was two grate objckshuns. Praps youre a Lutherin, says he. No, says I, I'm a Cristian, but it an't that—my scruples is irreligious. What's them, says he. Why, then, says I, its backer and garlick. And it aut pleasant to have a sweathart as can't come nigh won without yure being fumigatid. So my gentilman took miff—but wheres the true luve if a luver won't give up a nasty puffy habbit?

TO DOCTOR TRUBY, BECKENHAM, KENT.

DEAR DOCTOR,

As the post-mark will show, wo are at Cologne, whereby you have won the Hock wine, and I think I see you on the broad grin, and cracking your finger joints. . Well, let those laugh that win. It was a very near thing, and you all but lost ten times over. Not to name other warnings by land and sea, there was Nimeguen, so near a finish, that I

was dead and gone up to the knees. But that you won't
believe, or at least you won't own to it.   But I am no
Methuselah for all that.   It's my firm belief I shall never go
out of Cologne alive.   What signifies a man's eating, and
drinking, and sleeping ?   All one's nourishment goes for
nothing, if once sudden death has got insidiously into the
system.   My stamina is gone.   My constitution broke up a
matter of six years ago ; and as for my organs and functions,
they're not worth a straw.   You know that as well as I do,
but because I haven't exactly got apoplexy or epilepsy, or
atrophy, or any of your regulation diseases, you won't allow
me to have anything at all.   Mayhap, it's a new case, or a
complication of all the old ones, and beyond medical skill.
That's my own impression, but I needn't repeat the symptoms,
for you never could or would enter into my inward feelings.
We shall see which is right.   There was poor Bromley, with
much such a complaint as mine—nobody believed *he* was
going till he was gone, and it's my notion some people had
their doubts even then.

Regarding our foreign travels, you will hear all about them
from Bagster, excepting the night-bólt, which is at the
bottom of the river Rhine.   The very first time I tried it,
there was a night alarm in the hotel, and between a new-
fangled article and the dark, I might have been burnt or
suffocated in my bed-chamber before I could unscrew myself
out.   So much for what, by your leave, I call your Infernal
Machine.

As yet, I have not seen much of Cologne.   I did try one
or two strolls by myself, with one of the church-steeples for
a guide ; but what with the loftiness of the houses, and the
narrowness and crookedness of the streets, I soon lost my
landmark, and came to so many faults and checks, that I
never went out but I lost myself like a Babe in the Wood,

and had to be showed home by a little boy. That has put
an end to my rambles for the present, for I can't bring my
mind to the foreign fashion of going about with a lacquey-de-
place at my heels, like a mad gentleman and his keeper. But
I learned from my walks that Cologne has no Paving Board,
nor Commissioners of Sewers. Every yard you go is like
winding a pole-cat, and the roads are paved with rough
stones, where the horses skate and slip about, on shoes as
high-heeled as Queen Bess's. I happened to see one going
to be shod in the Beast Market, and it was a sight to draw
old Joe Bradley's eyes out of his head. By what I've seen of
the German cattle, they are far from remarkable for spirit or
vice, though, to judge by the blacksmith's contrivances, you
would suppose the whole breed was by Beelzebub, out of the
Devil's Dam. There was the horse, what you or I should
call a Quaker's nag, shut in a cage like a wild beast, with
a wooden bar to keep his head up, and another to keep it
down, and a bar over his back, in case of his rearing, and one
under his belly, to prevent his lying down, and a bar or
chain behind him, to hinder his lashing out. If all that
ceremony is fit and proper, thought I, — for one of our
English farriers to take a horse's hoof into his lap, mayhap a
young spicy colt, without a bar, or a chain, or anything, can
be nothing else but a tempting of Providence.

I have seen the famous Cathedral, which is a fine building,
but not half finished, and as such, an uncomfortable sight,
for it looks like a broken promise to God. But they do say
the King of Prussia is very anxious to complete it, which,
being a Protestant, is a liberal feeling on his part, and deserved
a better return from the Catholic Archbishop of Cologne than
flying in the face of his Majesty, who, by what I hear, gives
fair play to both religions. The more pity he was led to act
harshly by his Jewish subjects, and point them out by law for

mockery and ill-usage, even to forbidding them the use of
Christian names; for, as I was told by a Jewish gentleman
from Coblence, they were obliged to call their children after
the Heathens and Pagans—Diana, and Flora, and Cerberus,
and so forth, just like so many hounds.   The very worst way
in the world to make a Jewish father or mother say as Agrippa
did, " Almost thou persuadest me to be a Christian."

From the Cathedral we went to St. Peter's Church, where
I had a warning.   But on that subject, as I said before, I
shall hold hard, though it was a serious one for all that, and
decidedly apoplectic.   On my way home I looked in at several
Catholic places of worship.   In most of them service was
going on, in which I joined, for although it was a foreign
tongue, I felt it was in praise of the Almighty, just as well as
I knew that the music was a psalm tune and not a jig.
Thank God, Popery is none of my bugbears.   I am not like
old Mrs. Twisleton of Beckenham, who never closed her eyes
for a week after Catholic Emancipation, for fear of being con-
verted in her sleep.   To my thinking, it's too late in the day
for a Guy Faux or a Bloody Mary.   If we ever see a bonfire
in Smithfield, it will be to roast an ox whole, and not a martyr.
On the contrary, it's my firm belief that an *auto da fé* now-
a-days would be called a burning shame by the Papists themselves.   Roasting martyrs has gone by, as well as drowning of
witches ; and when one fashion is expected to turn up again,
it's time for our old women to quake in their shoes for fear of
the other.   However, some folks think otherwise, and are as
panic-struck by their own fancies as old Farmer Phillpotts,
who was well-nigh scared to death, one moonshiny night, by
a scarecrow made out of his own old clothes.   So in one of
the churches here I met with a fellow-traveller who came over
by the Lord Melville, a hot-tempered man, with a face as
red all over as Carbuncle's nose, and a mighty broil he was in

when the priests and singing-boys came past us in procession, with their candle-sticks and banners—"There," said he; "there's pomps and vanities, as we say in our Catechism; there's mummery! there's a gabble for you," when the priest began his Latin prayers. By-and-by a bell rang, and that sent him into a fresh tantrum. "What on earth has a little muffin-bell to do with religion?" Next, the priest held up the glory, or whatever it is called, which set the red-face pulling as many wry mouths as if it had been a bottle of horse physic. At last I fairly expected to see him go into convulsions like a mad dog, for he got a sprinkle of the holy water on his coat sleeve, but he brushed it off in as great a hurry as if it had been drops of vitriol. "Renounce me," says he, "if I can put up with it!" and off he flounced into the aisle, which only made matters worse. "Here's more of their humbug," says he pointing up at a black board that was hung to a pillar, and covered all over with little legs, and arms, and hands, and feet, in wax-work. "All miraculous cures, of course," says he; "but mayhap, sir, you believe in miracles? I don't, and no more did my father before me; and what's more, sir, he wouldn't have knelt down with a Papist on the same pavement—he wouldn't to save his soul." As that was a lash out at me, I spoke up, and made bold to ask if he approved of family worship? "I hope I do," said he, "we have it at home every night of our lives." "Because," said I, "it's my notion that all Christians are of one family, and as such, I can't understand how a friend to family worship can want to narrow the circle by shutting out any of his relations. To my mind Christianity was meant to be represented by our good old Christmas dinners, where we tried to assemble all that belonged to us round one hospitable board, down to our nineteenth cousins. Mayhap, I'm not quite orthodox," said I, "but I'm sincere, for they're the sentiments

F

of a dying man." Well, it will be a laugh against me down at
Beckenham, but you must have the end of the story.   At last,
from one thing to another, we got to high words in a whisper,
when up comes a beadle, or verger, or policeman, or somebody
in authority, and, not understanding English, takes quite the
wrong side of the case.   It's my belief, that, finding the other
party the warmest of the two in his looks, and the highest in his
voice, he thought he was defending instead of attacking the
Catholic religion,—whereby showing the red-faced fellow into
a seat right in front of the altar, he civilly beckoned, and
signed, and wheedled me down the aisle, and then fairly
bowed and scraped me out of the church-door.

To tell the truth, Doctor, standing, as one may say, on the
brink of the grave, and only comforted by a firm belief in my
own persuasion, it shocks me to find men putting so little
faith in the steadfastness and durability of their own church.
It's surely a melancholy thing, but, as we see at Exeter Hall
and elsewhere, those that most cry up Protestantism, and its
truth, and beauty, and reasonableness, and excellence, and its
being built of the solidest of all foundations, the rock of the
Gospel itself, are the most down-hearted and desponding about
its case.   Instead of trusting to its own nature, or to Providence to support it, they go about crying that Protestantism
is in danger, and, forsooth! give it over, just because, by
their own accounts, it has the best constitution, namely, a
divine one,—the best climate, namely, England,—the best
diet, namely, the reading of the Bible,—the best exercise,
namely, missionaries and itineranting,—the best physicians,
namely, Archbishops and Bishops,—the best apothecaries,
namely, poor curates,—the best nurses, namely, the speechifiers themselves,—and the blessing of God to boot.   Now, in
my humble opinion, a Christian man ought to put some
confidence in the virtue of his religion, as well as in his wife's;

for it's paying but a sorry compliment to either to be always expecting them to be corrupted and seduced—and what's worse, corrupted and seduced by an ill-favoured, misbegotten monster, as the speechifiers themselves paint his portrait, as ugly as Buckhorse.

To return to ourselves, in my own state of health there is no amendment, but, as you know in your own heart, there was none to be looked for. I have only been sent up the river Rhine, as other patients in a desperate way are packed off to Madeira, that their funerals may not rise up against their Doctors. My sister Kate, as usual, talks of not surviving poor George; but as yet, I am glad to say, shows no constitutional symptoms of going after him. As for my Nephew, he is well and hearty, and enjoys his foreign travelling so much, I am quite grieved for his sake, poor fellow, to reflect how soon and suddenly it may be brought to a close. But after all, our life below is only a tour that ends by returning to the earth from whence we came. As such, I have reached my own last resting place, and whenever you hear of the city of Cologne, I feel sure, dear Doctor, you will remember your old and very faithful friend,

RICHARD ORCHARD.

P.S—.The medicine-chest you took such a spite at was left behind in a hurry at Rotterdam, and never missed till last night, when I wanted a tea-spoonful of magnesia. I hope and trust I shall be able to get medicine in Germany; but Frank says, if their physics are like their metaphysics, a horse oughn't to take them without good advice.

TO GERARD BROOKE, ESQ.

My dear Gerard,

To borrow the appropriate style of a bulletin of health, " our Hypochondriac has passed a bad night, but is free from fever, and hopes are entertained of his speedy convalescence."

The truth is, this morning we were rather alarmed by the prolonged absence of the head of the family. The breakfast appeared—the tea was made, and stood till it was cold—but no uncle. As he is naturally an early riser, this circumstance excited, first surprise, then anxiety, and then apprehension. My aunt looked astonished, serious, and at last terrified, lest her brother fulfilling his own prophecy, should have really departed in earnest. In the end, I became nervous myself, and took the liberty of entering the bed-chamber of the absentee, when a sight presented itself which I cannot now recall without laughing.

Imagine my worthy uncle lying broad awake, on his back, in a true German bedstead—a sort of wooden box or trough, so much too short for him, that his legs extended half-a-yard beyond it on either side of the foot-board. Above him, on his chest and stomach, from his chin to his knees, lay a huge squab or cushion, covered with a gay-patterned chintz, and ornamented at each corner with a fine tassel,—looking equally handsome, glossy, cold, and uncomfortable. For fear of deranging this article, he could only turn his eyes towards me as I entered, and when he spoke, it was with a voice that seemed weak and broken from exhaustion. " Frank, I've passed a miserable night," Not a doubt of it, thought I, with a glance at his accommodations. " I haven't—slept—a

A Spare Bed on the Rhine.

wink." Of course not (mentally). "Did you ever see such
a thing as that?" with a slight nod and roll of his eyes
towards the cushion. I shook my head. "If I moved—it
fell off; and if I didn't, I got—the cramp." Here a sort of
suppressed groan. "Frank,—I've only turned once—all
night long." I ventured to suggest that he would have done
well to kick off the incumbrance on purpose, and the words
had hardly left my lips when off flew the variegated cushion
to the floor. The action seemed to relieve him, as if it had
actually removed a weight from his bosom : he drew a long
breath, and raised himself up on his elbow. " You're right,
Frank ; I've been a fool, sure enough—but that comes of
foreign customs one never met with before ; I suppose poor
Kate was scared by my not coming down ?" I nodded assent.
"Yes—I shall go that way, some day, no doubt. Why, these
beds are enough to kill one. It's impossible to sleep in 'em
—but it's my suspicion the Germans sit up smoking all night.
Anyhow, I'll stake my head there's not such a thing as a
slug-a-bed in the whole country."

As he now showed an inclination to rise, I left him for
the breakfast-table, where he soon joined us ; and when he
was seated, and had buttered his roll, he returned to the
subject. "Frank, I've been thinking over the sleeping
business, and my mind's made up. Take my word for it,
the German beds are at the bottom of the German stories.
They're all full of hobgoblin work and devilry, as if a man
had written them after bad dreams. Since last night I
think I could make up a German romancical story myself,
like 'the Devil and Dr. Faustus.' I'm convinced I should
have had the horrors, and no need to eat a raw-pork supper
neither, like Mr. What's-his-name, the painter ;—that's to
say, provided I could only have gone to sleep. There's
that outlandish cushion on your stomach—to my mind it's

a pillion—it's nothing but a pillion for the nightmare to sit
upon." "And then," chimed in my aunt, "the foreign
bedsteads are so very short—to stretch yourself is out of
the question. Besides, mine was quite a new one, with a
disagreeable smell I could never account for till this morning." "As how, Kate?" asked my uncle. "Why, it's an
unpleasant thing to mention," said my aunt, "but when I
awoke, I found myself sticking with both my soles to the
foot-board, by the varnish."

So much for our sleeping accommodations at Cologne.
Perhaps, Gerard, as you are of a speculative turn, you will
think my uncle's theory of diablerie worth working out.
To my own fancy, sundry passages of the "Faust,"—read
aloud in the original language,—sound suspiciously like a
certain noise produced by uneasy lying; indeed, I think it
very possible to trace all the horrible phantasmagoria of the
Walpurgis Night to the inspiration of a German bed, and its
"nightmare's pillion."

The rest of the day was spent in seeing the Lions—and
first, the Cathedral, the mere sight of which did me good,
both morally and physically. Gerard, 'tis a miracle of art,
—a splendid illustration of transcendentalism ; never perhaps
was there a better attempt, for it is but a fragment, to imitate
a temple made without hands. I speak especially of the
interior. Your first impression on entering the building is of
its exquisite lightness ; to speak after the style of the Apostle
Paul, it seems not "of the earth earthy," but of heaven
heavenly, as if it could take to itself wings and soar upwards.
And surely if angelic porters ever undertake to carry
Cathedrals instead of Chapels, (as we have seen a promise
below of "messuages carefully delivered,") the Dom Kirche
of Cologne will be their first burden to Loretto. The name
of its original architect is unknown in the civic archives, but

assuredly it is enrolled in letters of gold in some masonic
record of Christian faith. If from impression ariseth expression, its glorious builder must have had a true sense of the
holy nature of his task. The very materials seem to have
lost their materialism in his hands, in conformity with the
design of a great genius spiritualised by its fervent homage
to the Divine Spirit. In looking upward along the tall
slender columns which seem to have sprung spontaneously
from the earth like so many reeds, and afterwards to have
been petrified, for only nature herself seemed capable of
combining so much lightness with durability, I almost felt,
as the architect must have done, that I had cast off the
burden of the flesh, and had a tendency to mount sky-
wards. In this particular it presented a remarkable contrast
to the feelings excited by any other Gothic edifice with
which I am acquainted. In Westminster Abbey, for instance,
whose more solid architecture is chiefly visible by a " dim
religious light," I was always overcome with an awe amounting to gloom ; whereas at Cologne, the state of my mind
rose somewhat above serenity. Lofty, aspiring, cheerful,
the light of heaven more abundantly admitted than excluded,
and streaming through painted panes, with all the varied
colours of the first promise, the distant roof seemed to re-
echo with any other strains than those of that awful hymn
the "Dies Iræ." In opposition to the Temple of Religious
Fear, I should call it the Temple of Pious Hope. And now,
Gerard, having described to you my own feelings, I will not
give you the mere description of objects to be found in the
guide-books. From my hints you will be, perhaps, able to
pick out a suggestion that might prove valuable in the
erection of our new churches. Under the Pagan mythology,
a temple had its specific purpose ; it was devoted to some
particular worship, or dedicated to some peculiar attribute of

the Deity : as such, each had its proper character, and long
since the votaries and the worship have passed away,
travellers have been able to discriminate, even from the
ruins, the destination of the original edifice.   Do you think,
Gerard, that such would be the case, were a future explorer
to light on the relics of our Langham Place, or Regent
Street temples ; would an antiquarian of 2838 be able to
decide, think you, whether one of our modern temples was a
Christian church, or a parochial school, or a factory? Had men
formerly more belief in wrong than they have now in right ?
Was there more sincerity in ancient fanaticism than in
modern faith ?   But I will not moralise ; only as I took a last
look at the Cathedral of Cologne, I could not help asking
myself, "Will such an edifice ever be completed—shall we
ever again build up even such a beginning?" The cardinal'
Virtues must answer the question.   Faith and Charity have
been glorious masons in times past—does "Hope's Architecture" hold out equal promise for the future ?

The fees demanded by the guardians of the Dom Kirche
have been complained of by sundry travellers besides Grundy.
For my own part I should not object to their being higher,
provided they were devoted to the repairs of the building, or
even towards a more appropriate altar.   The present one is
in such a style of pettiness and prettiness, that it looks like
a stall at a religious fancy fair.   But then, as a set off, there
is a picture—the Adoration of the Virgin and Child—which
is a lay miracle !   It is very old ; but only proves the more,
that as Celestial Wisdom may come from the mouths of
babes and sucklings, even so was Heavenly Beauty produced
by Art in its very infancy.

Our next visit was to the Church of St. Peter, passing,
by the way, the house of Rubens, with his well-known effigy
painted over the door   The altar-piece, representing the

crucifixion of his patron-saint, is a wonderful picture—. though it possibly derives a portion of its interest from the extraordinary position of the main figure. The face of the Martyr Saint is particularly fine ; and, in order to aid the effect, the exhibitor produces a wooden machine, through which you look at the picture, stooping so that your own head is nearly in the same position as that of the Apostle ; —and thereby hangs a tale. My uncle had scarcely adjusted himself in the required attitude, and taken a glimpse at the painting, when he abruptly rose upright, muttering, in an under-tone, "That's done it at last—all my blood's gone to my head !" and withal walked off, and seated himself on a chair in the aisle, where he remained for some minutes, with his eyes closed, perfectly motionless and silent. As usual in such cases, we allowed the circumstance to pass unnoticed ; and by and by, as I anticipated, two or three exprimental hems, followed by a sonorous blowing of his nose, announced that our Hypochondriac had come, of his own accord, to himself. In fact, he soon stood again beside us, and pulling his hand from his pocket, presented a handsome gratuity to our attendant. "There, Mister ; it's no doubt a very fine painting, though to my mind rather an uncomfortable object ; as for that wooden invention," at the same time saluting it with a hearty kick to the utter astonishment of our little Sacristan, "it ought to be indicted ; it's nothing more nor less, sir, than a trap for the apoplexy !"

After this characteristic exhibition we parted, my uncle preferring to return to the hotel, and leaving me to visit and report on the other sights of Cologne. Amongst the rest was the Masquerade Room, devoted to the Carnival balls. It is a fine room as to size, and supported in the middle by columns, intended to represent huge champagne glasses, whence the painted characters and groups which

cover the walls and ceiling are supposed to effervesce. The
idea, however, is better than the execution—the intent
surpasses the deed. The designs display a good deal of
dull pantomime and trite allegory, such as a heart put up to
auction, and the like. But the Germans, even of Cologne,
on the strength of a Roman origin, ought not to attempt a
Carnival. The Italian Genius and the Teutonic are widely
asunder—as different as macaroni and sausage. Polichinello
is quite another being to Hans Wurst—he is as puff paste to
solid pudding. The national spirit is not sufficiently volatile,
airy, or mercurial. The wit of the Germans is not feather-
heeled; their humour is somewhat sedate. The serious
fantastic, the grave grotesque, is their *forte*, rather than the
comic. In short, their animal spirits, like their animal
frames, are somewhat solid; and I could not help fancying
that the frolics of their Saturnalia must resemble the
ponderous fun described by Milton :—

> " The unwieldy Elephant,
> To make them mirth used all his might, and wreathed
> His lithe proboscis."

In my way homeward I was struck by a voice that seemed
familiar to my ear, and looking in at a shop-door I saw what
would be a subject for a picture of domestic interest. On
one side of the counter stood my aunt, looking wonderfully
blank and discomposed; on the other, was a grave broad-
faced German, with his shoulders up to his ears, his eyebrows
up to his crown, and the corners of his mouth down to his
chin. On the counter itself, nearest my aunt, lay a small
parcel of her purchases, with a sovereign intended to pay for
them, while, next to the opposite party, were arranged three
or four Prussian dollars and some smaller coins; the
difficulty, whatever it might be, had evidently come to a

Pantaloon.

dead-lock. My aunt cast her eyes upward, as if the case was beyond mortal arrangement. The shopkeeper gravely shook his head, and had recourse to his snuff-box. A glance towards your humble servant made my aunt look in the same direction, and in an instant I was clutched by the arm and hauled into the shop. " I'm so glad you're come, Frank ; I was never so served in my life." And hastily gathering up the Prussian dollars, she banged them singly down again, each after each, on the counter, with a vehemence little in keeping with her character. " There," said she, when the operation was finished,' " one can't be deceived in that ; there's no more ring in them than in so many leaden dumps." Of course I guessed the matter at a glance, but having met with somebody that could understand her language, my aunt was more disposed to talk than to listen. " But my dear aunt, it's the case with all the currency." " I know it is. I have rung the small pieces too, and they're no better than brass farthings. Mr. Grundy was quite right, they all cheat the English if they can." " Pooh, pooh, it's the proper currency of the country." " Nonsense, Frank ! look here, they're only washed over like bad sixpences, anybody can see that ! The man must have taken me for a perfect fool." All this time the German had kept looking alternately in our faces as each happened to be talking, but now he inquired if I could speak his language, and without waiting my answer, began anxiously explaining his own share in the transaction. The change he said, was correct, he had counted it ten times over with the lady, but still she was dissatisfied ; and as for the money, it was the standard coin of the country. All of which I duly interpreted to my aunt, who, at last, was prevailed upon to exchange her good sovereign for the bad dollars ; and catching up her purchases she departed, compelled but unconvinced. Her secret opinion, indeed, tran-

spired as she stepped from the threshold :—"Well, I must
say, Frank, it's the first time I ever heard of a King being a
common coiner of bad money, and what's worse, obliging all
his own subjects to pass it off!"

By a curious coincidence, on entering the Hotel, we found
my uncle engaged in precisely similar speculations. "Here
Frank," said he, holding out to me a small document, "look
at that. Talk of rag-money! I wish old Cobbett was alive
again, or that his ghost would come up the river Rhine,
just to hear what he'd say on the subject. Why, here's
Mercury, and the Royal Arms, and the Spread Eagle, and
Hercules, and all sorts of engine-turning, and filagree-work,
and crinkum-crankums, and the value in three different
languages, French, English, and High Dutch, and after all
it's nothing but a three-shilling note!" "It's about as good
as their German silver," murmured my aunt, as if talking to
herself. "At least the Prussian money," said I, "has one
convenience?" "And what's that?" asked my aunt, rather
tartly; "it's both bad and heavy, as I know by my bag."
"I alluded," said I, "to its almost infinite sub-division : no
small consideration to your amateurs of cheap charity. In
England, for instance, there are plenty of professedly bene-
volent persons who would, no doubt, contribute their '*mite*,'
as it is called, to any charitable object, provided there were
any real coin of that denomination." "Cologne swarms
with objects sure enough," said my good aunt, with a very
sincere sigh for the multitudinous miseries she was unable to
relieve. "You have the comfort," said I, "my dear aunt,
that with twelve pfennings to a groschen, you may give to
nine beggars out of the dozen at the cost of -an English
penny."

Of course this was only banter, but the subject set me
thinking of the comparative misery of being poor in a rich

country. For example, to give a pauper in England a
farthing, which in Germany would purchase *something*, is
literally to give him nothing at all. I am not aware of any
article to be obtained at the price ; what used to be, and is
called a farthing candle, fetches a halfpenny. Still, I am not
quite convinced but that the cheapest country may prove
generally the dearest one ; the difficulty of spending money
alone must not be taken into account, but also the difficulty
of obtaining it. Hence, it seems to me that the real dear-
ness or cheapness of a country can only be properly weighed
by a native. But I am no political economist, and besides, I
think it as well to defer my local conclusions till I have had
some experience of the premises. So, lest you should think
my letter as long as an Eau de Cologne bottle without its
spirit, I shall here close. The verses are for Emily, the
sketch for yourself, with all loving remembrances from,
dear Gerard,

Yours ever truly,

FRANK SOMERVILLE.

TO * * * * *

WITH A FLASK OF RHINE WATER.

The old Catholic City was still,
In the Minster the vespers were sung,
And, re-echoed in cadences shrill,
The last call of the trumpet had rung ;
While, across the broad stream of the Rhine,
The full Moon cast a silvery zone ;
And, methought, as I gazed on its shine,
" Surely that is the Eau de Cologne."

G

I inquired not the place of its source,
If it ran to the east or the west;
But my heart took a note of its course,
That it flow'd towards Her I love best—
That it flow'd towards Her I love best,
Like those wandering thoughts of my own,
And the fancy such sweetness possess'd,
That the Rhine seemed all Eau de Cologne!

TO MISS WILMOT.

MY DEAR MARGARET,

Since my last, we have passed from Holland into
Prussia, but, alas! a change of country has only brought a
change of troubles. As I foretold, there was a plot against
the Dutch linen, which, by my brother's and nephew's contrivance, was seized at the German frontier. I suspect they
thought it would be an incumbrance; but, if so, it would
have fallen only on my unfortunate self. It's so different to
poor George, who never cared, in travelling, how he was
loaded. Heaven knows the packages, and boxes, and bundles,
we have taken only on a thirty miles' journey, without a
murmur on his part, or an objection. Indeed my course from
Rotterdam to Cologne has been marked by a series of mis-
fortunes: and, in particular, a most mortifying adventure on
board the steam-boat, which I do not like to trust on paper,
—but you shall hear it when we meet.

Only this very morning, I met with something that hurt me
very much, not merely on my own account, but for the sake of
human nature. It always shocks one to meet with ingratitude,
selfishness, and hard-heartedness in any body, but especially

in one of our own sex, and above all, a lady of birth and
breeding, who ought to possess more refined and delicate
feelings. I allude to Lady de Farringdon, who came over with
us in the Lord Melville, and was nearly washed away whilst
sitting in her own carriage on the deck. Providentially she
was released from her perilous situation, and carried down to
the ladies' cabin, but in a most deplorable state. She was
drenched from head to foot, and so terrified and sick, it
made me forget my own distresses to see her, and particularly when one reflected on the delicate nature of her
bringing up, and all the elegant comforts and luxuries, and
the devoted attention she had been accustomed to from her
infancy. Her own maid and the stewardess being quite
incapable, from fright and sickness, I felt it my duty to try
to alleviate the poor sufferer's afflictions, and can only say
she could not have received more assistance from me had
she been my own sister. To do her ladyship justice, she
expressed herself in the most handsome and grateful terms
—indeed, in such warm and affectionate language, and her
manner was so winning and friendly, even to kissing me,
that I felt as if we had known and loved each other for
years instead of only a day's acquaintance. In short, I quite
grieved at parting with her, on the quay at Rotterdam,
perhaps never to meet again in this world. You may fancy
my delight, then, at recognising the carriage and liveries at
a milliner's door in Cologne ; and seeing her ladyship in the
shop, I went in, and endeavoured to recall myself to her
remembrance. But, instead of the warm reception I
expected, after taking what I must call a rude stare at me
through her glass, all she said was, "O, I suppose you are
one of the persons who came over in the Lord Melville ?"
I told her I was, and hoped she had recovered from the
effects of that awful storm. "O, of course," she said, very

coolly; "we soon get over those things on shore;" and
then, turning away from me to the shopwoman, went on
bargaining for a piece of lace.   I was so shocked and hurt,
I hardly know how I got out of the shop, or if I even
wished her ladyship a good morning.   But it was really too
much;—to think that the same woman who had clung to
me, and rested her head on my shoulder; who had received
my best assistance, even in undressing, for she was as helpless
as a child; who had begged me to hold her hands, to feel
for her, and even to pray with her—could treat me in so
cruel a manner!   I confess I could not help shedding tears,
and almost made a vow never to attach myself to any one
again.   Indeed, my brother warned me from the beginning,
and told me, in his style, that I was "hooking on to the
wrong train."   But oh, Margaret! what is this world worth,
if we cannot trust to our first impressions?   But I must not
repine; for, at all events, I was not deceived in poor George.
As for Frank, he only laughs, and reminds me of the saying
of Mr. Grundy, which I took at that time for ill-nature,
"When you are abroad," said he, "you will meet with great
folks, or would-be great folks, on their travels, who will suck
all the information they can out of you, make use of you in
every possible way, and then cut you dead in the street the
next morning."

To-day I dined, for the first time, after the foreign fashion,
at a table-d'hôte; it was entirely by Frank's persuasion, as I
am not fond of eating in public, and to any one in spirits it
would, no doubt, have been an amusing scene.   The master
of the Hotel took the head of the table, which accommodated
about fifty persons.   As I had stipulated beforehand, my
brother sat on one side of me and my nephew on the other.
Directly opposite was a Prussian officer in a blue and red
uniform, and nearly a dozen little crosses and medals hanging

from the breast of his coat. Next to him was a fellow-
traveller from London; Frank calls him a Cockney, who
dreadfully alarmed us at Nimeguen by letting off pistols in
the night; on the other side of the officer was an empty
chair, with its back turned to the table to show that the
place was bespoke. The rest of the company was made up
of foreign ladies and gentlemen, and at the bottom of the
table a person so very outlandish that I must try to describe
him. Personally he was a large man, but from the breadth
of his face and the size of his head, which looked all the
bigger from a great quantity of hair that fell over his
shoulders, he ought to have been a giant. His features were
rather coarse and vulgar,—they could never have been handsome, and yet could never look ugly, with such an expression
of good-humour. But to my fancy it was the good-humour
of one who had never had anything to try it. He seemed
always ready to smile at something or nothing,—but not as
if from having cheerful thoughts, but from having no thoughts
whatever to trouble him, good, bad, or indifferent. The only
idea he seemed to entertain was of his dinner, in expectation
of which he had hold of his fork rather awkwardly, with his
third and fourth fingers over the handle, and the others
under it, so that the prongs came out beyond his little finger.
As for his dress, it set at defiance all rules as to colours that
go well together. His coat was chocolate brown, with a
pompadour velvet collar,—his waistcoat so gay with all the
hues of the rainbow, that it resembled a bed of tulips—and
then plum-coloured pantaloons. Across his bosom he wore
several gold or gilt chains, to one of which hung a very large
watch-key in the shape of a pistol; and his shirt was fastened
with mosaic studs, besides a complicated sort of brooch, that
looked like two hearts united together by little chains.
Besides these ornaments, his hands were covered with rings,

his right forefinger always sticking straight out like that on
a hand-post, as the joint could not bend for an immense ring,
with an amethyst as big as a shilling. Frank whispered that
he was travelling for Rundell and Bridge, but I suspect that
was only a quiz.

In the meantime a dinner-bell kept ringing by way of invitation to all the town, but as no more guests appeared, the
ceremony began. First came the soup, very like barley
broth (supposing rice instead of barley) and then the beef
which had been boiled in it, of course very insipid. It reminded me of the patent Pimlico bread I once tasted, when,
as poor George said, they had extracted all the spirit and left
nothing behind but the corpse of a loaf. I was obliged to
leave it on my plate, where, as it got cold, it turned almost
as white as a piece of wood. But you would have admired
the dexterity of the waiters. One of them brought a large
pile of clean plates, holding one between each finger, and
dealt them out to us as if they had been cards. The worst
is, the plates and dishes are all stone cold, and as, instead of
a bill of fare, every course is put on the table to show you
what you are to expect, and is then taken off again to be
carved, the hottest of their hot dinners is only like a hasty
attempt in warm weather at a cold collation. But what
most surprised me was the order of the eatables, so different
to any established by Mrs. Glasse or Mrs. Rundell. After
the soup, &c., came in a monstrous dish of asparagus, with a
sauce made of oiled butter and hard-boiled eggs. Next appeared a capon and salad, then a very sweet pudding, and
then some very sour krout. The next dish that went its
rounds, like a novel in a circulating library, was of very small,
very waxy, kidney potatoes (Frank called them "Murphy's
thumbs"), and then followed some unknown vegetable, with
a very unpleasant smell, in a brown sauce, looking, according

to Frank, like "sailors' fingers stewed in tar." Next we had
salmon and perch, in jelly, and cold, and last, and certainly
not least, a great solid piece of roast veal. My brother, who
partook of everything, was amused at this putting the cart
before the horse. "Egad! Kate," he whispered, "I have
eaten the wrong end of my dinner first, and suppose, to digest
it properly, I must stand on my head." Indeed, I came in
for my own share of novelties, for what seemed a pickled wal-
nut was so sweet, that the mere surprise made me return it
rather hastily to my plate. I was provoked enough, and
especially as the Londoner thought proper to notice it,
"Just like them Germans, ma'am," said he, "they arn't even
up to pickled walnuts!" But what followed was worse, for
after helping himself to what looked like preserved plums,
but proved to be sour, he spluttered one out again without
any ceremony, calling out loud enough for the whole room to
hear him, "Pickled bullises, by jingo!" As you may suppose,
I made up my mind to dine no more at a table-d'hôte, and
especially as I did not know in what tavern doings it might
end, for, on asking Frank the meaning of something painted
up in large letters on the wall at one end of the room, he
told me it was that gentlemen were requested not to smoke
during dinner! In fact, when dinner was nearly over, who
should walk in, and seat himself in the vacant chair just
opposite me but, *a common soldier!* Of course such an occurrence is usual, for no one objected to his company; on the
contrary, the officer conversed, and even hobnobbed with the
new-comer. But as trifles serve to show low breeding, I was
not surprised to observe the private helping himself first to
the wine : it was only after partly filling his own glass that
he recollected himself and helped his superior. Every
moment I grew more uncomfortable, for this young fellow
showed a great inclination to address me, and the Londoner

got still more vulgar and fault-finding; in short, I had just
resolved to rise and make my retreat, when all at once,—
pity me, my dear Margaret,—the door flew wide open, and
there stood Lady de Farringdon, with her horrid glass up to
her eye! I could have dropped off my chair! Instead of
coming in, however, her Ladyship contented herself with a
haughty stare round the table, and then departed, with a
last glance at myself, and a scornful sneer on her face, that
seemed plainly to say—"Yes, there you are, at an Inn-
keeper's ordinary, with all kinds of low company, and a
common soldier for your *vis-à-vis*." Without waiting for the
dessert I——

*　　*　　*　　*　　*　　*

MY DEAR MARGARET,—The above was written last night.
The occasion of my breaking off so suddenly was rather an
odd one, and has raised a pretty laugh at my expense.
Imagine me writing up in my own bed-room, by the light of
a single wax candle, but which was not above half burned
down, when all at once out it went, and left me in utter
darkness. I instantly rang the bell, but the hour was so late,
or the Germans were so early, or both, that I found I could
make nobody hear without disturbing the whole hotel; so I
undressed and groped into bed. This morning has explained
the mystery. The wax-ends, it appears, are somebody's per-
quisites, and in order to make sure of handsome ones, the
candles are fabricated on purpose with only a certain length
of wick. Frank says he was forewarned of this German trick
upon travellers by Mr. Grundy.

Besides the secret of the wax-candles, I have learned some
particulars that make me a little ashamed of my precipitation
at the ordinary dinner. The German hotel-keepers, I understand, are respectable persons, who always take the head of

the table ; and as for the common soldier, he was a young Prussian Baron, who, as every native must be a soldier, had volunteered into the line. The helping himself first, to a little wine, and then the officer, was only a customary politeness, in case there should be any dust or cork in the neck of the bottle. It will be a warning to me for the future not to be so rash in my judgment of foreigners, and foreign customs.

I have said nothing of Cologne Cathedral, and the Sepulchre of the Three Kings ; but to *me* tombs only bring painful reflections ; and instead of the Cathedral, I would rather have seen a certain village spire, rising above the trees, like a poplar turned into a steeple. But a broken spirit always yearns towards home. As to health, we are in our usual way ; except Martha, who has low crying fits that I cannot, and she will not, account for. Adieu. My Brother and Nephew unite in love to you, with, dear Margaret, your affectionate Sister,

CATHARINE WILMOT.

P.S.—There is a great stir here about a religious agreement that some hundreds of young Catholic females have signed, binding themselves not to marry unless to one of their own persuasion. A very tragical affair has happened in consequence, which Frank has made into a poem. I enclose a copy. To my taste it is rather pretty ; but my Brother says it is not good poetry, for it does not sing well to any tune that he knows.

THE ROMANCE OF COLOGNE.

'Tis even—on the pleasant banks of Rhine
The thrush is singing, and the dove is cooing,
A youth and maiden on the turf recline
Alone—And he is wooing.

Yet woos in vain, for to the voice of love
No kindly sympathy the Maid discovers,
Though round them both, and in the air above,
The tender Spirit hovers !

Untouch'd by lovely Nature and her laws,
The more he pleads, more coyly she represses ;—
Her lips denies, and now her hand withdraws,
Rejecting his caresses.

Fair is she as the dreams young poets weave,
Bright eyes, and dainty lips, and tresses curly ;
In outward loveliness a child of Eve,
But cold as Nymph of Lurley !

The more Love tries her pity to engross,
The more she chills him with a strange behaviour ;
Now tells her beads, now gazes on the Cross
And Image of the Saviour.

Forth goes the Lover with a farewell moan,
As from the presence of a thing inhuman ;—
Oh ! what unholy spell hath turn'd to stone
The young warm heart of Woman !

*   *   *   *   *

'Tis midnight—and the moonbeam, cold and wan,
On bower and river quietly is sleeping,
And o'er tho corse of a self-murdered man
The Maiden fair is weeping.

In vain sho looks into his glassy eyes,
No pressuro answers to her hand so pressing;
In her fond arms impassively ho lies,
Clay-cold to her caressing.

Despairing, stunn'd by her eternal loss,
She flies to succour that may best beseem her;
But, lo! a frowning Figuro veils tho Cross,
And hides tho blest Redeemer!

With stern right hand it stretches forth a scroll,
Wherein sho reads in melancholy letters,
Tho cruel fatal pact that placed her soul
And her young heart in fetters.

"Wretch! Sinner! Renegado! to truth and God,
Thy holy faith for human lovo to barter!"
No moro she hears, but on the bloody sod
Sinks, Bigotry's last Martyr!

And sido by sido the hapless Lovers lio:
Tell me, harsh priest! by yonder tragic token,
What part hath God in such a Bond, whereby
Or hearts or vows are broken?

TO GERARD BROOKE, ESQ.

My dear Gerard,

        Yesterday at an early hour, we bade adieu to the old Roman colony, and embarked in the Princess Marianne. Instead of any improvement, however, in the scenery, we soon found ourselves between low banks and willows ; as if, by some "stop her" and "back her" manœuvre, her Highness, with reversed paddles, had carried us into Holland.   But I am none of those fastidious travellers, who, in the absence of the picturesque, throw themselves back in the carriage, and go to sleep.   Although for some distance there was nothing alongside but a flat plain, yet lark after lark, "weary of rest," kept springing up from the dewy grass, and soared aloft on twinkling wings, that seemed, like its song, all in a quiver with delight.   The air was breezy, and bright, and balmy, and floated visibly against the horizon ; the sky was beautifully blue, and the feathery white clouds fluttered across it like summer butterflies.   The grass waved, the flowers nodded. the leaves danced,—the very water sparkled, as if it felt a living joy.   Even our Hypochondriac owed the genial influence of the time, and his sister resumed some of the spirits for which she was noted in her girlhood.   The truth is, there was a charm in these humble ruralities, of which even the Cockney, of Nimeguen renown, was aware.   "Tame scenery, sir," remarked a saturnine-looking man, at the same time turning his back on the bank we were gliding past.   "Yes," answered the Londoner, with a cheerful smile ; "Yes—but it's natur."

        Amongst other peculiarities, nothing strikes a stranger more, in his course up the Rhine, than the German fondness for bowing.   Whenever the steamer passes, or stops at, a little

Barely Civil.

town, you see a great part of the population collected on the shore, ready to perform this courtesy. One or two, like fuglemen, go through the manœuvre by anticipation, as if saluting the figure-head ; then the vessel ranges alongside, and off goes the covering of every head—hats and caps of all shapes and colours, are flourishing in the air. Wet, or dry, or scorching sun, every male, from six years old to sixty, is uncovered. Some seize their caps by the top, others by the spout in front ; this gives his hat a wave to and fro, that saws with it up and down ; the very baker plucks off his white night-cap, and holds it shaking at arm's length. Meanwhile, their countrymen on board vigorously return the salute ; the town is passed, and the ceremony is over. But, no !—a man comes running at full speed down a gateway, or round the corner of a street, looks eagerly for the boat, now 100 yards distant, gives a wave with his hat or cap, and then, thrusting his hands into his pockets, returns deliberately up the street, or gateway, as if he had acquitted himself of an indispensable moral duty.

Remarking on this subject to an English gentleman on board, he told me the following anecdote in point :—"During a temporary residence," said he, "at Mayence, I made a slight acquaintance with one of the inhabitants, of the name of Klopp. He had much of the honesty and conscientiousness attributed to his countrymen, and though in practice a plain, straightforward, matter-of-fact person, was nevertheless addicted, like Germans in general, to abstruse studies. Subsequently, for the sake of the baths, I shifted my quarters to Ems, and was one morning sitting at breakfast, when a rapping at the door announced a visitor, and in walked Herr Klopp. After the usual compliments, I inquired whether he had come to Ems for pleasure merely, or on account of his health? 'For neither,' replied the honest German ; 'my

errand is to you, and I shall return home directly I have paid
off a little debt.' I was not aware, I told him, that we had
had any pecuniary transactions whatever. ' No,' replied Herr
Klopp, 'not in money ; but if you remember, on such a day
(giving me the day and date) we passed each other on the
Mayence Bridge. I had recently been reading Fichte, and
my head was full of speculations ; so that, though conscious
of your bowing to me, I omitted to return your salute. It
is true that I recollected myself in the cattle-market, and
indeed pulled off my hat, but that hardly satisfied my conscience. So the end is, I have come to acquit myself of the
debt ; and here it is'——And, will you believe it, sir? with
all the gravity of a Prussian sentry presenting arms, the
scrupulous German paid me up the salute in arrear ! "

To reward our patience, the blue crests of the Siebengebirge
at length loomed over the low land, to the left, and assured us
that our Pilgrim's Progress had brought us in sight of the
Delectable Mountains. We had been advised to stop at
Bonn, for the sake of some excursions in the neighbourhood,
and that ancient and learned city soon made its appearance.
Its aspect was quaint and inviting. As we neared the shore
it was crowded with spectators, amongst whom those *Bonny*
Laddies, the students, were gaily conspicuous. A great many
were dressed as Tyrolese, with ribbons and flowers in their
high-crowned hats ; and whatever a Quaker might have
thought of such vanities, a painter would assuredly have been
grateful for such very picturesque accessories to the foreground.
You may form some notion of their appearance from the
remark of my uncle—" Frank, they must have made a long
night at the masquerade, to be in their fancy dresses so late
in the morning." When I told him they were the students,
he made one of his wry faces. "Students ! What do they
study ?—Private theatricals ! Yes—there's a youngster

dressed up like Macready in William Tell ; and yonder's
another with a parasol straw hat, a nankeen jacket, and a
long pipe in his mouth, like the Planter in Paul and
Virginia !"

The moment the "Princess" came abreast of the pier, a
party of the Burschen sprang on board, of course with an
equal number of pipes, and formed a group on the deck.
Most of them were in costume "marvellously imaginative ;"
some seemed to have sought their Journal des Modes, or
Mirror of Fashion, in the pictures of Vandyke or Salvator
Rosa ; others appeared to have been clothed, in a fit of
enthusiasm, by a romantic tailor.. Indeed one of them
presented so very *outré* a figure, that I was not at all sur- ·
prised to hear the Cockney's exclamation of "What a Guy!"
No small portion of care and culture had been bestowed upon
their hair, moustaches, and beards, which strongly reminded
me of the Dutch hedges, that are trained and trimmed into
all sorts of grotesque and fanciful shapes. But in the midst
of these speculations the bell warned us to provide for our
own departure ; and winding in Indian file through the
motley crowd, we made the best of our way to the hotel.

After establishing ourselves in comfortable quarters we
strolled about the town, first taking a long gaze from the
Altezoll, across the broad Rhine, at the grand group of Seven
Mountains. We then scanned the façade of the University,
took a peep in at a church or two, and discussed a flask of
Ahrbleichart in the Vinea Domini. During this ramble, we
saw, of course, a number of the students, and it was amusing
to hear Nuncle guessing at the historical personages they had
selected for their models ;—for instance, Peter the Wild Boy
—Van Butchell—Don Quixote—Samson—Absalom—Esau
—Blackbeard the Pirate—Confucius—Henri Quatre—and
Bampfylde Moore Carew. One very dissimilar pair he chris-

tened Valentine and Orson! another "Junker," remarkably
unkempt and unshorn, he compared to Baron Trenck; and
" Egad ! " he cried, as we passed a square-set figure in an
antique dress, and fiercely moustached, "Egad! there's Pam."
Perhaps the most whimsical of these fancies was that of a tall
fellow, who, with sleekly-combed hair, a huge white collar
thrown back over his shoulders, and trousers that buttoned
to his jacket, stalked along like a Brobdignagian schoolboy ;
I was anxious to know my uncle's opinion of these oddities,
and contrived to extract it. "All theatrical mummery,
Frank ; all theatrical mummery ! But mayhap," said he,
after a pause, "it's like a breaking out on the skin, and serves
to carry off fantastical humours that are better out than in."

I am inclined to think this is nearly the truth of the case ;
for it is notorious that these Burschen come in, according to
the proverb, as Lions, and go out as Lambs—some of the
wildest of them settling down in life as very civil civilians,
sedate burgomasters, and the like.   Indeed, were it otherwise—were there as much real as mock enthusiasm under
these formidable exteriors, should we not hear more often
than we do of University riots and outbreaks—of Middle-
Age forays—with an occasional attempt to set fire to the
Rhine ? The worst is, as a great portion of these students
affect the uncouth and savage, mere Tybalts and Fire-eaters,
if they at all act up to their characters, they must be public
nuisances ; and if they do not, they hardly allow themselves
fair play.   Many of them, doubtless, are good-hearted lads
and industrious scholars, and as such, sure it would better
become them to appear like what they are, ambitious of a
place in the political, literary, artistic, or scientific annals of
their country, rather than as candidates for a niche in its
Eccentric Mirror or Wonderful Magazine.

These vagaries in dress form, by the bye, a curious anomaly

in Prussia; where, in conformity with the military pendant of the King, all public bodies, excepting the learned ones, are put into uniform. Thus, there are the Post officials with their orange collars, the Police with their pink ones, the Douane with their blue ones, the Bridge-men with their red ones : — postilions, prisoners, road-makers, all have their liveries and their badges. But there is no *regulation* academical costume, and the students, by indulging in such eccentric *habits*, are possibly only making the most of their unique independence.

At one o'clock, we dined at the table-d'-hôte, and then rode off in a carriage to the Kreutzberg. At the top of the hill we found a party of French travellers, three gentlemen and a lady, enjoying the fine prospect. Had they been country-folk, it is probable that we should never have exchanged a word—for, as Marshal * * * said, "the advanced guard of an Englishman is his reserve,"—but with foreigners it is otherwise ; the strangers saluted us most courteously, and one of them addressing my Uncle, we all fell into talk. After commenting on the beauty of the view, we went *en masse* into the church, which formerly belonged to a Servite Convent. This edifice is considered as peculiarly sanctified, by possessing the steps which led up to the judgment-seat of Pontius Pilate, and which are said to be still stained by the blood-drops drawn from the brow of our Saviour by the crown of thorns. These sacred stairs, as you are perhaps aware, have the faculty, like Sir Boyle Roche's famous bird, of "being in two places at once." I ventured to hint this to the lively Frenchwoman, but instead of expressing doubt or vexation, she only answered with a "Vraiment ?" I then described the Scala Santa at Rome, but with as little effect. "Vraiment ?" she replied. "Quel miracle ! mais tout est possible au bon Dieu !"

Just at this moment we were startled by a loud exclamation in German from the attendant, followed by a slight
scream, and, to my astonishment, I saw my Aunt precipi-
tately scampering down the marble stairs! It seems she
had unconsciously stepped on the *tabooed* precincts, which
was no sooner perceived by the guardian of the place, than,
with a loud outcry that the stairs were sacred, he made a
snatch to draw her back by the arm. The abrupt voice, the
unknown tongue, the threatening gesture, and the angry
expression of a countenance by no means prepossessing, took
full effect on her weak nerves, and impelled her to escape as
from a madman. And now arose a serious difficulty. The
trespasser had stopped exactly half-way down the flight, to
set foot on which is sacrilege, but as she could not be
expected, nor indeed allowed, to stand there for ever, the
point was how to get her off. By going up them on her
knees, like a Catholic pilgrim, she would have gained a
plenary indulgence for a year; but this, as a staunch Protestant, she declined, and as a modest female she refused to
clamber over the double balustrade that separated her from
a common staircase on either side. Which would then occasion the least sacrilege, to ascend by the way she came, or to
descend and be let out at the great folding-doors, the number
of stairs to be profaned in either case being the same? It
was a question to pose the whole college of St. Omer? The
attendant was at his wits' ends how to act, and referred the
point to the French party, as Catholics and competent
advisers, but for want of a precedent they were as much
abroad as himself. The first gentleman he appealed to
shrugged his shoulders, the lady did the same; the second
gentleman shrugged his shoulders and made a grimace, and
the third shrugged his shoulders, made a grimace, and shook
his head. In the meantime, the trespasser looked alarmed

and distressed ; she had gained some obscure notion of the
case, and possibly thought, in her vague idea of the powers
of popery, that she had subjected herself to the pains and
penalties of the Inquisition. It was an awkward dilemma,
particularly as the attendant protested most vehemently whenever the culprit attempted to stir. Luckily, however, he
turned his back during his consultation, when, at a beckon
and a wink from my Uncle, my Aunt, not without trembling,
quietly slipped up the sacred stairs on the points of her toes !

This termination of so intricate a dilemma was a relief to
us all, and to none more than Martha, who now ventured to
draw out the handkerchief she had stuffed into her mouth,
by way of stopper to a scream. But the affair had so cowed
the unlucky transgressor, that when we visited the vault
underneath the church, to inspect the Mummies, she preferred to " sit out." And it was well she escaped a sight
which could not have failed to remind her of " poor George."
Imagine about two dozen of dead monks laid out, in their
habits as they lived, in open coffins, all in various stages of
decay, some almost as fresh and fleshy as might be expected
of an anchorite, after a long course of fasting and mortification ; others partly dropping, and dropped into dust ; and
here and there a mere skull, grinning like one of Monk
Lewis's spectres, from under its cowl. The cause of their
extraordinary preservation has given rise to much conjecture.
My own opinion is, that by way of pendants to the holy
stairs, and heaping " voonders upon voonders," the bodies
have been *Kyanized* by some secret process which was afterwards partially lost, as the more recent corses scarcely promise to keep so well as the more ancient ones. It was
impossible to stand amongst so many venerable relics of
humanity, some of them from three to four centuries old,
without entering into very Hamlet-like reflections. What

had become, during that long interval, of the disembodied
spirits? Had they slept in utter darkness and blank oblivion;
or had they a twilight existence, in dreams reflective of the
past? Did they still, perhaps, hover round their earthly
haunts and fleshy tenements; or were they totally entranced,
only to wake at the sound of the last trumpet? But these
are themes too awful for a gossipping letter. Suffice it, we
all felt the influence of the place and scene. In the neighbourhood of such objects, a strange mysterious feeling lays
us under a spell. By a sort of process of transfusion, the
vital principle that departed from the concrete form, seems
to have passed into an abstract figure:—Life is dead, but
DEATH is alive! and we breathe, and look, and tread, and
whisper, as if we were in his actual though invisible presence. Few words, therefore, were uttered as we stood in
that dreary avenue.—I remember but one exclamation from
the Frenchwoman, as she gazed on one of the most perfect
and placid of the faces—a wish, that the figure and features
of those we hold most dear, could always be thus preserved .
to us. It sounded like a natural sentiment, at the time,—
but it was little shared in by one of the spectators, who, as
we quitted the vault, drew me aside, with an air of great
solemnity. " Frank,—make me one promise. If I die in
these parts, don't let me be embalmed. It's all nonsense
and profanity. We're ordained to decay by nature, and
religion bids us try not to preserve our bodies, but to save
our souls. Besides, as to keeping one's face and person for
one's friends to look at, it's my notion they would soon give
over coming to see us, unless we could return the visits. No,
no! as Abraham said, 'let us bury our dead out of our
sight.' " " At least," said I, " the Mummies are a natural
curiosity." " Why, yes," he replied, with a smile, as we
stepped into the bright, brisk, open air, " and a political one,

too, Frank, to see so many of our representatives beyond corruption."

At the church-door we parted with the pleasant French people, who were going further inland ;—and then returned to our carriage. In our way home we halted at Poppelsdorf, to see the Botanical Garden, and the Museum, which contains abundant specimens of the mineralogy and geology of the Rhenish mountains, the Eifel, and the brown coal of Friesdorf. Amongst the fossils is a complete series of frogs, from the full-grown froggy that might a wooing go, down to that minute frogling—a tadpole. My uncle's remark on them was an original one, and deserves the consideration of our chemists. "Frank, if we could but find out a way of petrifying our great men, what a deal of money would be saved, in chipping statues ! "

But now, Gerard, good night. Fatigued and drowsy from our breezy rambles, a resolution has been moved and seconded, for retiring early, that I am too heavy-headed to oppose. "God bless the man who invented sleep ! " cries honest Sancho Panza, and Heaven be praised that he did not take out a patent, and keep the discovery to himself. My best love to Emily.

I am, my dear Gerard, yours very truly,

FRANK SOMERVILLE.

P.S.—Past one o'clock, and here I am, not couchant but rampant ! Yet have I been between sheets, and all but into the soft arms of Mr. Morpheus,—but oh ! Gerard, a night at Bonn is anything but a bonne nuit !

Never did I throw myself with such sweet abandonment into that blessed luxury, a bed. Sleep, the dear Eiderduck, was beginning to brood me with her downy breast and shadowy wings,—I was already swooning away into the delicious semi-oblivion that precedes the total forgetfulness, when crash! I was startled broad awake by the compound rattle of a vehicle that seemed to have twelve wheels, with four-and-twenty loose spokes in each, and a cast-iron horse! Students, of course, from their revels at Godesberg! Another and another followed—then a street squabble—and then " Am Rhein! Am Rhein!" arranged for any number of voices. Doze again—but no—another scrambling shandry-dan,—and then a duo—no, a trio,—no, a quart—no, a quint —no, a sext—zounds! a dozen were chiming in at the top-most pitch of their lungs! Partial as I am to music, I could not relish these outbreaks, nor did it comfort me a whit, that all who met, or overtook these wassailers joined most skilfully and scientifically in the tune!

> "I like your German singers well,
> But hate them too, and for this reason,
> Although they always sing in time,
> They often sing quite out of season."

In short, finding that it was impossible to sleep, I got up —rang for candles—cigars—and brandy and water, and then amused myself with the tale of *diablerie* I inclose. Mean-while the students have subsided—the streets are quiet— and once more, good night.

THE FATAL WORD.

A ROMANCE OF BONN.

THANKS to the merry company, and the good Ahrbleichart wine, at his Cousin Rudolph's, it was midnight ere Peter Krauss, the little tailor of Bonn, set out on his road home. Now Peter was a pious and a tender-hearted man, who would not hurt a dog, much less a fellow-creature ; but he had one master-failing, which at last brought him into a horrible scrape, and that was curiosity. Such was his itch for meddling and prying, that whatever business went forward, he was sure to look and listen with all his might. Let a word or two be pronounced in a corner, and you could fancy his ears pricking towards the sound, like the ears of a horse. Perhaps, if he had ever perused the tragical story of Blue Beard, he would have learned more prudence ; but, unhappily, he never read Fairy Tales, nor indeed anything of the kind, except some of the old Legends of the Saints.

Thus Peter Krauss, pipe in mouth, was trudging silently . homeward, through the pleasant valley between Rœttchen and Poppelsdorf, when all at once he heard something that brought him to a full stop. Yes,—there certainly was a talking on the other side of the bushes ; so giving loose to his propensity, he drew near, and listened the more eagerly as he recognised one of the voices as that of Ferdinand Wenzel, the wildest and wickedest of all the students at Bonn. The other voice he did not know, nor indeed had he ever heard one at all like it ; its tone was deep and metallic like the tolling of a great bell.

" Ask, and it shall be granted, if within my compass."

Peter, trembling, peeped through the thick foliage at the last speaker, and to his unutterable horror, descried a dreadful figure, which could only belong to one fearful personage —the Enemy of Mankind. Krauss could nearly see his full face, which was ten thousand times uglier than that of Judas in the old paintings. The Fiend was grinning, and dismally the moonlight gleamed on his huge hard cheek-bones, and thence downward to his mouth, where it gleamed awfully on his set teeth, which shone not with the bright bony whiteness of ivory, but with the flash of polished steel. Opposite to the Evil One, and as much at his case as if he had only been in company with a bosom crony, sat the reckless, daring, Ferdinand Wenzel, considering intently what infernal boon he had best demand. At last he seemed to have make up his mind ;—Krauss pricked up his ears.

"Give me," said the Wild Student, "the power of life and death over others."

"I can grant thee only the half," said the Fiend. "I have power to shorten human life, but there is only one who may prolong it."

"Be it so," said the Student; "only let those whom I may doom die suddenly before my face."

"All the blessed saints and martyrs forbid!" prayed Krauss in his soul, at the same time crossing himself as fast as he could. "In that case, I'm a dead man to a certainty! He will make away with all that is Philister—namely, with all that is good, or religious, or sober, or peaceable, or decent, in the whole city of Bonn!"

In the meantime the Evil One seemed to deliberate, and at length told the Wild Student that he should have his wish. "Listen, Ferdinand Wenzel. I will teach thee a mortal word, which if thou pronounce aloud to any human being, man, woman, or child, they shall drop down, stone-dead, as by a stroke of apoplexy, at thy very feet."

"Enough," said the Wild Student. "Bravo!" and he waved his arms exultingly above his head. "I am now one of the Fates. I hold the lives of my enemies in my hand. I am no more Ferdinand Wenzel, but Azrael, the Angel of Death. Come, the word—the mighty word!"

We have said that the topmost failing of Peter Krauss was curiosity,—it was rather his besetting sin, and was now about to meet with its due punishment. Where other men would have shut their eyes, he opened them; where they would have stopped their ears, he put up a trumpet. O

"Since then I'm doomed."

Peter, Peter! better hadst thou been born deaf as the adder than have heard the three dreadful syllables that made up that tremendous WORD. But Peter was wilful, and stretched out his neck like a crane's towards the sound, and as the Fiend, at Wenzel's request, repeated the fatal spell nine times over, it was impressed on the listener's memory, never to be forgotten.

"I have got it by heart," said the Wild Student, "and I know right well who shall hear it the first."

"Bravo!" said the voice that sounded like the toll of a death-bell.

The hair, long as it was, rose erect on Krauss's devoted head; every lock felt alive, and crawling and writhing like a serpent. He considered himself the doomed man. Wenzel owed him money, and debtors are apt to get weary of their creditors. Yes; his days were numbered, like those of the pig at the butcher's door. Full of these terrible thoughts, he got away as hastily as he could, without making an alarm, and as soon as he dared, set off at a run towards his home. On he scampered, wishing that his very arms were legs, to help him go at a double rate. On, on, on, he gallopped through Poppelsdorf, but without seeing it, like a blind horse that knows its way by instinct,—on, on; but at last he was compelled to halt, not for want of breath, for his lungs seemed locked up in his bosom; nor yet from fatigue, for his feet never felt the hard ground they bounded from; but because a party of students, linked arm in arm, occupied the whole breadth of the road. As soon as they heard footsteps behind them they stopped, and recognising the little tailor, began to jeer and banter him, and at length proceeded to push and hustle him about rather roughly. For some time he bore this rude treatment with patience, but in the end, even his good-humour gave way, and turned to bitterness.

"Ay, young and strong as ye be," thought he, "I know that, my masters, which could stiffen your limbs and still your saucy tongues in a moment." And why not pronounce the WORD then ?" said something so like a whisper, that Krauss started, expecting to see the Fiend himself at his elbow. But it was only the evil suggestion of his own mind, which, with some difficulty, he subdued, till the Burschen, tired of the present amusement, let go of their victim, and joining in a jovial chorus, allowed the tormented tailor to resume his race. "St. Remi be with me," murmured the frightened man, "and help me to restrain my tongue ! Oh that awful word, how nearly it slipped from me in my rage ! I shall do a murder, I know I shall—I shall be cursed and branded like bloody Cain !" and he groaned and smote his forehead as he ran. In this mood he arrived at his own door, where he let himself in with his private key. It was late ; his good wife Trudchen had retired to rest, and was in so sound a sleep that he forebore to awaken her. But that very sight, as she lay so still and so calm, only excited the most distressing fancies. "One word," thought he, "three little syllables, would make that sleep eternal !" Shuddering throughout his frame, he undressed and crept into his own bed, which was beside the other—but, alas ! not to rest. He dared not close his eyes, even for a wink. "If I sleep," thought he, "I shall dream, and as people always dream of what is uppermost in their minds, and moreover, as I am apt to talk in my sleep"—the mere idea of what might follow threw him into such an agony, that no opiate short of a fatal dose could have induced him to slumber for an instant. A miserable night he passed, now looking forward with terror, and then backward with self-reproach. A thousand times he cursed his fatal curiosity that had brought him to such a pass. "Fool, dolt, idiot, ass, long-

eared ass that I was, to listen to what did not concern me,
and to turn eaves-dropper to the Devil! I am lost, body
and soul! Oh that I had been born deaf and dumb!—Oh
that my dear mother, now in heaven,—Oh that my good
nurse, now in Munich,—had never taught me to speak! Oh
that I had died in cutting my first teeth! That detestable
word—if I could only get rid of it, but it is ever present, in
my mind and in my mind's eye! in the dark it seemed
written on the wall in letters of fire; and now the daylight
comes, they have turned into letters of pitch black!" Thus
he tossed and tumbled all night in his bed, with suppressed
moans, and groans, and sighings, and inward prayers, till it
was time to rise. Then he got up and opened his shop, and
afterwards sat down to breakfast; but he could not eat. If
he tried to swallow, the accursed word seemed sticking at
the bottom of his throat—sometimes it rose to the very tip
of his tongue, and then to taste anything was quite out of
the question. Life itself had lost its relish, like food with a
diseased palate. Conjugal and parental love, which had
been his greatest comforts, were now his uttermost torments.
When he looked at his good Trudchen, it was with a shudder;
and he dared not play with his own little Peterkin. "If I
open my lips to him," thought the father, "my child is dead
—in the midst of some nursery nonsense the WORD will slip
out, for it keeps ringing in my ears like a bell." In the
meantime his wife did not fail to notice his altered appearance, but it gave her little concern. The good Trudchen
was very fat and very philosophic, which some people call
phlegmatic, and she took the most violent troubles rather
softly and quietly, as feather-beds receive cannon-balls.
"Tush," said she, in her own full bosom, "he looks as if he
had not rested well, but he will sleep all the better to-night;
and as for his appetite, *that* will come-to in time." But tho

contrast only served to aggravate the sufferings of poor Krauss. To see his wife, the partner of his fortune, the sharer of his heart, his other self, so calm, so cool, so placid, grated on his very soul. There was something even offensive in it, like a fine sunny day to the mourners when there is a funeral in the house. His first impulse was to seek for sympathy, which generally implies making somebody else as miserable and unhappy as yourself; in fact, he was on the point of beginning the story to his wife, when one of those second thoughts, which are always the best, clapped a seal upon his lips. "No, no," he reflected, "tell a woman a secret? why, she'll blab it to the very first of her leaky gossips that drops in." In sheer despair, he resolved to bury himself over head and ears in his business, and accordingly hurried into his shop. But do whatever he would, his trouble still haunted him—he dreaded to see a customer walk in. "I am liable," said he, "as all the world knows, to fits of absence, and if I do not say the awful Word to somebody to his face, I shall perchance write it at the head of his bill." In the midst of this soliloquy, the little door-bell rang, as the door was thrown violently open, and in stalked the abominable Wenzel !

The devoted tailor turned as pale as marble, his teeth chattered, his knees knocked together till the kneepans clattered like a pair of castanets, whilst his hair again rose erect, like the corn after the wind has passed over it. But for once his fears were mistaken ; his unwelcome patron only came to order some new garments. "Heaven help me," thought the afflicted tradesman, " he is too deep already in my books, and yet 'if I make the least shadow of an objection, I am a dead man."

After turning over all the goods in the shop, the Wild Student selected a mulberry-coloured cloth, and then for the first time addressed himself to the proprietor. "Harkye, Peter Krauss, they tell me thou art a most notable listener."

The tailor's blood ran cold in his veins, and he gasped for breath; beyond doubt his eaves-dropping the night before had been discovered, if not known at the time by the Evil One himself. He was on the point of dropping on his knees to beg his life, when the next speech reassured him.

"You will please, therefore, to listen most attentively to my instructions."

The trembling Peter breathed again, whilst his customer went into a minute description of the frogs, and lace, and embroidery, with which the new garment was to be most elaborately and expensively trimmed. To all of which poor Krauss answered submissively, "Yes," and "Yes, certainly," in the plaintive tone of a well-whipped child. In the midst of this scene, two more students, inferior only to the first in bad repute, came swaggering into the shop, who, on the matter being referred to them, approved so highly of the mulberry-coloured cloth, that Wenzel at once bespoke the whole piece. "And now, Krauss," said the Wild Student, drawing his victim a little aside, "I have *one word* to say in your ear." At so ominous a speech, the little tailor broke out all over in a cold dew; that "one word" he guessed was his death-warrant; the ground he stood upon seemed opening under his feet like a grave. By a natural instinct he clapped both his hands to his ears; but they were almost instantly removed by the more vigorous arms of his enemy; he then, as a last resource, set up a sort of bull-like bellowing in order to drown the dreaded sounds, but the noise was as promptly stifled by the thrusting of his own nightcap into his open mouth. "Hist, thou listener," said the Wild Student, in an angry whisper, "those two gentlemen yonder are my most intimate friends; you will give them

I

credit for whatever they may choose to order, and I, Ferdinand Wenzel, will be answerable for the amount."

This was bad enough, but it might have been worse; and the little tailor was glad to assent, though he was now past speaking, and could only bow and bow again, with the tears in his eyes. Accordingly, his two new customers, thus powerfully recommended, began to select such articles as they thought proper, and gave ample directions for their making up. They then departed, Wenzel the last. "Remember," said he, significantly, holding up a warning finger, "remember—or else"—"I know, I know," murmured the terrified tailor, who felt as if relieved from an incubus, as the back of the Wild Student disappeared behind the closing door. But his grief soon returned. "I'm lost," he cried, in a doleful voice, "the more I'm patronised, the more I'm undone! They never will, they never can, pay me for it all. I'm a bankrupt—I must needs be a bankrupt—I'm a ruined man!" "Who is ruined?" inquired the comfortable Trudchen, just entering in time to catch the last words. "It's me," said the sorrowful tailor. "As how, Peter?" "How? Trudchen!—here has been that dare-devil, Ferdinand Wenzel, and brought two other scape-graces almost as bad as himself; and, besides heaven knows what else, he has ordered the whole piece of mulberry cloth." "He shall as soon have the mulberry-tree out of the garden," said the quiet Trudchen. "But he must have it," said the husband, with great agitation. "But he shan't," said the wife, quite collected. "I tell thee, Trudchen, he *must*," said the little tailor. "Well, we shall see," said the great tailoress, with the composed tone of a woman who felt sure of her own way.

Here was a new dilemma. Poor Peter Krauss plainly foresaw his own catastrophe; but to be pushed on to it, post haste, by the wife of his bosom, the mother of his sole child, was more than he could bear. "I tell thee, Trudchen, he *must* have it," repeated the doomed man. "You always try," said the phlegmatic Trudchen, "to have the last word." "And if I chose, I could make sure of it," retorted the now angry Peter. "Say the WORD to her at once," said the old whisper, which the affrighted husband no longer doubted was a suggestion from Satan in person. He was cool—nay, cold—in a moment ; and not daring to trust himself in his wife's presence, ran up to the little bed-chamber. The fat Trudchen stared awhile at this manœuvre, but as she reflected that persons, who go up stairs will, some time or other, come down again, she placidly resumed her knitting.

"Wretch! miserable wretch that I am!" sighed the disconsolate tailor, throwing himself on the bed with his face downwards. "I have been within an ace of murdering my own dear wife, the mother of my precious Peterkin! Oh! St. Mark! St. Remi! what mortal sin have I committed, to draw upon me such a visitation? Me, too, who could never keep a secret in my life! Then, again, if I take a glass extra of good wine, it is sure to set my tongue running. O what hundreds, thousands, of deaths will lie at my door! I shall be a Monster,—a Vampyre! Oh! I shall run mad—and then my head will wander—and I shall pronounce *it* in my ravings! It is sure to come out ! Cursed be the year, and the day, and the hour, and the minute, oh Peter Krauss! that thou wast born!"

"Alas!" (thus he continued) " the misfortune of a strong memory! The harder I try to forget it, the more it comes into my mind. If it had only been a long sentence—but a single word, that drops out like a loose tooth before one is aware. Ah! there is no being on my guard!" Having thus lamented, with many tears, by degrees he became more composed, and resolved to refresh his spirits by a walk in the

open air. But the tyrannical idea still pursued him with
its diabolical suggestions. For instance, he could not help
saying to himself, as a passenger passed by—"There's a tall
swaggering fellow, but I could strike him stone dead in an
instant. One WORD from me, and that flaunting maiden is a
corse." Moreover, the very demon, Curiosity, that first led
him to his guilty knowledge, now began to tempt him to its
abuse. "I wonder," thought he, "if it be true, or only a
juggle. Suppose I were to try it,—just one syllable,—on
that soldier, or that miller, or on his dog!" But remorse
soon followed. "Woe is me! I must fly the faces of my
kind! I must turn hermit,—or live like Roland on a bleak
rock, beyond speech with man, woman, or child!" As he
said this, he was run against by some one, blind with haste,
whom he caught by the arm. It was the maid-servant of
his old friend and neighbour, Hermann Liederbach. "Let
me go," cried the breathless female, struggling to get free.
"I am running to fetch the doctor to my poor master, who
has dropped down in a fit, if he is not dead."—"That's very
sudden," said Peter, as if musing. "Oh, like a gun!"
answered the maiden; "he was quite well and merry only
the minute before, talking and laughing with that Wild
Student, Ferdinand Wenzel."

  Poor Krauss was ready to drop down himself. However,
he contrived to get home, where he threw himself on his
knees behind the counter, and hid his face amongst the bales
of cloth. The horrid work was begun—but where would it
end? Nor were his fears in vain. On a sudden his attention
was excited by the trampling of numerous feet, and going to
the shop door, he saw a crowd following four men, who
carried a dead body on a hoard. "Hollo! what have you
there?" shouted an opposite neighbour from his upper
window. "It's poor Stephen Asbeck," answered several

voices; "he dropped down dead in the Market-place whilst squabbling with one of the students." Krauss stood rooted to the spot, till the whole procession had passed by. "It's dreadful work," said Mrs. Krauss, just entering from the back-parlour. "What is?" asked the startled tailor, with all the tremor of a guilty man. "To be cut off so suddenly in the prime of youth and beauty." "Beauty!" repeated Krauss, with a bewildered look, for in truth neither Lieder-bach nor Asbeck had any pretence to good looks. "Yes, beauty," replied Mrs. Krauss; "but I forgot that the news came while you were absent. Poor Dorothy has died sud-denly—the handsome girl who rejected that good-for-nothing Ferdinand Wenzel." Krauss dropped into a chair as if shot. His fat wife wondered a little at such excessive emotion, but remembering that her husband was very tender-hearted, went quietly on with her knitting.

Poor Peter's brain was spinning round. He who would not willingly hurt a dog, to be privy to, if not accomplice in three such atrocious and deliberate murders! His first im-pulse was to discover the whole affair to the Police: but who would believe so extraordinary a story? Where were his witnesses? Wenzel, of course, would confess nothing; and it would be difficult to call the Devil into court. Still his knowledge invested him with a very awful responsibility, and called upon him to put an end to the diabolical system. But how? Perhaps—and he shuddered at the thought—it was his dreadful duty to avert this wholesale assassination by the death of the assassin. As if to sanction the suggestion, even as it passed through the tailor's mind, the detestable Wenzel came into the shop to add some new item to his instructions. "Have you heard the news?" asked the Wild Student care-lessly; "Death is wondrous busy in Bonn." Krauss only answered with a mournful shake of the head. "Poor dear

Dorothy !" sighed Mrs. Krauss ; "so young, and so beautifuL" The Wild Student burst into a sneering laugh—
"There will be more yet," said he ; "they will keep drop,
drop, dropping, like over-ripe plums from the tree ? "

So fiendish an announcement was too much for even the
milky nature of Peter Krauss. His resolution was taken on
the spot. "Wretch ! Monster ! Were-Wolf ! " he said to
himself, "thou wert never of woman born. It can be no
more sin to slay thee than the savage tiger ! Yes,—thou
shalt hear the WORD of doom thyself ! " But the moment
he attempted to utter it, his tongue clave to the roof of his
mouth ; his throat seemed to collapse ; and when he had
regained the power of speech, the fatal word, that hitherto
had never ceased ringing in his inward ear, had vanished
completely from his memory ! However, such an oblivion
was in itself a blessing, as it removed any temptation to actual
. guilt ; but alas ! no sooner had the Wild Student departed,
than back came the hateful syllables, clear and distinct on the
tablets of Krauss's mind, like a writing in sympathetic ink.

As the vile Wenzel had predicted, the number of sudden
deaths rapidly increased. One after another, the most respectable of the inhabitants fell down in the street, and were
carried home. All Bonn was filled with lamentations and
·dismay. "It's the plague," said one. "It's the Black
Death," cried another. Some advised a consultation of
physicians ; others proposed a penitential procession to the
Kreutzberg.

In the meantime the unfortunate tailor again took refuge
in the bed-room, desperately closing his eyes and stopping his ears, against the melancholy sights and sounds that
were constantly occurring in the street. But the mortality
had become too frightful for even the apathetic temper of the
stout Trudchen, who for once, thrown into a state of violent

Tails from the German.

agitation, felt the necessity of comfort and companionship. Accordingly she sought eagerly for her husband, who, sitting as we have said, with closed eyes and ears, was of course unconscious of her entrance. Besides, he was grieving aloud, and his wife bent over him to catch the words.—" Miserable mortals," he groaned, " miserable frail mortals that we are ! —wretched candles,—blown out at a breath ! Who would have thought that such a cause could produce such a calamity ?—Who could have dreamed it ?—to think that such a hearty man as poor Liederbach, or poor Asbeck, could be destroyed by a sound—nay, that half a town should perish through simply saying —— " and the unconscious Peter pronounced the fatal WORD. It had scarcely passed his lips when something fell so heavily as to shake the whole house, and hastily opening his eyes, he beheld the comely Trudchen, the wife of his bosom, the mother of his darling Peterkin, in the last death-quiver at his feet !

The horrified Peter Krauss was stunned—stupified— bewildered ! With his eyes fixed on the victim of his fatal curiosity, he sat motionless in his chair. It was the shock of a moral earthquake, that shook his very soul to its founda-tions. He could neither think nor feel. His brain was burning hot, but his heart seemed turned to solid ice. It was long before he was even sensible of outward impressions ; but at last he became aware of a continued tugging at the tail of his coat. A glance sufficed—it was little Peterkin. " He will be the next !" shrieked the frantic father ; and tossing his arms aloft, he threw himself down the stairs and rushed out of the house. At the top of his speed, as if pursued by the unrelenting Fiend, he raced through the streets and out of the gates, into the open country, where he kept running to and fro like a mad creature, tormented by the stings of conscience. Over rocks, amongst thickets, through water, he leaped and crashed, and struggled; his flesh was torn and bleeding, but he cared not—he wanted to die.   At one time his course lay towards the Eifel, as if to end his misery in that scene of volcanic desolation, so similar to his own; but suddenly turning round, he scoured back to his native town, through the gates, along the streets, and dashing into the church of St. Remi, threw himself on his knees beside the confessional. The venerable Father Ambrose was in the chair, and with infinite difficulty extracted the horrible story from the distracted man. When it was ended, the priest desired to know the awful WORD which acted with such tremendous energy. "But, your reverence," sobbed Krauss, with a thrill of natural horror, "it kills those who but hear it pronounced."

"True, my son," replied the aged priest, "but all unholy spells will lose their power within these sacred walls."

"But your reverence ——"

"Peter Krauss!" said the priest, in a loud angry tone, "I insist on it, if you hope for absolution."

"Then, if I must ——"

"Speak, my son, speak."

'I will."

"Now!"

"Yes!"

"Come."

"Ah! ——"

"What is it?"

"Sancta Maria!"

"The word! the word!"

"POTZTAUSEND!" murmured Krauss, in a low tremulous voice, with a shudder throughout his frame, and a terrified look all round him. And lo! the ghostly father was a ghost indeed—the church of St. Remi had tumbled

All in one day.

into fragments, and instead of the holy tapers, a few strange lights were gleaming mysteriously in the distance. "Potztausend!" repeated Peter Krauss, giving himself a shake, and rubbing his eyes, "it's all the fault of the good Ahrbleichart; but I've certainly been sleeping and dreaming on the wrong side of the town-gate!"

TO REBECCA PAGE.

Dear Becky,

Missis being gone off to bed betimes, I take the oportunity to set up to rite to you how we get on. At this present we are at Bon, an old town with very good prospex, but dredful uproarus by reason of its Collidge, and so menny Schollards, witch as I've experenst at Oxford, always make more desturbans and hubbub then the ignorent and unlarned. To be sure wen the Germin ones are not making a noys, they sing bewtiful, witch is sum amends. Its been like a vocle consort all the evening in the streets. But then such figgers! It seems every won's studdy by dressing up and transmogrifying, to make himself as partickler as he can. Sum have square beerds, sum have triangle ones, sum have two mustaches, and sum contrive to have three, by sticking another on their chins. Thinks I, wen the hollydis cum, it must be a wise Father as nose his hone son!

But its the same in Garmany with the brute beastasses witch are no more left to natur than the human creturs. I mean the canine specious. One fine day, all at once, as if by command of the Lord Mare, lo and behold there was every Dog little or big, as had any hare, long or short on the scruff of his neck, mettimorfust into a Lion!

This arternoon we made a carridge incursion to a place
called the Krook's Burge.   After passing seven crosses,
before hand, you cum to a very holy Church on the top of a
hill, with the identicle flite of stares as led up to Poushus
Pilot's seat, and the drops of blud that fell from our Savior.
As such its the hite of wickedness to walk up them xcept on
your nees.   And oh Becky what do you think—I wouldn't
have had it happen to me, for pounds upon pounds, but
Missis was so thoghtless as stand upon the top stare, whereby
the parish clark called out quite horrifide, witch scard her so,
she scuttled a full half-way down.   Howsumever, it was
husht up, and she got over it—but if so be it had been *my*
case, I think my feet would often fly in my face.   Besides, I
have sinse heard a story that made my verry blud run could.
One day an Inglish lady stood on purpus on the top stare to
show her unbeleaf.   But a judgment fell upon her.   Afore
she could get back to Bon, her feet begun to ake and swell
as big as elifants, and partickly the soles as had sinned the
wust turned cole black and begun to mortify.   All the
Dockters in the place couldn't stop it, and she must 'have
died in tormints here and hereafter wen sumbody advized to
go up the holy stares on her bendid nees.   Accordingly
witch she did, and no sooner got to the tip-top wen lo and
behold her feet in a moment was as well and as sound as
ever !   In course she turnd Cathlick direckly, and in the
gratefulness of her hart she offered up too littel moddles of
feet in ivery, with the toe nails of goold.   Thats wat I call a
mirakel, tho sum pepel may chuse to dout.   But as a Party
you dont know says, what's faith ?   As for beleavin whats
only plain and probberble, and nateral, says he, its no beleaf
at all.   But wen you beleave in things totaly unpossible and
unconsistent and uncomprensible, and direct contrary to
natur, that is real true down-rite faith, and to be sure so it is.

And now, Becky, it must never go furder, but be kep a religus secret betwixt our two selves, but ever sinse Colon Cathedrul I have been dredful unsettled in my mind with spirituous pints.   It seemed as if I had a call to turn into a Roman.   Besides the voice in my hone inward parts, I've been prodigusly urged and advised by the Party you don't know, to becum a prostelyte, and decant all my errors, and throw meself into the buzzum of Rome.   Cander compels to say, its a very cumfittable religun, and then such splendid Churchis and alters and grand cerimonis, and such a bewtiful musicle service, and so many mirakles and wunderful relicts besides, plain Church of England going, partickly in the country parts, do look pore and mean and pokey after it, that's the truth.   To be sure theres transmigration, but even that I might get over in time, for we can beleave anything if we really wish to.   Its a grate temptation, and provided I felt quite certin of bettering meself, I would convert meself at once.   But Lord nose, praps its all the work of Satan at bottom awanting me to deny my Catkism and throw off the Minester I've set under so menny years.   Oh, Becky, its terribel hard wurk to argufy yureself out of yure own per-suasion !   You may supose with such contrary scrupples and inward feelings pulling two ways at once, what trubbles and tribbleation I go thro !   The wust is, my low fits and cryings cant be hid from Missis, who have questioned me very closely, but if she once thoght I was agoing to turn and alter my religun, it wood soon be, Martha, sute yureself, witch to be throne out of place in a forrin land would be very awkwurd ; and as such praps would be most advizable to put off my beleaving in anything at all, till our return to Kent. Besides, Becky, you may feel inclind, on propper talking to, to give up yure own convixions too, and in that case we can both embrace the Pope at the same time.   As yet no sole suspex xccpt Mr. Frank, who ketched me crossing meself by way of practis before the glass. Goodness nose what he ment, but ho, ho, Martha, says he, so you've got into the clutchis of the Proper Gander.

Besides the holy stares, theres another mirakel in the Volt under the Krooks burge Church, namely, abuv a skore of ded Munks, sum of them as old as fore hundred sentries, yet perfickly fresh and sweet. They say its the sanktimonious-ness of the place that has preserved them so long, witch is like enuff. But oh, Becky, its an awful site, and will set me dreeming of Ghostesses and Could Munks for a munth to cum. Our next stop was at Poplar's Dorf, where there is a British Museum full of all sorts of curiosities, such as oars from the Minors, wooden timber trees made of cole, and partickly sum peterfried frogs, witch I was told had been pelted till they turned into stone. The poor frogs do get sadly pelted that's certin.

After the museum we driv home, and a rare frite and narro escape we had by the way as you may judg. It was getting rather duskish, wen all of a sudden out jumpt a very ill lookin yung man from behind a tree, and begun running behind the carridge. He was drest xactly like a Banditty, such as you see in a play in Drewry Lane or Common Garden ; but besides, I 'overherd yung Master say he suposed he was one of Shiller's gang of Robbers. A pretty hearing for us females ! Howsumever as Missis didn't screech no more did I—but you may be shure I set and quacked all the way till we got safe into Bon.

The family is all in their ordnary way. Master as yushal talks of dying tho without goin off—but human natur will cling to this wurld like a puddon when you haven't butterd the dish. If anything, Missis takes on less than she used to about her poor dear late : and as for Mr. Frank, he's so

" And beauty draws us by a single hair."

harty he's quite a picter. Wishing you the same, and with luv to all enquiering frends, I remane, dear Becky, your luving frend till deth,

MARTHA PENNY.

P.S.—The fair sects have a hard place in Garmany. I forgot to say in our incursion we saw plenty of wimmin, a toilin and moilin at mens labers in the roads and fields. But thats not the wust, theyre made beasts of. Wat do you think, Becky, of a grate hulkin feller, a lolluping and smoking in his boat on the Rind, with his pore Wife a pullyhawling him along by a rope, like a towin horse on the banks of the Tems !

———◆———

TO GERARD BROOKE, ESQ.

MY DEAR GERARD,

AFTER the postscript of my last letter, you will not be surprised to hear, that a longer stay at Bonn was strongly objected to by my uncle, who, having "not many days to live," sets a peculiar value on his nights. Like myself, he had been annoyed by the nocturnal rattling and singing,— and indeed he declared in the morning that he would as lief reside "next door to Vauxhall."

The arrival of the first steamboat was therefore the signal for our departure; and bidding adieu to Bonn with an emphatic "*Peace* be with you," we embarked in the Prince William. It had brought a tolerable assortment of tourists from Cologne, and amongst the rest our old acquaintance the Red-faced man. For some reason he fought particularly shy of my uncle,—but with myself he was as communicative and complaining as usual. He gave me to understand that he had been prodigiously disgusted by the high Catholic mummeries at Cologne, and still more annoyed by the companionship of the "Yellow-faced Yankee," who, of course, to plague him, had taken up his quarters at the same hotel. "Renounce me," said he, "if I could get rid of him—for as we two were the only persons that spoke English in the house he *would* converse with me, whether I answered or not. Consume his yellow body! he stuck to me like a mustard plaster, and kept drawing my feelings into blisters;—however, I've got a good start of him, for he talked of staying a whole week at Cologne." But alas! for the pleasant anticipations of Mr. John Bowker! He had barely uttered them, when the turmeric-coloured American appeared running at full speed towards the steamboat, followed by a leash of porters! "Say I told you so!" exclaimed the petrified citizen—"he'll haunt me up to Schaffhausen—he will, by all that's detestable—yes, there he comes on board"—and even as he spoke the abhorred personage sprang into the vessel, followed by his three attendants. The Red-face could not smother a grunt of dissatisfaction at the sight, but what was his horror, when, after a few words with the conducteur, his old enemy walked straight up to him, and puffed a whiff of tobacco smoke into his very face! "It's an unpleasant sort of a fix," said he, "and in course only a mistake, but you've walked off with all my traps and notions instead of your own." "I've what?" gobbled the Red-face, its crimson instantly becoming shot with blue. "You've got my luggage, I guess," replied the Yellow-face, "and if it's all the same to you, I'll just take it ashore." The perplexed Bowker was too much agitated to speak; but hurrying off to the huge pile of bags and boxes, in front of the funnel, began eagerly hunting for his baggage. To his unutterable dismay he could not recognise a single article as his own. In the meantime

the American appeared to enjoy the confusion, and in a dry
way began to "poke his fun" at the unfortunate traveller.
"Mister Broker, is that 'ere your leather trunk?" "No,"
growled the other. "In that case it's mine, I reckon."
"Mister Broker, is that 'ere your carpet-bag?"—and in the
same provoking style he went through nine or ten packages
seriatim. "And where—where the devil is my luggage
then?" asked the bewildered Bowker. "The last time I see
it," said the Yellow-face, "it was in the passage of the
Mainzer Hof; and there it is still, I calculate, provided it
hasn't been shipped downwards to Rotterdam." "To Rotterdam!" shouted the Red-face, literally dancing with excite-
ment: "Gracious powers! what shall I do?" and then
hastily turning round to appeal to the nearest bystander,
who happened to be my aunt, "Renounce me, madam, if I have
even got a clean shirt!" "It's all right," said the American,
as the porters shouldered the last of his properties ;—"it's an
ugly job, that's the truth; but it might have been a considerable deal worse, and so I wish you a regular pleasant
voyage up the rest of the Rhine."

"Say I told you so!" repeated the discomfited Bowker,
after a long hyena-like grin at the receding object of his
aversion—"it was all as true as gospel—he *is* my evil genius
and nothing else!—If it hadn't been for his yellow face—
(here, you Sir, in the green apron—a glass of brandy and
water—hot, and strong!) if it hadn't been for his infernal
yellow face, I say, I should have looked after my luggage!
But he's my evil genius, sir—I know it: renounce me if I
don't believe he's the Devil himself! Why else don't his
jaundice kill him—I should like to know that—why don't it
kill him, as it would any one else?" Luckily his eloquence
was here interrupted by the hot brandy and water; and the
conducteur undertaking to forward the missing baggage to

Coblenz, the crimson face gradually grew paler, whilst his temper cooled down in proportion, from the red heat of Cayenne pepper to that of the common sort.

The bell now rang, forewarning the passengers and their friends that it was time to separate;.whereupon, to the infinite surprise of my aunt, two remarkably corpulent old gentlemen tumbled into each other's arms, and exchanged such salutes as are only current in England amongst females, or between parties of opposite sexes. To our notions there is something repulsive in this kissing amongst men; but when two weather-beaten veterans, "bearded like the pard," or like Blücher, indulge in these labial courtesies, there is also something ludicrous in the picture. It is, however, a national propensity, like the bowing; and to the same gentleman who told me the anecdote of Herr Klopp, I am indebted for a similar illustration.

"On the last New Year's Eve," said he, "being at Coblenz, I took it into my head to go to an occasional grand ball that was given at the civil Casino. The price of the tickets was very moderate; and the company was far more numerous than select. Indeed a Frenchman of the time of the republic might have supposed that it was a fête given in honour of the famous principle of Egalité—there was such a commixture of all ranks. At one step I encountered the master tailor who had supplied the coat on my back; at another, I confronted the haberdasher of whom I had purchased my gloves and my stock;—the next moment I was brushed by a German baron—and then I exchanged bows with his Excellency the Commander of the Rhenish Provinces. There was, however, a sort of West-end to the room, where the fashionables and the Vons seemed instinctively to congregate; whilst the bulk of the bourgeoisie clustered more towards the door. Dancing began early, and by help of relays of per-

The Omni-Buss.

formers, one incessant whirl of gown-skirts and coat-tails was
kept up until midnight, when, exactly at twelve o'clock, the
advent of another year was announced by the report of some
little cannons in an adjoining room. The waltz immediately
broke up, and in an instant the whole crowd was in motion,
males and females, running to and fro, here and there, in
and out, like a swarm of ants, when you invade their nest.
Whenever any two individuals encountered, who were friends
or acquaintance, they directly embraced, with a mutual
exclamation of 'Prosit Neue Jahr!' Bald, pursy old gentlemen trotted about crony-hunting—and sentimentally falling
on each other's waistcoats, hugged, bussed, and renewed their
eternal friendships for twelve months to come. Mature
dowagers bustled through the moving maze on the same
affectionate errands; whilst their blooming marriageable
daughters, seeking out their she-favourites, languished into
each other's fair arms, and kissed lips, cheeks, necks, and
shoulders,—none the less fondly that young, gay, and gallant
officers, and tantalized bachelors were looking on. I stumbled
on my tailor, and he was kissing—I came across my linen-
draper, and he was being kissed:—I glanced up at the
musicians, and they were kissing in concert! It was a
curious and characteristic scene; but remembering that I was
neither saluting nor saluted, and not liking to be particular, I
soon caught up my hat, and passing the doorkeeper, who was
kissing the housekeeper, I kissed my own hand to the Coblenz
casino, and its New Year's Ball."

And now, Gerard, could I but write scenery as Stanfield
paints it, what a rare dioramic sketch you should have of the
thick-coming beauties of the abounding river:—the Romantic
Rolandseck—the Religious Nonnenwerth—the Picturesque
Drachenfels! But "Views on the Rhine" are little better
than shadows even in engravings, and would fare still worse

in the black and white of a letter. Can the best japan fluid
give a notion of the shifting lights and shades, the variegated
tints of the thronging mountains—of the blooming blue of
the Sieben Gebirge? Besides, there is not a river or a
village but has been done in pen and ink ten times over by
former tourists. Let it be understood then, once for all,
that I shall not attempt to turn prospects into prospectuses,

"And do all the gentlemen's seats by the way."

I must say a few words, however, on a peculiarity which
seems to have escaped the notice of other travellers : the
extraordinary transparency of the atmosphere in the vicinity
of the Rhine. The rapidity of the current, always racing in
the same direction, probably creates a draught which carries
off the mists that are so apt to hang about more sluggish
streams—or to float lazily to and fro with the ebb and flow of
such tide rivers as the Thames : certainly it is, that the
lovely scenery of the "arrowy Rhine" is viewed through an
extremely pure medium. To one like myself, not particularly
lynx-sighted, the effect is as if some fairy euphrasy had conferred a supernatural *clairvoyance* on the organs of vision.
Trees and shrubs, on the crests of the hills, seem made out,
in the artist phrase, to their very twigs ; and the whole
landscape appears with the same distinctness of detail as if
seen through an opera-glass or spectacles. To mention one
remarkable instance : some miners were at work on the face
of a high precipitous mountain near Unkel ;—the distance
from the steamer was considerable, so that the blows of their
sledges and pickaxes were quite unheard ; yet there were the
little figures, plying their tiny tools, so plainly, so apparently
close to the eye, that it was difficult to believe that they were
of the common dimensions of the human race. Had those
dwarf miners, the Gnomes of German romance, a material as

well as a fabulous existence ?   Of course not : but I could
not help thinking that I saw before me the source whence
tradition had derived the Lilliputian mine-hunting elfins of
the Wisperthal, who constructed the Devil's Ladder.

I was rather disappointed at Bonn, by the first sight of
what sounds so poetically, a vineyard.   The stunted vines,
near at hand, are almost as prosaical as so many well-grown
gooseberry bushes—indeed a hop-ground beats a vineyard all
to sticks, or more properly, all to poles—as a picturesque
object : but in some degree the graperies have since re-
deemed themselves.   They serve to clothe the hills with a
pleasant verdure ; and at a distance give a *granulated* appearance to a blue mountain, which has something artistic about
it, like the tint on a rough drawing-paper compared with the
sleekness of the same tint on a smooth Bristol card-board.
In the autumn, when the leaves change colour, the vines
become still more pictorially valuable to the eye, as during
the season of their blossoming they are peculiarly grateful to
another sense by their rich fragrance.   Besides, there is
occasionally something morally interesting in the mode of
their culture : for instance, at the Erpeler Ley, where the
vines literally grow from baskets filled with earth, which are
carried up and planted in all practicable holes and corners of
the barren rock.   In other places, the precarious soil in terrace
under terrace, is secured from sliding down the shelving
mountain by dwarf walls of loose stones, which, at a distance,
look like petty fortifications.   Considering these toilsome
expedients, and their vinous product, one may truly exclaim,

"Hic, labor, *Hock* opus est !"

As you leave the open country around Bonn, the towns and
villages become more retired in their habits, the natives
creeping like earwigs and cockroaches into the cracks and

crevices of the land, where their habitations are crowded into
such narrow gorges and gulleys as to be only visible when you
are right abreast of these ravines.   You then discover a
huddle of houses, with dark high-pitched roofs, pierced with
two or three rows of port-holes—such dwellings presenting a
very quaint and picturesque but Doubly Hazardous appearance,—whole villages having, seemingly, been built by some
speculating timber-merchant, who found his staple was quite
a drug in the market. Accordingly every front, back, or
gable is profusely interlaced with beams and rafters, not in
conformity with any architectural rules, but stuck in as
uprights, cross-pieces, and diagonals, by mere chance or
caprice.   Imagine this intricate wood-work, either painted or
of sundry natural hues,—that the wall between is white-
washed (Hibernicé) with bluish, yellowish, reddish, or verdant
tints—pale pinks, lilac, salmon colour, bleu-de-ciel, pea-green,
and you may form some idea of the striped and motley aspect
of a Rhenish village.   A church spire generally rises above
the dark-clustered roofs ; and a number of little chapels, like
religious outposts, are perched on the neighbouring heights.

Amongst the churches, there is a steeple of common
occurrence, which, from a particular point of view, reminds
one of the roofs in certain pictures that are rather older than
the rules of perspective.*

A comfortable life the inhabitants of the Rhenish towns
and villages must have had under the sway of the Knight-
Hawks, whose strongholds invariably frowned on some adjacent
crag ! Can you imagine a timid female, with weak nerves, or
a mild gentlemanly sort of person, living at all in the Middle
Ages ? One of these noble robbers, the Count Henry of Sayn
mortally fractured the skull of a young boy by what was only

meant for a paternal pat of the head; it is easy to suppose, then, how heavily fell the gauntleted hand, when it was laid on in anger. What atrocious acts of perfidy, barbarity, and debauchery were openly or secretly perpetrated within those dilapidated castles! What fiendish contrivances for executing " wild justice !" The cruel Virgin-Effigy, whose embrace was certain and bloody death! The treacherous Oubliette, with its trap, whereon to tread was to step, like Amy Robsart, from Time into Eternity! But the Freebooters are extinct, and their strongholds are now mere crumbling ruins; not the less beautiful for their decay to the painter or to the moralist. It must wholesomely stagger the prejudices of a *laudator temporis acti* to muse on those shattered monuments and their historical associations; nor would the spectacle be less salutary to a certain class of political theorists— as was hinted by my uncle. "I'll tell you what, Frank, I do wish our physical-force men would hire a steamer and take a trip up the river Rhine; if it was only that they might see and reflect on these tumble-down castles. To my mind every one of them i like a gravestone, set up at the death and burial of Brute Force."

Verily, these are but sorry Pleasures of Memory to be illustrated by such enchanting natural scenery as Roland-seck, the Nonnenworth, and the Drachenfels! *Apropos* to which last, you will find enclosed a new version of ". Der Kampf mit dem Drachen." It may have less romance than the indigenous legends, but, perchance, all the more reality.

Along with these souvenirs of the " good old times," it was our fortune to have a sample of the good new ones. My uncle had been alluding to some rumoured insubordination amongst the Landwehr, encamped in readiness for the Autumnal Grand Manœuvres at Coblenz—when he was accosted by a stranger, who, apologising for the liberty, begged to caution him against touching on such subjects. "It may bring you, sir," said he,

"into serious trouble—and you might be required to produce
the parties, from whom you had the report." My uncle of
course thanked his informant, but with a wry face, and soon
fell into audible soliloquy : "Humph!—I thought it was
written, 'He that hath an ear let him hear'—but I suppose
even the Scriptures are forbidden in such despotical countries.
Well, it's all one to a dying man—or for my part I wouldn't
live under such a suspicious government for a week!" I
afterwards took occasion to inquire of the stranger if there
was really any ground for apprehension, or such a system of
espionage as his warning would seem to imply? "Ask Von
Raumer," was his answer,—"or rather his book. He will
tell you that the Prussian Police has been too busy in what
he calls *fly-catching*, and has even driven patient people—and
who so patient as the Germans?—to impatience. He will
tell you that the folly of a day, the error of youth, is recorded
in voluminous documents, as *character indelibilis;* and that
the long list of sins is sent to Presidents and Ambassadors,
that they may keep a sharp look-out after the guilty. Fly-
catching may sound like a mild term, sir, but not when you
remember that the greatest of all fly-catchers are Butchers."
" And pray, sir," I asked, "did any instance come under your
own observation?" "Yes,—the very night of my first visit
to Coblenz there was an arrest, and the Blue-bottle, the son
of a President, was carried off in a cart, escorted by gens-
d'armes, for Berlin. He has recently been pardoned, but under
conditions, and after two long years of suspense—a tolerable
punishment in itself, sir, for a little buzzing !"

Nothing further of interest (scenery excepted) occurred in
our progress. Passing ancient Andernach, Hoche's obelisk,
—and liberal thriving Neuwied, a standing refutation of all
intolerant theories, we at last approached the end of our
voyage. The sun was setting behind Ehrenbreitstein, and

whilst the massy rock and its fortress slept in solid shade, the opposite city of Coblenz, encircled by its yellow and loop-holed walls, shone out in radiant contrast,

"With glittering spires and pinnacles adorn'd."

The view is magnificent, especially when you command that "Meeting of the Waters," whence the city derives its name. The junction, indeed, is rather like an ill-assorted marriage, for the two rivers, in spite of their nominal union, seem mutually inclined to keep themselves to themselves. But so it is in life. I could name more than one couple, where, like the Rhine and the Moselle, the lady is rather yellow and the gentleman looks blue.

In a very few minutes the steamer brought up at the little wooden pier just outside of the town-gates ; and in as many more we were installed in the Grand Hotel de Belle Vue. You will smile to learn that our hypochondriac has conceived such a love at first sight for Coblenz, that, forgetting his "warnings," he talks of spending a month here ! Love to Emily from,

Dear Gerard, yours very truly,
FRANK SOMERVILLE.

P.S.—I have found here a letter for me, *poste restante*, that has thrown the head of the family into an unusual tantrum. It seems that, by previous arrangement between the parties, in default of my uncle's writing from Rotterdam it was to be taken for granted that he was defunct, in which case his old crony and attorney at Canterbury had full instructions how to proceed. The lawyer, not hearing from Rotterdam, has chosen to consider his client as "very dead indeed,"—and thereupon writes to advise me that he has proved the will, &c., &c., in conformity with the last wishes of my late and respected uncle. Between ourselves, I suspect it is a plot got

up between Bagster and Doctor Truby, by way of physic to a
mind diseased ; if so, the dose promises to work wholesomely,
for our hypochondriac is most unreasonably indignant, and
inconsistently amazed at having his own dying injunctions
so very punctually fulfilled !

THE KNIGHT AND THE DRAGON.

IN the famous old times,
(Famed for chivalrous crimes)
As the legends of Rhineland deliver,
Once there flourished a Knight,
Who Sir Otto was hight,
On the banks of the rapid green river !

On the Drachenfels' crest
He had built a stone nest,
From which he pounced down like a vulture,
And with talons of steel
Out of every man's meal
Took a very extortionate multure.

Yet he lived in good fame,
With a nobleman's name,
As " Your High-and-well-born " address'd daily—
Though Judge Park in his wig
Would have deemed him a prig,
Or a cracksman, if tried at th' Old Bailey.

It is strange—very strange !
How opinions will change !—

How antiquity blazons and hallows
Both the man, and the crime,
That a less lapse of time
Would commend to the hulks or the gallows !

Thus enthrall'd by Romance,
In a mystified trance,
E'en a young, mild, and merciful woman
Will recal with delight
The wild keep, and its Knight,
Who was quite as much tiger as human !

Now it chanced on a day,
In the sweet month of May,
From his casement Sir Otto was gazing,
With his sword in the sheath,
At that prospect beneath,
Which our tourists declare so amazing !

Yes—he gazed on the Rhine,
And its banks, so divine ;
Yet with no admiration or wonder,
But the *goût* of a thief,
As a more modern chief
Looked on London, and cried " What a plunder !"

From that river so fast,
From that champaign so vast,
He collected rare tribute and presents ;
Water-rates from ships' loads,
Highway-rates on the roads,
And hard poor-rates from all the poor peasants !

When behold ! round the base
Of his strong dwelling-place,
Only gained by most toilsome progression,
He perceived a full score
Of the rustics, or more,
Winding up in a sort of procession !

"Keep them out ! " the Knight cried,
To the warders outside—
But the hound at his feet gave a grumble !
And in scrambled the knaves,
Like feudality's slaves,
With all forms that are servile and humble.

"Now for boorish complaints !
Grant me patience, ye Saints ! "
Cried the Knight, turning red as a mullet ;
When the baldest old man
Thus his story began,
With a guttural croak in his gullet !

"Lord supreme of our lives,
Of our daughters, our wives,
Our she-cousins, our sons, and their spouses,
Of our sisters and aunts,
Of the babies God grants,
Of the handmaids that dwell in our houses !

"Mighty master of all
We possess, great or small,
Of our cattle, our sows, and their farrows ;

Of our mares and their colts,
Of our crofts, and our holts,
Of our ploughs, of our wains, and our harrows!

"Noble Lord of the soil,
Of its corn and its oil,
Of its wine, only fit for such gentles!
Of our cream and sour-kraut,
Of our carp and our trout,
Our black bread, and black puddings, and lentils!

"Sovran Lord of our cheese,
And whatever you please—
Of our bacon, our eggs, and our butter,
Of our backs and our polls,
Of our bodies and souls—
O give ear to the woes that we utter!

"We are truly perplex'd,
We are frighted and vex'd,
Till the strings of our hearts are all twisted;
We are ruined and curst
By the fiercest and worst
Of all robbers that ever existed!"

"Now by Heav'n and this light!"
In a rage cried the Knight,
"For this speech all your bodies shall stiffen!
What! by Peasants miscall'd!"
Quoth the man that was bald,
"Not your Honour we mean, but a Griffin.

"For our herds and our flocks
He lays wait in the rocks,
And jumps forth without giving us warning;
Two poor wethers, right fat,
And four lambs after that,
Did he swallow this very May morning!"

Then the High-and-well-born
Gave a laugh as in scorn,
"Is the Griffin indeed such a glutton?
Let him eat up the rams,
And the lambs, and theirs dams—
If I hate any meat, it is mutton!"

"Nay, your Worship," said then
The most bald of old men,
"For a sheep we would hardly thus cavil,
If the merciless Beast
Did not oftentimes feast
On the Pilgrims, and people that travel."

"Feast on what," cried the Knight,
Whilst his eye glisten'd bright
With the most diabolical flashes—
"Does the Beast dare to prey
On the road and highway?
With our proper diversion that clashes!"

"Yea, 'tis so, and far worse,"
Said the Clown, "to our curse;
For by way of a snack or a tiffin,

Every week in the year
Sure as Sundays appear,
A young virgin is thrown to the Griffin !"

" Ha ! Saint Peter ! Saint Mark !"
Roar d the Knight, frowning dark,
With an oath that was awful and bitter :
" A young maid to his dish !
Why, what more could he wish,
If the Beast were High-born, and a Ritter !

" Now, by this our good brand,
And by this our right hand,
By the badge that is borne on our banners,
If we can but once meet
With the monster's retreat,
We will teach him to poach on our manors !"

Quite content with this vow,
With a scrape and a bow,
The glad peasants went home to their flagons,
Where they tippled so deep,
That each clown in his sleep
Dreamt of killing a legion of dragons !

Thus engaged, the bold Knight
Soon prepared for the fight
With the wily and scaly marauder ;
But, ere battle began,
Like a good Christian man,
First he put all his household in order.

"Double bolted and barr'd
Let each gate have a guard"—
(Thus his rugged Lieutenant was bidden)
"And be sure, without fault,
No one enters the vault
Where the Church's gold vessels are hidden.

"In the dark oubliette
Let yon merchant forget
That he e'er had a bark richly laden—
And that desperate youth,   .
Our own rival forsooth !
Just indulge with a kiss of the Maiden !

"Crush the thumbs of the Jew
With the vice and the screw,
Till he tells where he buried his treasure ;
And deliver our word
To yon sullen caged bird,
That to-night she must sing for our pleasure !"

Thereupon, *cap-à-pie*,
As a champion should be,
With the bald-headed peasant to guide him,
On his war-horse he bounds,
And then, whistling his hounds,
.   Prances off to what fate may betide him !

Nor too long do they seek,
Ere a horrible reek,
Like the fumes from some villanous tavern,

Set the dogs on the snuff,
For they scent well enough
The foul monster coil'd up in his cavern !

Then alighting with speed
From his terrified steed,
Which he ties to a tree for the present,
With his sword ready drawn,
Strides the Ritter High-born,
And along with him drags the scared peasant !

"O Sir Knight, good Sir Knight !
I am near enough quite—
I have shown you the beast and his grotto : "
But before he can reach
Any farther in speech,
He is stricken stone-dead by Sir Otto !

Who withdrawing himself
To a high rocky shelf,
Sees the monster his tail disentangle
From each tortuous coil,
With a sudden turmoil,
And rush forth the dead peasant to mangle.

With his terrible claws,
And his horrible jaws,
He soon moulds the warm corse to a jelly ;
Which he quickly sucks in
To his own wicked skin
And then sinks at full stretch on his belly.

Then the Knight softly goes
On the tips of his toes
To the greedy and slumbering savage,
And with one hearty stroke
Of his sword, and a poke,
Kills the beast that had made such a ravage.

So, extended at length,
Without motion or strength,
That gorged serpent they call the constrictor,
After dinner, while deep
In lethargical sleep,
Falls a prey to his Hottentot victor.

"'Twas too easy by half!"
Said the Knight with a laugh ;
" But as nobody witness'd the slaughter,
I will swear, knock and knock,
By Saint Winifred's clock,
We were at it three hours and a quarter ! "

Then he chopped off the head
Of the monster so dread,
Which he tied to his horse as a trophy ;
And, with hounds, by the same
Ragged path that he came,
Home he jogg'd proud as Sultan or Sophi !

Blessed Saints ! what a rout
When the news flew about,
And the carcase was fetch'd in a waggon ;

What an outcry rose wild
From man, woman, and child—
"Live Sir Otto, who vanquish'd the Dragon ! '

All that night the thick walls
Of the Knight's feudal halls
Rang with shouts for the wine-cup and flagon ;
Whilst the vassals stood by,
And repeated the cry—
" Live Sir Otto, who vanquish'd the Dragon !"

The next night, and the next,
Still the fight was the text,
'Twas a theme for the minstrels to brag on !
And the vassals' hoarse throats
Still re-echoed the notes—
" Live Sir Otto, who vanquish'd the Dragon !"

There was never such work
Since the days of King Stork,
When he lived with the Frogs at free quarters ;
Not to name the invites
That were sent down of nights,
To the villagers' wives and their daughters !

It was feast upon feast,
For good cheer never ceased,
And a foray replenish'd the flagon ;
And the vassals stood by,
But more weak was the cry—
" Live Sir Otto, who vanquish'd the Dragon !"

Down again sank the sun,
Nor were revels yet done—
But as if ev'ry mouth had a gag on,
Though the vassals stood round,
Deuce a word or a sound
Of " Sir Otto, who vanquish'd the Dragon !"

There was feasting aloft,
But through pillage so oft
Down below there was wailing and hunger ;
And affection ran cold,
And the food of the old,
It was wolfishly snatch'd by the younger !

Mad with troubles so vast,
Where's the wonder at last
If the peasants quite alter'd their motto ?—
And with one loud accord
Cried out " Would to the Lord,
That the Dragon had vanquish'd Sir Otto !"

TO PETER BAGSTER, ESQ., CANTERBURY.

My DEAR PETER,

    . I am not a man to be easily shocked, but I don't
know when I've been more struck of a heap, since my pitch
off Jupiter into the gravel-pit, than by your precious letter
to my nephew. Suppose you did not hear from me, what
then ? A hundred things might turn up to prevent my
taking pen in hand—but no,—dead I was to be, and dead I
am, and I suppose stuck into all the newspapers, with a

flourish about my Xtian fortitude and resignation. I know
I named Rotterdam, but why didn't you wait for my letter
from Nimeguen? I cannot help thinking that, as an old
friend, you might have stayed a post or two, and hoped for
the best, instead of taking a flying leap to such a melancholy
conclusion. Even as an old sportsman you ought to have
known better than to cry who-oop before I was fairly run
into. God knows I am but too likely to die every day and
hour of my life, without being killed before my time. If it ·
had been a first warning, there was some excuse for giving
me over—but you know as well as any one how many fatal
attacks I have pulled through in the most miraculous
manner. Go I must, and suddenly, but owing to a wonderful original constitution, as you are well aware of, I die
particularly hard. Besides, you and Truby were always
incredulous, and even if you had seen me laid out in my
coffin, it's my belief you would both have sworn it was all
sham Abram. I must say, Peter, it has gone to my heart.
Five-and-twenty years have we been hand and glove, more
like born brothers than old friends, and here you knock me
on the head with as little ceremony as a penny-a-line fellow
would kill the Grand Turk or the king of France. Hang
me, Peter, if I can believe you are your own man. As for
proving the Will, and so forth, it's the first time I ever
knew you to be prompt in law business instead of quite the
reverse ; for, asking your pardon, you did not get the nick-
name of " Lord Eldon " for nothing amongst your clients in
Kent. Then to put the whole house into mourning ! I
don't mind expense ; but it goes against the grain to be
made ridiculous and a laughing-stock, which I shall be
whenever I get back to Woodlands after being made a ghost
of to my own servants. A rare joke it will be amongst them
for John to be sent by a dead and gone master for a jug of

ale ! Besides, who knows but I may be run after by all the fools in the parish, and kissed and sung hymns to, and made a prophet of, for coming back out of my own grave, as you know your idiots down at Canterbury expected about Mad Thom !

But that is not the worst. You not only kill me out of hand, but, forsooth, you must take away my character to my own nephew. In your Burking letter to him you say, " and so, those gloomy forebodings which, amongst your late worthy uncle's friends, were looked upon as mere nervous fancies and vapourish croakings, have, alas ! been sadly fulfilled." Croakings indeed ! I always knew I should die suddenly, and I always said so, and proved it by my symptoms and inward feelings ; but is a man for that to be made out a complete hypochondriac, which I never was in my life ! I don't wish to be harsh, but if anything *could* frighten and flurry such a poor hypped croaking creature as you have made of me, out of this world into the other, it would be just such an undertaker's black pall as you have chucked over me in the shape of a condoling letter ! Luckily my own nerves are of a tougher texture, but poor Kate cried and sobbed over your infernal black-edged funeral sermon› with its comfortings and sympathisings, as if I had been fairly dead and buried in the family vault. However, I shall now drop the uncomfortable subject, hoping you will not take amiss a few words of serious advice, namely, not to treat an old friend like a defunct one, just because he don't write by every post that he is alive.

This plaguy business has so put me off the hooks, that you must excuse particulars as to our foreign travels. But I writ to Truby from Cologne, and what's better, I sent the Hock wine I bet him, and if you ride over, mayhap he will let you look at a bottle and the letter at the same time.

"O Fye, let us a' to the Bridal."

M

At this present we are at Coblenz, where we have taken lodgings for a month. The truth is, it is all on poor Kate's account, for foreign travelling is harder work than in England for females—and I shall not be sorry myself to fetch up my sleep, for between shipboard and outlandish short beds, and strange bedding, and the musical disturbances at Bonn, I have never had one good night's rest since I left the Tower Stairs.

But you must not go to suppose, old friend, from the month's lodgings, that I have better hopes of myself, or of a longer run; but there were no apartments to be had for a shorter time, and I was sick of the bustle of the hotel. If I was foolish enough to try to forget my dispensation, I should have been reminded by two German funerals that passed this very morning to the parish church of St. Castor's, hard by. As you may like to know the ceremony—the hearse, very like a deer-cart, was covered by a black pall with a large white cross, and the letters B.S., which I suppose meant Burial Society; for, besides a cross-bearer and a flag-bearer, there were about a score of regular attendants, all carrying lighted tapers and singing a hymn, though the solemnity of the thing was a little put out of sorts by the jerking antics of one man who kept rolling his head about like a harlequin with St. Vitus's dance. The mourners walked behind the hearse, with a prodigious long train of friends and towns-folk; but after the service, they all dispersed at the church door, whereby, the ground being a good mile out of town, the poor old gentleman went to his grave with only a boy with a cross before him and nobody at all behind him; just as if he had gone off in a huff, or been sent to Coventry by all that belonged to him. The same, to our English notions looking rather neglectful and dis-respectful, and to my mind not in character with such a

romantical, feeling, and sentimental people as the Germaus,
—whereby I have made Frank promise to go to the ground
and see the last of me till I am fairly earthed. And it won't
be long, poor fellow, before he is called to his sad duties. I
feel sensibly worse since beginning this letter, and as such,
old friend, your card of condolement was only wrong in point
of date, and by the time this comes to hand may be a true
bill, down to the hatbands and gloves.

          ✱   ✱   ●   ●   ✱

Since the above there has been another guess-sort of
procession to old St. Castor's Church—namely, a marriage.
Having lived single so long, without enlarging on my opinious
of wedlock, you may guess their nature by what I may call
my silent vote on the subject. But to judge by the young
fellow who played bridegroom I must have been wrong all
my days, for there must be as great difference of quality
between single blessedness and the other, as between single
Gloster and Stilton. Frank has sketched him off with his
"tail,"—but blacklead pencil can give no notion of his action
and moveable airs. Zounds! you would have thought a
Benedict was as much above a bachelor as a thorough-bred
to a cart-horse. And mayhap so he is; but for my part, as
Frank said, I could not make myself such a walking object
in public for the best of women. What's more, I cannot even
guess how a bashful young fellow could get over a German
courtship if it's at all such a before-folk affair as is described
by the Old Man in his Book of Bubbles—namely, a lover
taking a romantic country walk with his intended, and eight
or ten of her she-cronies singing, laughing, and waltzing after
her heels. Without being particularly sheepish or shame-
faced as a young man, I don't think I could have gone
sweet-hearting with half a score of bouncing girls ballad-

Pig Coursing.

singing and whirligigging along with me, all agog, of course, to see how love was made, giggling at my tender sentiments, and mayhap scoring every kiss like a notch at cricket, provided one could have the face to kiss at all in such a company. But foreign love-making is like foreign cookery; an egg is an egg all the world over, but there are a hundred ways of dishing it up.

And now, old friend, God bless you and all your family, by way of a last farewell from your old and faithful friend,

RICHARD ORCHARD.

I wish you could see the breed of pigs in these parts. They are terribly long in the legs, and thin in the flanks, and would cut a far better figure at a Coursing Meeting than a Cattle Show. Some of them quite run lean enough for greyhounds.

———————

TO GERARD BROOKE, ESQ.

MY DEAR GERARD,

You will not be sorry to receive tidings of a person whose mysterious disappearance, some two or three years back, cost us both some speculation. Yesterday, whilst looking at the monument of Cuno of Falkenstein, in the venerable church of St. Castor, I was accosted by name, and with some difficulty recognised, under a German cap and kittel, our old friend Markham. In answer to my inquiries, he told me a new edition of the old story—of "becoming security for a friend," &c.; in short, he had come abroad to retrench, and selected this bank of the Rhine for his saving-bank. From what I could learn, the experiment had not answered his expectations. "You remember," said he, "our laughing at a written notice stuck up at the Opera House in London, enforcing certain exclusive regulations, in consequence of the great *affluence* of strangers behind the scenes! In the same sense, the great affluence of strangers up the Rhine has not only had the effect of raising the price of every article, but with its proper meaning, the supposed affluence of the English travellers has generated a proportionate spirit of rapacity and extortion. I reckon, for instance, that I am charged a third more than a native on my whole expenditure, so that you see there is not so much room left for saving."

Of course the opinions of a disappointed man must be received *cum grano salis*,—but in the main Markham's statements agree with those of Grundy, and though his remarks have occasionally a splenetic tone, yet he "gives his reasons." On some topics his outbreaks are rather amusing. Thus, when I asked if he did not find the natives a very good, honest sort of people, he replied to my question by another— "Do you expect that the descendants of our Botany Bay convicts will be remarkable for their strict notions of *meum* and *tuum?*" "Of course not," said I; "but the honesty of the German character has been generally admitted." "Granted," said he, "but there is such a thing as giving a dog a good name as well as a bad one, upon which he lives and thrives as unjustly as another is pitch-forked or shot with slugs. That the Germans are honest as a nation I believe, as regards your Saxons, Bavarians, Austrians, or north-countrymen,—but as for your Coblenzers, and the like, whence were they to derive that virtue? Was the *rara avis* hatched in any of the robbers' nests so numerous in these provinces? Was it inculcated by the ministers of their religion? An Archbishop of Cologne, when asked by one of

his retainers how he was to subsist, significantly pointed out,
that the Knight's castle overlooked four highways, and hinted
to his vassal that, like Macheath, he must take to the road.
No, no,—if the Rhinelanders be particularly honest, they
were indebted for their education, like Filch in the Beggars'
Opera, to very light-fingered schoolmasters. Why, every
Baron in the land was a bandit, and half the common people,
by a regularly organised system, were either Journeymen
Robbers or Apprentices. That's matter of history, my boy !
At any rate, if Rhenish honesty be a fact, our prison philan-
thropists are all wrong ; and Mrs. Fry and the sheriffs, who
are so anxious to separate the juvenile convicts from the
accomplished thieves, ought immediately to take a trip up
the Rhine. Instead of classification and moral instruction,
the true way would be something like this :—take a clever
boy, bring him up like a young Spartan—reward him for
successful picking and stealing—strike the eighth command-
ment out of his catechism—send him to school in Newgate,
and let Bill Soames be his private tutor ; do all this, and
expect eventually to discover him the Honest Man that
Diogenes couldn't find with his lantern !" "Do you speak,"
I asked, "from theory or from experience ?" "From both,"
said he ; "and comparing the Middle Ages with the modern
ones, I cannot help thinking that an extortion of some 30 per
cent. on all foreign travellers on the Rhine, has a strong
smack of the old freebooting spirit."

On leaving St. Castor's we saw, directly opposite the porch,
the well-known fountain with its celebrated inscriptions :—

"ANNO 1812.

"Mémorable par la Campagne contre les Russes, sous la
Préfecture de Jules Douzan."

"Vu et approuvé, par nous Commandant Russe de la Ville
de Coblentz, le 1ᵉʳ Janvier, 1814."

"There !" said Markham, pointing to the graven words,
"there are two sentences which have caused far more
cackling than they deserved. The adulation of mayors and
prefects is too common, for the erection of a monument on
any occasion, or no occasion at all, to be a matter of
wonder. But the mere undertaking an expedition against
Russia, *was* a memorable event in the career of Napoleon,
whatever its ultimate result. As for the Russian General,
he might naturally be astonished and delighted to find himself in command of a city on the Rhine, and its obelisk ; but
his comment, if it points any moral at all, chiefly recalls the
uncertainty of all human calculations. As a sarcasm it is
feeble, with a recoil on himself ; for where is St. Priest now,
or who hears his .name ? Whereas, the spirit of the French
Emperor still lives and breathes on the banks of the Rhine—
aye, in Coblenz itself—in his famous Code !"

Our old acquaintance volunteering to be my guide, we
made the round of the sights of the town, which are not very
numerous, as the valets-de-place are well aware when they
eke out their wonders with an old barrack or a street-pump.
So having seen the new Palace, the house that cradled Prince
Metternich, the Jesuits' Church with its surprising cellars,
and some other local " Lions " and cubs, we adjourned to
Markham's lodgings, where, after ascending a dark, dirty,
circular staircase, we entered an apartment with a visible air
of retrenchment about it ; for, with mere apologies for
window-curtains, it had given up carpets, and left off fires.
The only ornamental piece of furniture, for it certainly was
not useful, was the sofa, which on trial afforded as hard and
convex a seat as a garden-roller. " Rather different from my
old snuggery in Percy Street," said my host with a dubious
smile. " There is not, indeed, much sacrifice to show," I
replied, " but perhaps the more solid comfort." " Comfort,

my dear fellow !" cried Markham, "the Germans don't even
know it by name ; there's no such word in the language!
Look at the construction of their houses ! A front door and
a back door, with a well staircase in the middle, up which a
thorough draught is secured by a roof pierced with a score or
two of unglazed windows ; the attics by this airy contrivance
serving to dry the family linen. Make your sitting-room,
therefore, as warm as you please, with that close fuming,
unwholesome abomination, a German stove, and the moment
you step out of the chamber door, it is like transplanting
yourself, in winter, from the hot-house into the open garden.
To aggravate these discomforts, you have sashes that won't
fit, doors that don't shut, hasps that can't catch, and keys
not meant to turn ! Then, again, the same openings that
let in the cold, admit the noise ; and for a musical people,
they are the most noisy I ever met with. Next to chorus
singing, their greatest delight seems to be in the everlasting
sawing and chopping up of fire-wood at their doors ; they
even contrive to combine music and noise together, and the
carters drive along the streets smacking a tune with their
whips ! "

The conversation was here interrupted by the entrance of
Mrs. Markham, a handsome, but careful-looking personage,
to whom I was cordially introduced. Indeed she confessed
to trouble, especially a severe illness of her husband soon
after their arrival at Coblenz—not to mention all the minor
annoyances and inconveniences of living in a foreign country
without any knowledge of the language. "But those little
trials," she said, "are now things to laugh over, although
they were sufficiently harassing at the time." "My chicken,
for instance," cried Markham, with a chuckle at the remembrance. "You must know, that Harriet here took it into
her kind head that, as I was an invalid, I could eat nothing

but a boiled fowl. The only difficulty was how to get at it,
for our maid does not understand English, and her mistress
cannot speak anything else. However, Gretel was summoned,
and the experiment began. It is one of my wife's fancies
that the less her words resemble her native tongue, the more
they must be like German ; so her first attempt was to tell
the maid that she wanted a cheeking or a keeking. The
maid opened her eyes and mouth, and shook her head. 'It's
to cook,' said her mistress, 'to coke—to put in an iron thing
—in a pit—pat—pot.' 'Ish verstand nisht,' said the maid
in her Coblenz patois. 'It's a thing to eat,' said her mistress,
'for dinner—for deener—with sauce—soace—sowse.' But
the maid still shrugged her shoulders. 'What on earth am
I to do?' exclaimed poor Harriet, quite in despair, but still
making one last attempt. 'It's a live creature—a bird—a
bard—a beard—a hen—a hone—a fowl—a fool—a foal—it's
all covered with feathers — fathers — feeders — fedders!'
'Hah, hah!' cried the delighted German, at last getting
hold of a catchword, 'Ja! ja! fedders—ja wohl!' and away
went Gretel, and in half an hour returned triumphantly with
a bundle of stationer's quills!"

The truth of this domestic anecdote was certified by Mrs.
M. herself. "But I was more successful," she said, "the
next morning ; for on Gretel opening her apron, after mar-
keting, out tumbled a long-legged living cock, who began
stalking about, and chuckling with surprise to find himself
in a drawing-room. At last, on the third day I succeeded,
for I did obtain a dead fowl, and reckoned myself fortunate, even though it came in, after all, roasted instead of
boiled."

"But now you know something of the language," said I,
"you fare sumptuously, of course, for it's a luxuriant country."
"To the eye," so replied Markham, "it is lovely indeed ;

Beer with a Body.

and, at a first-rate hotel, where you enjoy the choicest of its
productions, it may keep its promise. But for a private
table, just listen to our bill of fare. Indifferent beef—veal
killed at eight days old—good mutton, but at some seasons
not to be had—poultry plentiful, but ill-fed—game in
moderation. No sea-fish—yes, oysters, as big, shell and all,
as a pennypiece, and six shillings a hundred. You hear of
salmon-fisheries, but the steamers have frightened away
the fish. I have seen about six here in two years, and
have been asked two dollars a pound ; perch 3*d.* and
4*d.* per pound ; and worthless chub and barbel *ad libitum.*
No good household bread—it is half rye—and wheaten flour
is only to be bought at the pastrycook's ; good vegetables,
but the staple one, potatoes, small and waxy, such as we
should call *chats* in England, and give to the pigs. Fruit
abundant, but more remarkable for quantity than quality,
and often uneatable from vermin,—for example, cherries,
fine to look at, but every one containing a worm. For
foreign fruit, you may have indifferent oranges at 4*d.* to
5*d.* each. Coffee reasonable and good—tea as dear and bad.
Then for wine, the lower sorts of Rhenish and Moselle are
cheap and excellent; but the superior kinds are easier to
procure in London than on the Rhine. Foreign wines you
may have at pleasure—for your honest Rhinelanders have
little to learn in the arts of adulteration and simulation.
Thus you have Bavarian beer brewed at Coblenz ; West-
phalia hams cured in Nassau ; Florence oil extracted from
Rhenish walnuts ; French Cognac, Bordeaux, and Champagne,
made from German potatoes and grapes ; English gin distilled
at Düsseldorf; and Gorgona anchovies caught in the Rhine.
Perhaps you are not aware, that in addition, the Germans are
the most notorious poison-mongers in Europe ?"

I stared, as you may suppose, at such an assertion. "It

is true, however," said Markham; "some of their physicians
have detected an active poison in their national blood-
sausages ;—a little while back there were proclamations in the
papers against poisonous-coloured sugar-plums ; Mr. Kraus
of Düsseldorf found their potato-brandy so poisonous, as to
attribute to its use most of the crimes committed in Rhenish
Prussia ;—and of course you are aware of the experiments
in London with the poor finches and the poisonous German
candles ! "

"Now he is too bad—isn't he ? " interposed Mrs. Markham, with a smile. "But it is half a joke and whim. Would
you believe it, sir, he has set me against all the beer in the
place, on account of an establishment facing the Moselle,
inscribed, oddly enough, ' Baths and Beer Brewery.' He will
have it, that as hot malt is recommended in some cases by
the German doctors, the two businesses are only brought
under one roof for the natives to bathe in the beer ! "

"And why not ? " said Markham. "Does not Head say,
that at Schwalbach they bathe in the mulligatawny soup,
and at Wiesbaden in the chicken-broth ? But to return to
our subject, the advantages of living in Coblenz. It may be
otherwise, elsewhere in Germany ; but as a general principle
take my word for it, the grand difference is not in the cost,
but in the manner of living. As for retrenchment, on the
same plan it might be effected in London. Lodge in a second
floor—dispense with a carpet,—have as little and as plain
furniture as possible—burn wood in a German stove—keep a
cheap country servant—buy inferior meat, chats, and rye-
bread—drink Cape and table-beer—see no company—dress
how you please—above all go to market, as you must do
here, with your ready-money in your hand—then sum up at
the year's-end, and I verily believe the utmost saving. by
coming to such a place as this, would be some 10*l.* or 20*l.* to

Persecuted according to Law.

set off against all the deprivations and disadvantages of expatriation."

You will perceive a little sub-acid in Markham's statements; but allowing for that ingredient, his remarks seem deserving of consideration. I suspect it would require more philosophy than most persons possess, to reside in London with the indifference as to caste, appearances, and fashion, which his scheme requires; but that persons of limited incomes might live in the provinces, or in Scotland, as cheaply, and more comfortably, than on the Continent in general, appears to me very probable, and on various accounts highly desirable; especially as experience proves that a residence abroad is as injurious, as foreign travelling is beneficial, to the English character.

Wishing to make Markham known to my uncle, I induced him to return with me to my lodgings. In our way we passed through the Place-d'Armes, a small square, surrounded by lime-trees. "Here," said my companion, "is the scene of a recent and successful insurrection!"—"Indeed!" I could not help exclaiming—"then it had but a small theatre, which I presume was the reason why the performance did not get into the English journals."—"May be so," said he, "but here is the play-bill;" and taking a small slip of paper from his pocket-book, he read to me the following manifesto:—

NOTICE.

"The warm weather of spring now returning, it is again a common duty to clear the trees and bushes of caterpillars. Notice is therefore given to all possessors of trees and bushes to clear them from caterpillars and to exterminate these destructive vermin. This clearing of the trees, &c., must be done *thoroughly* until the 10th of April. Any neglect in this respect will incur the punishment dictated by the laws of the police.

(Signed) "THE OBER-BURGERMEISTER."

"There," said Markham, "there's the proclamation! Now look up at those bare lime-trees, stripped of almost every leaf —was there ever such a practical quiz on a despotic government? It has quelled the Frankfort rioters—it has dispersed the Heidelberg students—it has bridled and curbed young Germany, and tamed the Burschenschaft—but it cannot put down the Raupenschaft! Think of a Prussian Ober-Burgermeister beaten by a blight! Imagine the first magistrate of the capital of the Rhenish provinces foiled by a secret society of grubs! Fancy the powerful prying police defied by an association of maggots,—and absolutism itself set at nought by a swarm of proscribed vermin! Nature at all events will not stand dictation; and so far from the insects being exterminated, they have got so much a-head in some parts of the country, that the proprietors of fruit-trees and bushes have had serious thoughts of cutting them all down!"

"Possibly," said I, "the authorities neglected to enforce their mandate by personal example. A police director might think it beneath his dignity to arrest a maggot; and a mounted gendarme would probably disdain to pursue a creeper."—"Yes," added Markham, "and a ponderous Head-Burgomaster might naturally decline to swarm like ''possum up a gum-tree' after an illegal caterpillar."

This conversation brought us to our lodgings, where we found my uncle just recovering from a "warning," which had been accompanied by rather singular circumstances. It appears at the Civil Casino, to which foreigners are liberally admitted, he had formed an acquaintance with a Mr. Schwärmer, who spoke a little English, and had offered to be

Easy Does It.

his Cicerone to the Kuhkopf, the highest hill near Coblenz, and celebrated for the splendid view from the top. Probably our hypochondriac was a little blown by the steepness of the ascent, or rendered rather dizzy by the height : however, feeling some unusual sensations on reaching the summit, he immediately took it for granted that he was "going suddenly ;" accordingly, deliberately preparing himself for his departure, first by sitting and then by lying down, he "composed his decent head to breathe his last." His calmness and business-like manner, I suppose, gave him an appearance of wilful premeditation to the act ; for, according to Nunkle's account, he had no sooner intimated to his companion what was about to happen, than the other, falling into one of those suicidal fits of exultation, so prevalent in Germany, burst out with, "It is one sublime tort !—and here is one sublime place for it ! I shall die too !" Whereupon, without more ceremony, he pulled a little phial of Prussic acid or some other mortal compound from his waistcoat pocket, and was proceeding to swallow the contents, when the dying man, jumping up, knocked down the bottle with one hand and Mr. Schwärmer himself with the other, and then, totally forgetting his own extremity, walked off in double quick time, nor ever stopped till he reached his own door. Two full hours had elapsed since the occurrence, but between the walk home and his moral indignation he had hardly cooled down when we arrived. "I'll tell you what, Frank," he said, on ending his story, " I never liked the four cross-roads and the stake through a suicide's body in England; but when I saw Mr. Swarmer going to drink the deadly poison, hang *me* if I wasn't tempted to drive my own walking-stick into his stomach !"

" Perhaps, sir," said Markham, " you are not aware that there was formerly a Club of Suicides in this very country.

They were bound by a vow not only to kill themselves, but
to induce as many persons as they could to follow their
example. I have not heard that they made any proselytes,
but they all died by their own hands—the last blew out
his brains, if he had any, in 1817."—"They ought to have
been hung in effigy," said my uncle. "A great many
suicides," continued Markham, "were attributable to Wer-
ther, who brought *felo-de-se* quite into vogue."—"That
Vairter," said my uncle, "ought to have been ducked in a
horse-pond."—"He was a mere fiction, sir, a creature of
Göethe's," said Markham. "Then I would have Gooty
ducked himself," said my uncle. "Even at this day," said
Markham, "there is Bettine, an authoress, who proclaims
that one of her earliest wishes was to read much, to learn
much, and to die young."—"And did *she* kill herself, sir?"
asked my aunt. "No, madam, she married instead; but
her bosom-friend, dressed in white with a crimson stomacher,
stabbed herself in such a position as to fall into the Rhine.
Then again there was Louisa Brachmann, *alias* Sappho, so
inclined to die young, that at fourteen years of age she threw
herself from a gallery, two stories high."—"And was killed
on the spot, of course?" said my aunt, with a gesture of
horror. "No, madam,—she lived to throw herself, five-and-
twenty years afterwards, into the Saale."—"How very dreadful!" shuddered out my aunt. "Yes, madam, to English
notions; but her German Biographer, or rather Apologist,
says, that her first flight in her fourteenth year was only a
lively poetical presentiment of that which weighed her down
in her fortieth, namely, the beggarliness of all human
pursuits compared with the yearnings of the soul."—"She
must have been a forward child of her age," remarked my
uncle, "to have seen and known the world so soon."—"Now
I think of it," said my aunt, "I remember reading in the

work of a female traveller in America, that on describing to
a lady her emotions at the sight of Niagara, the other asked
her if she did not feel a longing to throw herself down, and
mingle with her mother earth ?"—" That was a German
lady, you may be sure," said Markham, "or at least of
German origin. The fact is, these people kill themselves for
anything or nothing : for instance, I should be loth to trust
a sentimental Prussian with himself, with his pipe out and an
empty tobacco-bag. Young or old it is all one. Only the
other day there was a reward offered in the Rhein-und-Mosel-
Zeitung for the body of an aged gray-haired man, describing
his cap, his suit of hoddan gray, his blue woollen stockings,
and buckled shoes. One would have thought that such a
John Anderson might have had patience to 'toddle down'
the hill of life like a Christian ; but no—at the end of the
advertisement there was an intimation, that he was supposed
to have thrown himself into a neighbouring river ! Talking
of drowning—the same element is fatally used, as I have
been well informed, in a very different manner. As ball-
cartridge is not always to be got at, a common soldier
inclined to self-murder, after loading his musket with powder,
pours a quantity of water into the barrel ; by which his
head, provided it be held close to the muzzle, is frightfully
blown to atoms. One fact more and I have done, for it
literally out-Herods Herod. A Doctor, whose name I forget,
but it was given in the newspapers, not only determined to
kill himself, but to bury himself into the bargain ! With this
view he dug a grave, in which he shot himself ; the pistol, at
the same time, firing a sort of mine filled with gunpowder,
by the explosion of which, though the experiment only
partially succeeded, he expected to be covered with earth and
sand."—" And, for my part," began my uncle, "if I had been
the Coroner for Germany"—" In Germany, my good sir, there

is no Coroner."—"Egad! I thought as much," cried my uncle, "and, as it seems to me, no Schoolmaster or Clergyman either, or the people would know that, as Shakspeare says, the Almighty has fixed a canon against self-slaughter."

"Seriously," said Markham, "this propensity to suicide is a reproach which the Germans have to wipe away before they can justly claim the character of a moral, religious, or intellectual people. The more so, as it is not the vulgar and ignorant, but the educated and enlightened,—Scholars, Doctors, Literati,—men that would be offended to be denied the title of Philosophers,—women that would be shocked not to be called Christians—who are thus apt to quench the lamp of life in unholy waters, or to shatter with a profane bullet 'the dome of thought, the palace of the soul.'"

And now, Gerard, as a sermon concludes the service, these grave strictures shall end my letter. My best love to Emily and yourself.

Yours ever truly,
F. SOMERVILLE.

P.S.—We kept Markham to dine with us, after which he and I took a stroll to the other side of the Moselle Bridge, where the sight of a little chapel brilliantly lighted up, led to a conversation on the religious characteristics of the natives. According to our friend there is a good deal of bigotry extant in Coblenz, and a very active Propaganda, with a professional layman or two at its head, who aim at conversions wholesale and retail. "As an instance," said he, "there was an English family residing here, all Protestants. The head of it was occasionally absent on his travels, and one fine day at his return home—hey presto!— he found his wife, her aunt, and all his children, Roman Catholics!" By a whimsical coincidence, the anecdote had

scarcely left his lips, when, turning a corner into the high
road, who should we come upon plump, trudging up the hill
at her best pace, with a huge unlighted wax ‚taper in her
hand, but Martha, my aunt's maid! The surprise pulled us
all up short; but, before I could utter a word, she pitched
her candle into the hedge, wheeled right-about with the
alacrity of a Prussian soldier, fairly took to her heels, like a
mad cow, and, aided by the descent, was out of sight in "no
time at all." Markham, who understood the matter, burst
into a loud laugh, and then explained to me the whole
mystery; for which, if you are curious on the subject, you
may consult the enclosed verses.

OUR LADY'S CHAPEL.

A LEGEND OF COBLENZ.

WHOE'ER has cross'd the Mósel Bridge,
And mounted by the fort of Kaiser Franz,
 Has seen, perchance,
Just on the summit of St. Peter's ridge,
A little open chapel to the right,
Wherein the tapers aye are burning bright;
So popular, indeed, this holy shrine,
At least among the female population,
By night, or at high noon, you see it shine,
A very Missal for *illumination !*

Yet, when you please, at morn or eve, go by
All other Chapels, standing in the fields,
Whose mouldy, wifeless husbandry but yields
Beans, peas, potatoes, mangel-wurzel, rye,
And lo ! the Virgin, lonely, dark, and hush,
Without the glimmer of a farthing rush !

But on Saint Peter's Hill
The lights are burning, burning, burning still.
In fact, it is a pretty retail trade
To furnish forth the candles ready made ;
And close beside the chapel and the way,
A chandler, at her stall, sits day by day,
And sells, both long and short, the waxen tapers
Smarten'd with tinsel-foil and tinted papers.

To give of the mysterious truth an inkling,
Those who in this bright chapel breathe a prayer
To "Unser Frow," and burn a taper there,
Are said to get a husband " in a twinkling :"
Just as she-glowworms, if it be not scandal,
Catch partners with *their* matrimonial candle.

How kind of blessed saints in heaven—
Where none in marriage, we are told, are given—
To interfere below in making matches,
And help old maidens to connubial catches !
The truth is, that instead of looking smugly
　(At least, so whisper wags satirical)
The votaries are all so old and ugly,
　No man could fall in love but by a miracle.

However, that such waxen gifts and vows
Are sometimes for the purpose efficacious,
　　　　In helping to a spouse,
Is vouch'd for by a story most veracious.

A certain Woman, though in name a wife,
　　Yet doom'd to lonely life,

Her truant husband having been away
Nine years, two months, a week, and half a day,—
Without remembrances by words or deeds,—
Began to think she had sufficient handle
To talk of widowhood and burn her weeds—
Of course with a wax-candle.
Sick, single-handed with the world to grapple,
Weary of solitude, and spleen, and vapours,
Away she hurried to Our Lady's Chapel,
  Full-handed with *two* tapers—
And pray'd as she had never pray'd before,
To be a *bonâ fide* wife once more.
"Oh Holy Virgin ! listen to my prayer !
And for sweet mercy, and thy sex's sake,
Accept the vows and offerings I make—
Others set up one light, but here's *a pair !*"

  Her prayer, it seem'd, was heard ;
For in three little weeks, exactly reckon'd,
  As blithe as any bird,
She stood before the Priest with Hans the Second ;—
A fact that made her gratitude so hearty,
To "Unser Frow," and her propitious shrine,
She sent two waxen candles superfine,
Long enough for a Lapland evening party !

  Rich was the Wedding Feast and rare—
  What sausages were there !
Of sweets and sours there was a perfect glut :
With plenteous liquors to wash down good cheer
Brantwein, and Rhum, Kirsch-wasser, and Krug Bier,
And wine so *sharp* that ev'ry one was *cut.*

Rare was the feast—but rarer was the quality
Of mirth, of smoky-joke, and song, and toast,—
When just in all the middle of their jollity—
With bumpers fill'd to hostess and to host,
And all the unborn branches of their house,
Unwelcome and unask'd, like Banquo's Ghost,
    In walk'd the long-lost Spouse !   .

        What pen could ever paint
The hubbub when the Hubs were thus confronted !
The bridesmaids fitfully began to faint ;
The bridesmen stared—some whistled and some grunted :
Fierce Hans the First look'd like a boar that's hunted ;
Poor Hans the Second like a suckling calf :
Meanwhile, confounded by the double miracle,
The two-fold bride sobb'd out, with tears hysterical,
" Oh Holy Virgin, you're too good—*by half !* "

MORAL.

Ye Cóblenz maids, take warning by the rhyme,
And as our Christian laws forbid polygamy
        For fear of bigamy,
Only light up *one* taper at a time.

TO REBECCA PAGE.

Dear Becky,

    At long and at last here we be at Coblinse.   It's a
bewtiful Citty and well sekured all round with fortifide stone
walls with eyelet holes to shoot thro, besides being under
the purtection of a grate Castel on the other side of the

river as can batter the town all to bits in a minit. I thoght
as well to rite and let you no we have took loggings here for
a munth, but by wats to do it will be ni a fortnite afore we
are domestically setteld. Missus has hired a Gurmin Maid
to assist—her name is Catshins witch stands for Kitty and
she can talk bad inglish perfickly. As a feller servent she is
companionable and good humerd enuff, but dredful slow and
dull headed. Wat do you think she did this blessid
morning? Why kivered a panful of skalding hot milk with
the plate as held the fresh lump, witch in coarse soon run
into meltid butter! But in sich dilemmys she only hunches
up her sholders to her ears and says "hish viso nit," and
theres an end. Howsumever she's very obleeging and
yuseful to me in my new religun, such as teachin me to
cross meself the rite way and wat I'm to do when I'm in a
high Mess. I have practist fasting a littel by leaving off
lunchis but Lord nose wat I'm to do on the Fish Days for
theres nothink but stockfish and cabble yaw. But won
comfort is if it don't come too hi for my pockit the Bishup
will sell me a dispensary.

Between you and me I am going this evening to Virgen
Mary's Chapel for if so be you present a wax candle at her,
and pray with all yure hart and sole, they do say yure as
shure of a Bo as if you had him in yure hone pantry. Any
how its wurth the trial; Besides the hole town is chuck full
of officers and milentary agin the Grate Sham Fites and
Skrimmages, and as Mirakels don't stick at trifles who nose
but I may be Missis Capting? But I hear Missus Bell.

Last nite the Germins being very parshal to dancing I
went along with Catshins Cosen to a Grand Ball. There
was moor than abuv a hundred of us in won Assembly room,
but am sorry to say smoaking was aloud, witch quite spiled

the genteel.   Catshins Cosen askcd me to dance and seeing
several steddy lookin elderly women, jest such sober boddies
as our Cook or Housekeeper standing up I made bold to
accept, when all at once the music struck up and my Partner
ketching me by the waste, willy nilly, away we went on one
leg spinning like pegtops and wirligiggin at such a rate I'm
shure if my pore brains had been made of cream they would
have turned into butter !   All I could do was to skreek at
the tiptop of my voice, but noboddy minded so I broke loose
out of the ring and set meself down on the flore jest like
frog in the middle, wile the rest waltzed round and round
me steddy elderly boddies and all—but it was sich a constant
wirlin and twirlin the very room seemed running round and
my head begun to swim so I was obleeged to lay down flat
on my back and shut both my eyes.   To add to my
suffrings, afore going to the Ball I had my hair dressed by a
reglar dresser, who drew it up alla Chinese, and tied it so
tite atop that after gettin more and more paneful every
minit I felt at last like being scollupt by a Tommy Hawkin
wild Ingian !   Howsumever, when the dance was over, my
Partner cum and pickt me up and refreshed me with a glass
of sumthing verry nasty, called snaps, but what with the
frite and the giddiness and my headake and the snaps and
the fumes of the filthy tobacker I was took with a faintness
and afore I could be assisted out of the assembly room I was
as sick saving yure presence as a dog.   That spiled me a
good gownd allmost new besides loosing my best hankicher
in the bussle; but I mustn't grudge the xpense, considring
us sarvents don't often get a nite's pleasure.   Now I must
brake off agin—but it isn't Missis this tim—but Catshins
wanting to teach me my beeds.

Catshins sister has jest cum in with her babby.   I do wish

A Chrysalis.

O

you could see it—such a littel figger rolled and twistid up like a gipsian mummy! The wust is of sich tite swaddling if so be you don't put their pore little lims into the bandages quite strate, it follers to reason they will come out crookid— witch I supose is the way theres so many bandy boys about the streets—for I never see so menny rickitty objex in my born days. Why its called the Inglish Krankite by the Gurmins is best none to themselves; but I will say for the Kentish babbies they are well nust and strate in their legs, and what's more a Kentish woman wouldn't let her littel boys run about all unbuttond behind like so many Giddy Giddy Gouts, just as if they had no mother to *look after them.*

Catshins sister says there has been a shockin axident this morning in our naberhood. The climing boys in this town are grown up men instead of littel urchings as about Lonnon. Well, one of the men was sent for, to sweep a chimbley built up after the Inglish fashion, when by sum piece of bad luck or stupid-headness a fire was lited under him and down he came tumbling quite stiffled and sufocated with the smoak. So a Doctor was fetched in a hurry, and the moment he clapt eyes on the pore sutty object, wat in the wurld Becky do you think he said! "O says he, I can do nothing for him—he's black in the face!" To be sure a Doctor knows best—but for my part I never saw a chimbly sweep's face of any other culler!

Oh Becky, I've had such a flustration! After asking Missus for an hour or so for going out in the evening I was jest on my road to the chappel I told you of, when afore I knowed where I was I almost ran full butt agin Mr. Frank. What becum of my bewtiful wax candle, whether I chuckt it away or yung Master took it out of my hand, I know no

moor then the man in the moon I was in such a quandary.
I verily beleave I run all the way home without feeling
the ground! As yet Missus hasn't said a word; but I think
by way of preventive I shall give her warning. My nerves
is too quivering to rite furder, xcept luve to all kind frends
at Woodlands; I remane, dear Becky, yure luving frend
forever and ever,

MARTHA PENNY.

TO MISS WILMOT, AT WOODLANDS.

MY DEAR MARGARET,

With any one else I should feel ashamed and
alarmed at my long silence; but you well know the state of
my nerves and feelings, and will give me credit for not
wishing to disturb your happier thoughts with the effusions
of my own bad spirits. Besides, I have met with so many
annoyances and disagreeables! However, you will be glad
to hear that I am getting more reconciled to foreign travelling: it is very fatiguing; but the lovely scenery, since
we left Bonn, has almost repaid me for all my troubles by the
way. I will not attempt to describe the beautiful mountains,
the romantic old castles, and the pretty outlandish villages,
—but whenever you marry, Margaret, pray stipulate for a
wedding excursion up the Rhine. One painful thought,
indeed, would intrude—if *he* could have enjoyed the scenery
with me—for you remember poor George's fondness for
picturesque views and sketching—but I must not be so
ungrateful as to repine whilst our tour has brought such
relief to my own mind, as well as amendment to my health.
Even my brother seems to have benefited by the change of

"Out of sight out of mind."

air and scene,—he is decidedly less hypped, and his warnings come at longer intervals. I even think he is getting a little ashamed of them, they have failed so very, very often—and especially since a letter from Mr. Bagster to Frank, supposing his uncle to be deceased :—but above all, after a warning he had on the top of a mountain, when a ridiculous German offered to die along with him, which turned the tragedy into such a comedy, that my poor brother, as Frank says, threw up the part, and we have hopes will never perform in the piece again. He almost expressed as much to me in relating this last attack. "I'm afraid, Kate," said he, "you will begin to think that I am as fond of dying over and over again as the famous Romeo Coates."

I am delighted with Coblenz, where we have taken lodgings for a month. For some days after our arrival we dined at the table-d'hôte, but I cannot say that I like the style of cookery. Somebody declares in his travels, that when a German dish is not sour it is sure to be greasy, and when it is not greasy it is certain to be sour ; but the cook at our hotel went a step further in his art, for he contrived to make his dishes both sour and greasy at the same time. Luckily there were other things more English-like in their preparation —such as roast beef, though it was rather oddly introduced to me by the waiter—" Madame ! some roast beast ? "

Our cookery is now done at home under the superintend- ence of Martha, who agrees better than I expected with the German maid whom I have engaged. Perhaps there is some cause in the back-ground for this unusual harmony, but as yet it is only a suspicion : in the meantime, you will be amused with a scrape which poor Martha's allspicy temper got her into this morning as we were passing over the Rhine bridge. There is a toll on all provisions brought into the town, even to a loaf of bread ; and men are stationed at each

of the gates to collect it. We had often seen these officers,
in a green uniform, stopping the country-people, and peeping
into their baskets and bundles, with a rather strict vigilance ;
but I was hardly prepared to see one of them insisting on
searching a baby. The poor mother loudly remonstrated
against such an inspection, and hugged the infant closer
to her bosom ; but the man was inflexible, and at last seized
hold of the child's clothes in a very rough manner. A
struggle immediately took place between the officer and the
woman, who was almost overcome, when she suddenly met
with very unexpected assistance. Since the seizure of my
unfortunate Dutch linen, the custom-house people have never
been any favourites with Martha,—but besides this dislike,
the assault on the baby aroused all her womanly feelings,
and she flew to the rescue like a fury. In a very short time
she had almost regained the little innocent, when to her
inexpressible horror, as well as my own, owing to the violence
of the scuffle, the body of the poor baby slipped through
its clothes, and actually rolled some seconds on the ground,
before we could feel convinced that it was only a fine leg of
mutton !

It seems that the frequent visits of the supposed infant to
Coblenz, in all weathers, had first excited suspicion ; and
one of the Douaniers remarked besides that the little dear
came rather plumper from the country than it went back
again from the town. Hence the *dénouement*, which raised
an uproarious horse-laugh from the spectators, and not a
little you may suppose at the expense of my magnanimous
maid.

There is no accounting for foreign customs, but it seems
to me a very odd proceeding for the heads of a town to lay
a tax on the persons who bring it victuals. I am sure food
is not over plentiful here, to judge by the poor of the

place. This morning, a wretched famished-looking woman came to the kitchen, Martha tells me, to beg for "the broth that the ham was boiled in!" But oh! Margaret, in spite of their own wants and misery, how kind are the poor to the poor! At the next door, in an upper room, there is a harmless crazy woman, who, either from the poverty or the niggardliness of her relatives, is but scantily supplied with food. From the back of the house where she is confined there runs a row of meaner dwellings, wholly occupied by common mechanics with their families,—and amongst the rest a sickly-looking weaver, so thin and sallow that he looks like a living skeleton. At the height of the first floors there is a sort of wooden gallery, common to all the inhabitants of the row, and on this platform, which is overlooked by my bed-room window, I often see her needy but kindly neighbours standing to talk to the unfortunate maniac, and thrusting up to her, on the end of a long stick, some morsel of food, such as a carrot or a potato, saved out of their own scanty meals. A rather comely young woman, who has several hungry-looking children, is one of the foremost in these daily charities. The first time I saw it, the sight so affected me, that I sent directly for all the bread in the house, and contrived to make myself understood by holding up a roll in one hand, and pointing to the mad woman's window with the other. The young wife was the first to observe the signal, and never, never shall I forget the delighted expression of her countenance! It brightened all over with a smile quite angelical, as she clasped her hands together and uttered the word "Brod!" in a tone which convinced one that bread was a rarity in her own diet. In a minute the good warm-hearted creature was round at our door, to receive the rolls and some cold meat, which she took as eagerly, and thanked me for as warmly, as if they had been intended for herself. her lean

husband, and her hungry children. But my commission was
faithfully performed : and I had soon afterwards the gratifi-
cation of hearing the poor crazy woman singing in a very
different tone to her usual wailings. Of course I did not forget the young wife—but what are the best of our gifts—the
parings of our superfluities—or even the Royal and Noble
Benefaction, written up in letters of gold, to the generous
donations of the humbler Samaritans, who, having so little
themselves, are yet so willing to share it with those who have
less ! As I have read somewhere, " The Charity which Plenty
spares to Poverty is human and earthly ; but it becomes
divine and heavenly when Poverty gives to Want."

On the back of this occurrence I had a rather different
scene. A woman, of the lower class, very shabbily dressed,
found her way up to my room, and, by her manner, intimated
to me that she came to beg. I was so impressed with the
notion that she could want nothing but food, that I directly
offered her some victuals there happened to be on the table,
but which to my astonishment she declined. So I summoned
Kätchen, our German servant, to interpret, and after some
conversation with the stranger, she told me in her broken
English that the thing wanted was some " white Kleiden,"
at the same time pointing to her own gown. As the woman
had made a motion with her finger round her head as if
describing a fracture, it occurred to me that the white
kleiden might be wanted for bandages, and going to a store
of old linen which I always keep in reserve for such purposes,
I made up a bundle of it for the poor creature, but, after a
slight inspection, she rejected it, as it seemed to me, with no
small degree of contempt. But I could get no better explanation—Kätchen still referred to her gown, and the woman
waved her hand round her head. All at once the truth
flashed across me—the secret was baby linen—a little night-

Confirmation strong.

gown and a nightcap—but I had no sooner suggested the
notion to Kätchen, who repeated it to the other, than they
both began to laugh. At last I sent for an old friend in
need, the "German and English Dictionary," and by its help
I managed to learn, that the woman wanted a white muslin
frock for her youngest daughter to be confirmed in ; and the
motion round her head signified a wreath of artificial flowers.
Although rather surprised by the nature of the object, I gave
a trifle towards it; and in return, the woman brought me
the girl to look at in her holiday costume. By dint of
gifts and loans she was decked out like a figurante, in
a white muslin dress, white cotton stockings, and light-
coloured shoes, with a wreath of artificial lilies-of-the-valley
on her head, and a large white lace veil. During the
morning the street swarmed with similar figures, besides
as many boys in full suits of black, with large white
collars, white gloves, and a white rose at the button-hole.
They all seemed to have a due sense of the unwonted smart-
ness of their appearance—the little girls especially looked so
clean, so pretty, and so very happy in their ephemeral finery,
I could not help grieving to reflect, that on the morrow so
many of them would be pining again in their dirt and rags.
Even their little day was abridged ; for towards noon it came
on to rain, and to save the precious white kleiden from spot
or splash, the wearers were obliged to hurry home, as the
Scotch people say, particularly "high kilted."

Frank has discovered an old acquaintance here, a Mr.
Markham ; and I have been introduced to his wife. She
would be an acquisition merely as a companion and a countrywoman ; but she is really a pleasant and warm-hearted
person, and, in spite of the warning of Lady de Farringdon,
we are already sworn friends. They came here to retrench,
and she makes me sigh and smile by turns with her account

of their great and little troubles in a foreign land. Their worst privation seems to have been the separation from all friends : my heart ached to hear her relate their daily walks to see the packet discharge its passengers, in the vain hope of recognizing some familiar face : but the next moment she made me laugh, till the tears came, with her description of a blight in her eyes, and her servant's uncouth remedy. What do you think, Margaret, of having your head caught in a baker's sack, hot from the oven,—then being half suffocated under a mountain of blankets and pillows,—and at last released, quite white enough, from the heat and the loose flour, for a theatrical ghost !

I have purchased two head-dresses to send you, as samples of the costume of the place. One, to my taste, is very pretty, a small black silk cap, embroidered with gay colours at the top of the head, and from the back hang several streamers of broad black sarcenet ribbon. The other cap is also embroidered or beaded, but two plaited bands of hair pass through the back, and are fastened up with a flat silver or gilt skewer, in shape like a book-knife. Adieu. Love to all from all, including, dear Margaret, your affectionate Sister,

CATHARINE WILMOT.

P.S.—I open this again to tell you that my suspicions about Martha were wrong ; but they had better have been correct. She is not in love—but has turned a Roman Catholic ! I think I see you all lifting up your hands and eyes, from the parlour to the kitchen ! But it is too true. Frank, it appears, met her two evenings ago, with a taper in her hand posting to a chapel, where the Coblenz single women go to pray for husbands ! This, then, accounts for her frequent absences both of body and mind. I fancied her goings out were to meet some sweetheart, but it was to

Cavaliers and Roundheads.

attend at Mass ·or confession, and all her wool-gatherings were from puzzling over the saints on her beads and her new catechism. I consulted with my brother on the subject, but all he said was, "that Martha's religion was her own concern, and provided she did her duty as a servant, she had a right to turn a Mussulwoman if she pleased." When I taxed Martha herself, she owned to it directly, and, as usual, in all dilemmas, gave me warning on the spot. *That* of course goes for nothing, but I shall never be able to keep her. As they say of all new converts, she runs quite into extremes, and I firmly believe is more of a Catholic than the Pope himself. For instance, there are several masses, at different hours of the day, to suit the various classes of people; and, will you believe it? she insists on going to them all. But this comes of foreign travelling. Well might I wish that I had never left Woodlands.

TO GERARD BROOKE, ESQ.

My dear Gerard,

This morning I again called on our friend, and found him in company with a little man of such marked features, that between his physiognomy and his London-like pronunciation of English, it was impossible to disconnect him with old clothes, and oranges, Holywell Street, and the Royal Exchange. He was, however, a Prussian, and had simply carried the German pronunciation of W—which· is identical with the Cockney way of sounding it—into our own language.

I had scarcely been introduced to this Mr. Isaac Meyer, when another visitor was announced, who was likewise

P

"extremely proud and happy to make my acquaintance ;"
but just in the middle of his pride and happiness, a glance at
the little man stopped him short like a stroke of apoplexy.
All his blood seemed to mount into his head ; the courteous
smile vanished ; his eye glistened ; his lip curled ; his frame
trembled ; and with some difficulty he stammered out the
rest of his compliment.   In anticipation of a scene, I looked
with some anxiety towards the other party, but to my
surprise he was perfectly calm and cool ; and was either
unconscious of the other's perturbation, or took it as a matter
of course.   Any general conversation was out of the question ;
after a very short and very fidgetty stay, during which he
never once addressed the object of his dislike, the uncomfortable gentleman took his leave, and the other soon
after concluded his "visit."   When they were gone, Markham
explained the phenomenon.   "The little man," said he, "is
of the Hebrew persuasion ; and the big one belongs to a
rather numerous class, described by Saphir—whose satirical
works, by the bye, I think you would relish,—in short he is
a Jew-hater—one of those who wish that the twelve tribes
had but a single neck.   You saw how he reddened and
winced !   As Shakspeare says, 'some men there are love not
a gaping pig, some that are mad if they behold a cat,' and
here is this Herr Brigselbach quite set aghast, and chilled
all over into goose-skin, at the sight of a human being with
black eyes and a hook nose !"

"But surely," said I, "such a prejudice is rare, except
amongst the most bigoted Catholics and the lower orders !"

"Lower orders and Catholics !—quite the reverse.   I
presume you heard of a certain freak of Royal authority,
forbidding the Hebrews the use of Christian names, and
enjoining other degrading distinctions.   Such an example in
such a country was enough to bring Jew-hating into fashion,

if it had not been the *rage* before. But you must live in
Germany to understand the prevalence and intensity of the
feeling. You will not rank the editor of a public journal, or his
contributors, in the lower and ignorant class : nevertheless my
little Isaac the other day lent me a local paper, and the two
very first paragraphs that met my eye were sarcastic anecdotes
against his race. One of them was laughable enough, indeed
I laughed at it myself; but in this country such stories are
circulated more for malice and mischief than for the sake of
the fun. It ran thus :—A certain cunning old Jew had lent
a large sum of money, and charged interest upon it at nine
per cent. instead of six, which was the legal rate. The
borrower remonstrated ; and at last asked the usurer if he
did not believe in a God, and where he expected to go when
he died ?—'Ah,' said the old Hebrew, with a pleased twinkle
of the eye and a grin—'I have thought of that too—but
when God looks down upon it *from above*, the 9 will appear to
Him like a 6.'"

"And what does Mr. Meyer say," I inquired, "of such
attacks on his brethren ?"

"Little or nothing. When I alluded to the paragraphs
and expressed my indignation, he merely smiled meekly, and
said a few words to the effect that 'suffering was the badge
of all his tribe.' In fact they are used to it, as was said of
the eels. By the bye, Von Raumer speaks of a Prussian
liberal, who abused Prussia, as no better than a beast ;—but
he surely forgot this oppressed portion of his countrymen.
As to love of country in general, he is right—but has the
degraded inhabitant of Juden Gasse a country ? To look for
patriotism from such a being, you might as well expect local
gratitude and attachment from a pauper without a parish !
No, no,—that word, so dear, so holy, to a German, his
Fatherland is to the Jew a bitter mockery. He has all the

duties and burthens, without the common privileges of the
relationship—he is as heavily taxed, and hardly drilled, as
any member of the family ; but has he an equal share of the
benefits—does he even enjoy a fair portion of the affection of
his brothers and sisters ?   Witness Herr Brigselbach.   As
for his Fatherland, a Jew may truly say of it as the poor
Irishman did of his own hard-hearted relative—'Yes, sure
enough he's the parent of me—but he trates me as if I was
his Son by another Father and Mother !' "

By way of drawing out our friend, who, like the melan
choly Jaques in his sullen fits, is then fullest of matter, I
inquired if the bitterest writers against the country were not
of Meyer's persuasion.

"Yes—Heine abused Prussia, and he was a Jew.   So did
Börne, and he was a Jew too, born at Frankfort—the *free*
city of Frankfort, whose inhabitants, in the nineteenth
century, still amuse themselves occasionally, on Christian
high days and holidays, with breaking the windows of their
Hebrew townsmen.   What wonder if the galled victims of
such a pastime feel, think, speak, and write, as citizens of
the world !   As Sterne does with his Captive, let us take a
single Jew.   Imagine him locked up in his dark chamber,
pelted with curses and solider missiles, and trembling for his
property and his very life, because he will not abandon his
ancient faith, or eat pork sausages.   Fancy the jingling of
the shattered glass—the crashing of the window frames—
the guttural howlings of the brutal rabble—and then picture
a Prussian Censor breaking into the room, with a flag in
each hand, one inscribed Vaterland, the other Bruderschaft
—and giving the quaking wretch a double knock over the
head with the poles, to remind him that he is a German
and a Frankforter !   Was there ever such a tragi-comical
picture !   But it is not yet complete.   The poor Jew, it may

be supposed, has little heart to sing to such a terrible accompaniment as bellows from without; nevertheless the patriotic Censor insists on a chaunt, and by way of a prompt-book, sets before the quavering vocalist a translation of Dr. Watts's Hymn of Praise and Thanksgiving for being born in a Christian Land!"

Amused by Markham's *extempore* championship of the twelve tribes, by way of jest I insinuated that during his admitted scarcity of cash, he had perhaps been supplied with moneys by means of his clients. But he took the jest quite in earnest. "Not a shilling, my dear fellow,— not a gros. But I am indebted to them for some kindness and civility : for they certainly hate us far less than some sects of Christians hate each other. It's my firm belief that the Jews possess many good qualities. Why not? The snubbed children of a family are apt to be better than the spoiled ones. As for their honesty, if they cheat us now in retail, we have plundered them aforetime by wholesale, —and like master like scholar. But there's little Meyer, a Jew every inch of him, and with the peculiar love of petty traffic ascribed to his race. He will sell or barter with you the books in his library, the spoons in his cupboard, the watch in his fob, and yet in all my little dealings he has served me as fairly as if he had flaxen hair, blue eyes, and a common journey-work nose, with a lump, like a makeweight, stuck on the end. The extortions and cheating I have met with were from Christians; and what is singular, the only time I ever had my money refused in this country, it was by Jews. There are many poor Hebrew families in Bendorf, and other villages on the banks of the Rhine, and it is a pleasant sight to behold, through the windows of their cottages, the seven candles of their religion shining— like the fire-flies of a German night—the only lights in their darkness, to an outcast people in au alien laud. In one of these humble dwellings at Sayn, I once left my hat and coat in exchange for a cap and kittel, preparatory to a broiling hot excursion farther up the country. During my metamorphosis, I happened to take notice of a sickly-looking crippled boy, about nine years old, who was sitting at a table in the corner of the room ; and the mother informed me, with a sigh too easy to interpret, that he was her first-born, and her only son. On my return I resumed my clothes, and offered the poor people a trifle for their trouble, but they had already been overpaid by a common expression of sympathy, and refused my money so pertinaciously, that I could only get rid of the coin by pressing it into the wasted hand of the helpless child. Poor little fellow ! I wish I could hope to give him another,—but he was already marked for death, and his thin, sharp, sallow face, seemed only kept alive by his quick black eyes ! "

"In England," continued Markham, "we have seen a Jewish sheriff of London ; but I verily believe if anything could excite a rebellion in these provinces, it would not be the closing of the coffee-houses, and the suppression of the newspapers, but the making a burgomaster of the race of Israel. However, all other brutal sports and pastimes are falling into decadence with the progress of civilisation : bear-baiting is extinct ; badger-drawing is on the wane ; cock-throwing is gone out ; cock-fighting is going after it ; and bull-running is put down : so put on your hat, my dear fellow, and let us hope; for the sake of Christianity and human nature, that Jew-hating and Jew-running will not be the last of the line ! "

Our first stroll was through the market-place, which was crowded with countrywomen, many of them afflicted with *goître*. It has been supposed to arise from drinking snow-

The Truck System.

water; but as this country abounds in excellent springs, such a theory can scarcely be entertained. In Markham's opinion it is caused by the sudden stoppage of perspiration, and contraction of the pores, by keen blasts from the mountains, whilst the women are toiling bare-necked in the heat of the sun. I asked him if the accounts were correct of the unremitting industry and hard labour of the Germans. "In the towns," said he, "perhaps not : the men are either more indolent, or have less physical strength than the English. I have frequently seen three or four fellows carrying or drawing loads that would be a burden for only one or two in London. Sometimes you see a leash harnessed to a small truck of wood; perhaps there is a woman along with them, and I have remarked that *she* is always in earnest, and, like the willing horse, does more than her fair share of the work. Indeed the softer sex has the harder lot here, for, besides what are with us considered masculine employments, in the fields and on the water, they have all the in-door duties of a woman to perform. As regards the peasantry, great labour is a matter of necessity : by the hardest labour, the land being highly taxed, they only procure the hardest fare ; and there being no poor-rates to fall back upon, they must either work hard or starve. You may read in their faces a story of severe toil and meagre diet. Look at those country girls, poor things—"

"Nay," said I, pointing to a group, "I see round ruddy faces and plump figures, and, thanks to the shortness of their petticoats, that they have very respectable calves to their legs."

"Phoo! phoo!" replied Markham, "those are nurses or nursery-maids, and come, witness their peculiar dress, from another country; Saxony, perhaps, or Bavaria. But look at those yonder, with their wrinkled foreheads, and hard

sharp features, more resembling old mothers, than young
daughters; observe the absolute flatness of their busts,
and the bony squareness of their figures, making them look
so like men in women's clothes. And no wonder—the toil
they go through for a trifle, is sometimes painful to con-
template. Last summer we purchased a small cask of wine
from a woman who owns a little vintage : and when it was
delivered, we were shocked to find that she had carried it
from her village, a league distant, on her head! In fact,
time and trouble, so valuable elsewhere, seem here to go for
little or nothing ; and the waste in both is occasionally quite
surprising. For instance, it is nothing unusual in the streets
of Coblenz, to see a big man, a big dog, and a big stick, all
engaged in driving a week-old calf."

Luckily I have seen this illustration of Markham's and
made a sketch of it ; and will now attempt to describe the
toilsome and tedious operation. The Big Man with the
Big Stick goes first ; then comes Staggering Bob ; and
lastly, the Big Dog. In a very methodical manner the Big
Dog jumps about from side to side of the calf ; who with a
natural doubt whether these gambols are not meant for its
amusement, makes a dead halt, and indulges in an innocent
stare at its four-footed companion. As this stops proceedings, the Big Man immediately begins to haul at the rope,
as if he wanted to pull the poor creature's head off, which,
of course, drags backwards as lustily as it can. Thereupon
the Big Man gives up pulling, and going to the rear,
begins pushing with all his might ; but the only result is,
that after tottering a step or two to the right or left, the
Calf *jibs*, and suddenly appears with its head where its tail
ought to be ; namely, towards the place from whence it
came. Bob has then to be turned, and put straight again ;
an operation of considerable difficulty ; for during this

An Overdriven Calf.

manœuvre, the Big Dog sadly embarrasses matters, by jumping about and between both parties. Here, then, the Big Stick comes into play, which the Big Man shakes at the Big Dog, who scampers away some dozen yards—the Calf, in a sportive fit, runs after him—the rope winds round the other two calves, to wit, the Big Man's—and the whole affair is in a tangle! "Potztausend!" but at last all is clear. Still the perverse Calf, though strictly brought up on Temperance Principles, persists in staggering from one side of the street to the other, and finally refuses to stir a foot at all;—the Big Man gives it a poke with his Big Stick, and down it tumbles! So in despair the Big Man throws the live veal over his shoulder,—carries it till he is dead tired—then puts the Calf on its own legs again—then the Big Dog jumps about as before—and then—*Da Capo!*

To resume—I continued my queries to Markham, as to Prussia and its happy, free, proprietary peasantry. " Free!" said he, " how are they to be free, where no one else is, or can be, under the *Unitarian* rule of a single will? As for their happiness, you may judge yourself. Go into any of the villages that look so picturesque from the Rhine,—look in at an open door, and you will see a dark, dirty, squalid comfortless room, hardly furnished enough to invite an execution. Ask yourself what makes the gaunt, sallow, toil-worn faces, that gaze on you from the window, so gloomily phlegmatic— what renders the children about the streets so stunted, so spiritless, so prematurely old? On the Moselle, the proprietary peasantry are notoriously in a state of distress; and their wines, at a ruinous price, are bought up by the capitalists. But a remedy has been discovered," said Markham, with a bitter smile, " they are to give up wine-growing, and breed silk-worms! This notable plan has been strongly advocated in the 'Rhein-und-Mosel-Zeitung,' with grave cal-

culations of the great value of the raw material, and its still
greater value when manufactured into satins, sarcenets, and
gros-de-Naples. Only two points have escaped these sages :
mulberry trees are not of remarkably rapid growth, and how
are the poor peasantry to subsist in the meantime ? But
supposing the trees full-grown, the worms hatched, fed, trans-
figured, and inclosed in myriads of cocoons, is it not probable
that the same untoward causes and commercial obstacles which
denied them a profitable market in the wine trade will be
equally adverse to the sale of their silk ? Besides, Moselle
wine is only grown on the Moselle ; whereas in the other
article there will be a competition. But the system is in
fault, not the commodity ; and when a man does business on
a losing principle, it is all one whether he deals in figs or
tenpenny nails ! "

In our progress from the market, we arrived at a small
square, in the midst of which stood an extraordinary vehicle,
that, except for the inscription, might have been taken for a
Mammoth's travelling caravan. On measurement, it was
nine (German) feet wide, and thirty-six long. Markham
pointed at it with great glee. " That unwieldy machine,"
said he, " was the invention of one of the military con-
tractors, a Mr. Bohne, or Bean, who ought to be called Broad
Bean for the future. A fortnight ago it left Berlin, with
eleven thousand schakos, two thousand of which it has
delivered by the way, at Erfurt and Mayence ; the rest are
bound to Luxembourg. The Germans have a proverb, that
if you can get over the dog you can get over his tail ; but
in the present case the hitch was comparatively at the tail.
The Monster Machine had got over the greater part of the
journey, when it stuck in the gate of Baccharach, stopping
the eil-wagen, the extra-posts and every other carriage in its
rear. Next it was two whole days in getting through, or

A Broad Joke.

rather round, Boppart, for it had to be taken to pieces, and to circumvent the town by water—and now here it is, with a few more such difficulties, between itself and its ultimate destination. However, the thing carries a moral. Göethe charged the English with want of reflection, that they did not look backward enough; and here is a proof that the Germans do not sufficiently look a-head :—in short, whilst our object is pace, and our only cry is 'Hark forward!' they are perpetually trying back, with a cold scent, towards their great-grandfathers and grandmothers."

There! You have had a tolerable course of Markham; but you will be interested in the tone of his mind, as well as in the course of his fortunes. He afterwards took me up to Ehrenbreitstein, where we met with a friend of his, Captain Walton, an Englishman by birth, but in the Prussian service. On comparing notes with this gentleman, it came out that I was familiar with several of his friends in Kent; and from what I heard of him it is likely that we shall be intimates. From the Fortress, we proceeded to view an ancient Roman Tower, in the vicinity, where I picked up a hint for the story you will find inclosed. Love to Emily from

Yours ever truly,

FRANK SOMERVILLE.

THE LAST OF THE ROMANS.

A TALE OF EHRENBREITSTEIN.

THE night was breezy and cloudy, but the moon was at full, and as the opaque vapours flitted across her silver disk, that grand mass of rock and masonry, " the Broad Stone of

Q

Honor," gleamed fitfully or frowned darkly on the valley beneath. On the right, rose the mouldering, slender, round tower, of Roman origin; on the left, the wind moaned through the waving poplars on the height of Pfaffendorf; below, lay the snugly sheltered Thal Ehrenbreitstein, beyond which the broad rapid Rhine reflected the red and yellow lights of the opposite city of Coblenz.

The hour was late, for Germany; and the good Pfarrer Schmidt, aided by the steep descent, was stepping homeward at a good round pace, when suddenly a sound struck on his ear like a groan. He instantly paused to listen, and distinctly heard a rattling, which, to his surprise, seemed to come from the ancient tower, and in another minute a tall stalwart figure came stumbling down the dilapidated steps of the old gray building ; and, staggering like a drunken man towards our wayfarer, addressed him with a few words, in one of the dead tongues. The language, however, was not unknown, for it was the same in which the good Pastor repeated the offices of his religion—wherefore, replying to the stranger in Latin, they entered at once into discourse. But the conversation had not gone far, ere, suddenly recoiling three or four steps backward, the Priest began to mutter and cross himself with the utmost fervor. And little wonder ; for, by help of a glance of the moon, it was plain that the figure had no kind of clothing on its body, save an old rusty cuirass, which, with the extraordinary tenor of its last question—" And how fares the noble Cæsar ?" sufficed to convince the astonished Priest that he was communing with either a resuscitated Roman, or a Roman ghost !

At so awful a discovery it is natural to suppose that the Priest must have immediately taken to flight ; but in the first place, he had a strong belief in the efficacy of the exorcisms and other spiritual defences with which he was armed ;

and secondly, terror, which acts variously on different individuals, seemed to root him to the spot. In the meantime,
the figure, folding its arms, turned from side to side, cast a
glance at the dark modern citadel, then at the opposite
fort of Pfaffendorf, and then muttering the word "Confluentia," took a long, long look across the glittering river.
Again and again the apparition rubbed its eyes as if doubtful
of being in a dream. At last, arousing from this reverie, the
figure again addressed the Pastor with great earnestness, at
the same time laying its hand upon his arm. The action
made the Priest start, and tremble excessively; but by a
very sensible pressure, it served to convince him that the
figure, whatever it might be, was not merely a phantom.
Wonder now began to mingle and struggle with fear, and by
degrees getting the mastery, the Priest, after a devout
inward prayer, took courage, and by a sign invited the
stranger to accompany him towards his home. The figure
immediately complied,—and walking parallel with each other
but with a good space between, they began to descend the
steep, the Priest noticing with secret satisfaction, as the
moon shone out, that his mysterious companion, like a solid
body, threw a distinct shadow across the road.

Arrived at the parsonage, which was not far distant, the
Pastor conducted his strange guest into his study, and carefully closed the door. His next concern was to furnish his
visitor with decent garments; and with much difficulty and
persuasion, the Ancient was induced to put on a modern suit
of black. For some considerable time neither of them spoke
a word, each being absorbed in the same occupation of gazing
and marvelling at the other; and remembering that the host
was a Catholic Priest of the nineteenth century, and the
guest a contemporary of Julius Cæsar, it is easy to imagine
that they mutually found matter enough for admiration

to tie up their tongues. But at last, the stranger breaking
the silence, they again engaged in discourse, which was long
and earnest, as needs must have been where one party had
to be convinced that he had been dead and buried above a
thousand years. However, the hasty observations he had
made on the altered aspect of Confluentia and its vicinity,
helped to confirm the Roman that only a vast lapse of time
could have wrought the great changes he had remarked.
In reply to the Priest, he said he was a Centurion, by name
Paratus Postumus, of the 22d Legion, who had accompanied
Julius Cæsar in his second passage across the Rhine to make
war on the Catti :—that he was subject to fits, and had once
or twice been on the point of premature interment whilst he
lay in a trance. Thereupon, as if recollecting himself, he
suddenly started up on his feet, and eagerly inquired for the
nearest temple, that he might go and offer up his grateful
vows for his wondrous revival. Such a question made the
pious pastor look extremely grave, and he again crossed
himself very fervently, on being thus vividly reminded that
the stranger introduced beneath his roof, was in verity a
heathen ! However, on reflection he comforted himself with
the hope of the glory that would accrue to himself and to
his church, by making so miraculous a convert ; and to this
end, after giving a rapid sketch of the decline and fall of
Paganism, he began to unfold and extol the grand scheme of
Christianity, according to the interpretations of the Council
of Trent. But to this latter part of his discourse, the
Roman listened with impatience, and finally ceased to listen
at all. The downfall of his own multifarious faith—the
destruction of its temples and altars, under Constantine,
alone engrossed his thoughts, and, to judge by the workings
of his rugged countenance, gave him singular pain and
concern. For some time he remained buried in meditation,

but at length suddenly raising his arms towards heaven, and lifting his eyes in the same direction—"O great Jupiter!' he exclaimed, "it cannot be! There must be some relics of that glorious theogony still left upon earth,—and I will wander the whole wide world through till I discover where they exist!" So saying, he pointed to the door with so stern a look that the trembling Priest, giving up all hope of his miraculous convert, was fain to obey the signal; which was again repeated at the outer gate. For a moment the Figure paused at the threshold, and then, after a gracious expression of thanks, strode forth into the blank darkness and disappeared!

*   *   *   *   *

Years had rolled away, and in their course had wrought further changes on the Rhine and on its banks. Shooting past the slow barge, with its long team of horses, toiling against the stream, the gay smoking steam-boat now rushed triumphantly up the arrowy river, freighted with thousands of foreigners, who haunted the healing springs, the vine-clad mountains, the crumbling fastnesses, and romantic valleys of the lovely provinces. The pious Pastor Schmidt, now old and infirm, was one evening sitting dozing in his ample and high-backed elbow chair, when the door of his little study abruptly flew open, and uninvited and unannounced, an unceremonious visitor stepped boldly into the room. The eyes of the good priest were somewhat dimmer than afore-time, but a single glance sufficed to recognise the unmistake-able Roman features of the Centurion. He was clothed, however, in a costume very different to the old suit of black: and his countenance had undergone a still greater alteration than his dress. Instead of the stern settled melancholy that had darkened it at the close of his former visit, the expression

of his countenance was now complacent, and even cheerful.
After mutual salutations, being both seated opposite to each
other, the Centurion began as follows; not, however, in Latin,
but in passable German :—"Holy father, congratulate me !
As I predicted, my ancient religion, in some degree, is still
extant!" The Pastor pricked up his ears. He was a bit of
an antiquarian, and a classical scholar to boot, and the
announcement of the Pagan Polytheism being still in
existence, raised his curiosity to the highest pitch. "Was it
in India, in Persia, or by the Egyptian Pyramids; in
Numidia; at Timbuctoo; amongst the savage islands of the
Pacific ; or in Peru, the country of the Incas?" "Father,"
replied the Centurion very coolly, "I have not travelled out
of Europe." The Priest was dumbfounded. Except one
portion devoted to Mahomet, the whole spiritual empire of
that quarter of the world was divided, he knew, between the
Greek Patriarch, the Levitical Priesthood, Luther, and the
Pope. The Centurion continued—"You told me, I think,
that the people called Christians worship only one God?"
The Priest nodded an assent. "But I tell you they have
almost or quite as many gods as we had in our ancient
mythology." The Priest stared, and shook his head. "Yes,
I tell you," said the Centurion, vehemently, "their altars
and rites are as various—their divinities as numerous as our
own. Look, for example, at Britain." "The English are
Protestants and heretics," said the Priest, making the sign of
the Cross. "But they are Christians," retorted the Centurion. "Yes, and as such," said the Priest, "they worship
the same God that I do,—the one and indivisible,—whatever
mortal errors otherwise belong to their doctrines." "At
least so they profess," said the Centurion : "But tell me, is
the Deity whom one sect bows to, in reality the very same
that is ʻreverenced by another? No, verily—with one God

there would-be but one worship offered up in the same
spirit ! "

" Alas ! alas ! " said the pious Pastor, " it was the accursed
schism of Martin Luther that led to such discordances. After
separating from the holy Mother Church, the fallers-off
became again split and divided amongst themselves ! "

The Centurion took no notice of this lamentation, but
resumed his discourse. "I have visited their temples—I
have stood before their altars—I have witnessed their rites
and listened to their doctrines, and what wide diversities do
they all present ! In one temple, I heard groans and yells
and female shrieks ; in a second, a full-toned organ, and
melodious choristers ; in a third, I heard nothing, not even a
word : and was I to blame if I looked round for a statue of
Harpocrates ? Then, again, in one temple I saw infant
children sparingly sprinkled with water ; in another grown
men and women were wading up to their chins in a sort of
Frigidarium, or cold bath. Under one sacred roof the
votaries leaped and shouted like the Bacchantes and Cory-
bantes ; in a neighbouring fane, they stood, and sate, and
knelt, by turns, with the steady uniform precision of soldiers
at drill. In one rustic temple, standing amidst the fields,
they played upon fiddles, oboes, bassoons, flutes and clarionets ;
in another, in North Britain, Euterpe was dethroned, and all
musical instruments were accounted profane, except the
human larynx and the human nose. Then the sacred
buildings themselves, how different ! Here a very Temple
of the Muses, adorned with painting and sculpture, and the
most gorgeous architecture ; there, a sordid structure, as
plain and unadorned as a stable or a barn. Even the priests
displayed the same incongruities. One wore an elaborate
powdered wig and an apron ; another, the natural hair,
combed in long lank locks down the forehead and cheeks

Some prayed uncovered, some in a broad-brimmed hat;—
here prayed a minister in a white robe—yonder prayed
another in a black one; a third wore his every-day clothes.
In short, there was no end to these varieties."

"It is even so," said the priest, shaking his gray head.
"So many heresies, so many new modes. Yet these are
mostly external matters. Whatever the form may be, the
worship of all Christians is offered up to the same one and
indivisible God!"

"The same! one and indivisible!" almost shouted the
centurion. "Tell me, and as thou art a religious man and a
Christian priest, answer me truly—Is it the same universal
God that the parish pauper must only address from a
wooden bench, and the proud noble can only praise from an
embroidered velvet cushion? Is it the same Providential
Being that the lowly peasant thanks for his scanty hardly-
earned daily bread, and the rich man asks to bless his riotous
luxury and wasteful superabundance? Is the merciful
Father, of whom the weeping child on bended knees begs
the life of its sick and declining parent, the same, the very
same, as the God of Battles invoked by the ambitious
conqueror, on the eve of slaughtering thousands of his
fellow-men? Is the Divine Spirit, who gave his only Son
in atonement for the sins of the whole world, the same God
of the Gospel, whose name is paraded as the especial patron
of exclusive pious factions—of uncharitable bigots and
political partisans? Is there anything in common between
the fierce vindictive Creator wrathfully consigning the
creatures he has made to everlasting and unutterable torments, as depicted by the gloomiest of fanatical sects, and
the beneficent Jehovah, silently adored by the Quaker, as
the God of peace and good-will towards men? Is it the
same Divine Author——" "Enough, enough," interposed

the priest, with a deprecating wave of the hand. "Nay, but answer me," said the centurion. "Have I described one God, or many? In the list I have only partly sketched out, can you find nothing answerable to our plurality—to Plutus, to Mars, to Mercury, and Jupiter Tonans? Is the Christian Deity indeed one and indivisible, or made multiform, like Jove of old, by the separate impersonation and worship of his various attributes?"

"You have at least broached a curious theory," answered the Catholic priest, with great placidity, for his own particular withers were as yet unwrung. "But where," he asked, "would you find your great host of inferior deities, your Dii Minores, your demi-gods and demi-goddesses and the like?" "Where!" cried the centurion—"where else but close at hand? They are only disguised under other names. For instance, we had our Vertumnas and our Pomona, the patron of orchards—our Bona Dea; Hygeia, the goddess of health; Fornax, the goddess of corn and of bakers; Occator, the god of harrowing; Runcina, the goddess of weeding; Hippona, the goddess of stables and horses; and Bubona, the goddess of oxen. Now, we need only go into the Eifel——"

"Sancta Maria!" exclaimed the priest, reddening to his very tonsure—"Do you mean to adduce our blessed saints!"

"Exactly so," replied the calm centurion. "They are your Dii Minores—your demi-gods and demi-goddesses, and so forth, answerable to our own, and appointed to much the same petty and temporal offices. Have you not St. Apollonica for curing the tooth-ache, St. Blaize for sore throats, and St. Lambert for fits? Is not St. Wendelin retained to take care of the cows and calves, and St. Gertrude to drive away rats?"

The indignant priest could bear no more: it was like

being compelled to swallow the beads of a rosary, one by
one. "Anathema Maranatha!" he exclaimed in a paroxysm
of anger. "Accursed pagan! libellous heathen! Begone!
You shall no longer profane my dwelling! Hence, I say!"
—and extending his arm to give force to the mandate, the
venerable pastor thrust his attenuated fingers into the flame
of the candle and started up broad awake!

TO REBECCA PAGE.

DEAR BECKEY,

  Thenk hevin the storm I tould you of has blowed
over; but I believe I may thank master for it, who was so
kind as say I mite turn a Turk or a Hottenpot, if so be it
agreed with my conshense. As for missus, she looks grumpy
enuff at my new devotions—but let her look, I mayn't
always be her servent to be tried xperiments on, as was the
case this blessed morning. Complaining, as usual, of her
weak state of nerves, she was advized by Mrs. Markhum to
try the Rine baths, as being verry braceing; and missus was
so considderrit as to let poor me make the fust trial. The
baths are kep in a floting house, witch is made fast to the
Rine Bridge, of boats; and a pretty rushin and rampagin
the river makes between them, like a mill race. But there
was no help for it, as bathe I must; and was all crudling,
and shakin, and shiverin, in the tearing could water; when
before one could say lawk deliver us, a nasty grate barge
come. spinning down the river, and by sum mismanigement
the towin rope hung too low down, and jist ketching the
bath house, wipt off the hole roof in a jiffy! There was a
hawful crash, you may suppose; and at that very minit I

had duckt my head under, and wen I come up agin, lo and
behold! there was nothin at all up abuv, xcept the bare sky.
In course it was skreek upon skreek from the other rooms;
and thinks I, if tops comes off, so may bottoms, and in that
case, down sinks the floting baths, and were all drownded
creturs as sure as rats. So out I run on to the bridge of
boats, jist as I was, with nothin on but my newdity; but
decency's won thing, and death's another. The rest of the
bathing ladies did the same; and some of them, pore things,
fainted ded away on the boards. Luckly, none of the mail
sects was passing by, for xcept won Waterloo blue bonnit, we
were all in a naturalized state, like so menny Eves. Most
fortunately, it was a hot sunny day, or we mite have kitcht
our deths; howsumever, I was gitting more composed, wen
hearing a tramp, tramp, tramp, I turned round my hed, and
wat should I see but a hole rigment of Prushian sogers a
marching over the bridge. In such an undelicate case,
staying was out of the question, so I giv a skreech, and roof
or no roof, it was won generil skuttle back into the littel
house. Then sich a skramble and hudling on of our close,
there wasn't a lady but looked as if her things had been put
on, as the saying is, with a pitchfork! As for the ones in
fits, the bath pepel carried them back! and as the best
and shortest way of bringing them to, popped them into the
water agin, witch had the effect. Thenk gudness, there was
no wus harm done; but Catshins says, wen the roof was
took off, I ought to have crost meself; and to be sure, so I
ought, as well as Sanctus Marius, instead of O Criminy!

So much for bathing afore missus. For my part, I don't
admire boat bridges. Give me good iron or stone wons, like
Southwurk, or Rochistir. Ony the other day, a grate mis-
guidid raft of wood driv agin the pinted end of an iland
called Over Work, witch split the raft in two; so one half

came down by the rite side of the iland, and the other by
the left; and betwixt them, they broke and carried away
both ends of the Rine bridge; and there was a pore old
woman and her cow, witch mite have been me, a dancing
about, well ni crazy with frite, on the bit of bridge as was
left in the middle of the river! Yesterday, Catshins took
me to visit at her old place; being twelve o'clock, the
fammily was jist going to dinner, and so I saw the hole
preparation. First there was soop, and Catshins said, the
cook said somebody said as how the English soop was so
pore, it was obleeged to be disgized and flavioured up with
pepper and spice; but I tould her, Lord help her, I never
see any soop in England, but wat, wen could, was a perfect
jelly, as might be chuckt over the house. Howsumever, I
tasted the Germin soop, and thinks I, there'd be jist as
much taste of the meat if a cow had tumbled into the Rine.
Then came the beef, with iled butter and sowr sarce; and
tell cook at home if she wants a new ornimentle dish, I'll be
bound she never thort of a bullock's nose in jelly. For
wegetables, small fried taters, and something green, as
looked like masht duck weed, besides a hole truss of sallet;
and instead of a fruit-pie, a flat cherry-tart, amost as big as a
tebord. As for the servents, the best part of their dinner
was ould cowcumbers as had crawled on the ground till they
was as yeller underneath as a toad's belly—sliced up in
winiger and shocking bad ile, along with monstrashious big
inguns. To be sure they do feed very queerly. Catshins
says, her missis was ill laterly with the morbus; and the
fust thing she begged for in the eating way was a veal cutlit
and a lot of bullises stewed in sour wine! As for desert,
they eat plums by the bushell, and pounds upon pounds of
cherris; and wat's more, swallow the stones!

Talkin of dinners, please God if I ever settle in Germiny,

there's three things I'll have out from England, a warmin pan, a plate-warmer and a knife-board ; for the knives here are never sharpt, and as we say of dill-water, are so innocent, you may give them to a new-born babby without the least danger. But lawk, if you was to send them out things, they don't know the rite use of them, and most likely they would fry pan-cakes in the warmin pan, and make a pantry of the plate-warmer, jist as they fetch water for drinkin in a tin pail as is painted red on the inside and green on the out. Nothing's used in its proper way. When we cum to the lodgins, I found in the drawing-room a square painted tin basket, exactly like an English bread-basket, and ever sinse I've put the rolls in it, but wen Catshins come she said it's to hold sand, and to be spit into—wat a forrin idear !

All together I shouldn't like to be a Germin servent ; but I'm sadly afeard I shan't stop long where I am. Missus gets very cross, and seems to think I never do enuff; but if she was in my shoes she would find I have more work than I can do, what with my new religion and gitting all the he and she saints by heart ; and to be taught nitting ; and practise waltzing and singing, and learn Germin besides, witch is very puzzling, for they say ve for we, and wisy wersy.

The grate Sham Fites is begun, and I've been to the Larger, as it's called, witch is full of shows and booths, and partikly wooden taverns and publick howsis, three to one. But the pitcht wite tents is a bewtiful site in the middle of a wide plane, with the blue mountings all round. I went with a party in a waggin, the same as to Fairlop Fair, and was very cumfittable till the cumming home, wen a Germin tailer, overtook with snaps, went to sleep in the bottom of the waggin with his lighted pipe among the straw. A pretty frite it was ! for the straw flamed up, and we were all obleeged to bundle out neck and crop. Thenk providens there was no personable axident, xcept to the yung man his self, who, when he sobered, was dreadfully put out to diskiver his faverit curl and all his back hare was singed off his head.

Now I must stop for want of candle, and besides Catshins snores so she puts me out. Give my luve to every boddy in Becknam, not forgetting yourself, and so as the Cathlicks say, Bendicity from

Dear Becky,
Yure luving Friend,
MARTHA PENNY.

P.S.—I've begun to confess a little, namely going to the Germin Ball in Missis's silk stockins. But I couldn't quite unbuzzum. But in course me and the Priest will get more confidential in time.

TO GERARD BROOKE, ESQ.

MY DEAR GERARD,

You must have wondered at the unusual pause in my correspondence, and I will at once proceed to show cause. Ten days ago, my uncle, after so many false alarms, was taken ill in earnest, without any warning at all. Just after breakfast, he was seized with violent cramp, or spasms, in the chest and stomach, and for some hours was in great pain, and even some peril. Very much against his will, for he persisted that nobody but Truby understands his constitution, we called in medical advice, and as the case was urgent, sent for the Doctor next at hand.

The *Pale* of Civilization.

Now that the danger is over and gone, it is curious to recall how much farce was mingled with proceedings that seemed so serious at the time. The Ex-Patient himself laughs heartily whenever he speaks on the subject, and especially of his medical treatment, which he says will be "nuts to Truby, when he gets back to Kent."

The truth is, however the philosophers and professional men of this country relish a despotic government, they are particularly fond of placing themselves under the tyranny of a ruling idea. Hence all kind of extravagance. As Markham says, "A German is not content to take an airing on his Hobby in a steady old gentlemanly sort of way. He gives it a double feed of metaphysical beans, jumps on its bare back, throws the bridle over its ears, applies his lighted pipe to its tail, and does not think' he is riding till he is run away with. At last, the horse comes to some obstacle, where there is a great gulf fixed. He naturally refuses to leap; but not so his master. No true German would give a doit for a ditch with a further side to it; so down he gets, takes a mile of a run, swings his arms, springs off with 'one bound that overleaps all bounds,' and alights on his head. quite insensible, somewhere 'beyond beyond.'"

Their physicians afford striking examples of this ultraism. Thus Hahnemann, having hit on the advantage of small doses, never rested till he had reduced them to infinitesimals. In the same manner, Herr Bowinkel, having convinced himself that bleeding, in some cases, is improper, ends by scouting Phlebotomy altogether; whilst Herr Blutigel, in the next street, arrives at quite the opposite extreme, and opens every vein he can come at with his lancet. In short, your German is fond of fiddling, à la Paganini, on one string.

One of these empirical professors it was our fortune to

call in to my uncle, in the person of Doctor Ganswein, who, after a very cursory inquiry into his patient's malady, pronounced at once that it was a case for the Wasser-Kur. How this cure was to be effected you will best understand from a conversation which took place between the Physician and my Aunt. I must premise that my Aunt began the colloquy in French, as it was taught in Chaucer's time at Stratford atte Bowe; but after having puzzled the Doctor with sundry phrases, such as "son habit est si plein," meaning, "he is of such a full habit," she betook herself to her mother-tongue.

Aunt. And as to his eating, Doctor?

Doctor. Nichts; noting at all.

Aunt. And what ought he to drink?

Doctor. Kalt Wasser.

Aunt. Would it be well to bathe his feet?

Doctor. Ja——mit Kalt Wasser.

Aunt. And if he feels a little low?

Doctor. Low?—vat is dat?

Aunt. Out of spirits; a little faint like.

Doctor. Faint—ah!—So?—you shall sprinkle at him viz some Kalt Wasser.

Aunt. And nothing else?

Doctor. Ja—— I shall write something (*he writes*). Dere! you shall send dis papier to de Apotheke in de Leer Strasse, almost to de Rondel. Your broder shall drink some flasks of Kissingen.

Aunt. Kissingen—what's that? Is it any sort of wine?

Doctor. Wein! nein! It is some sort of Kalt Wasser.

Aunt. Oh, from the Baths?

Doctor. Ja! ja!—it shall be goot to bath too—in Kalt Wasser. (*To my Uncle*) Sare, have you read my leetle boke?

Uncle (*in pain*). What's it—about—Doctor?

Doctor. De Heilsamkeit of de Kaltes Wassers. I have prove de Kalt Wasser is good for every sickness in de world.

Uncle. Humph! What for—water in the head?

Doctor. Ja—and for wasser in de shest. And for wasser in de—what you call him? de abdomen. It is good for every ting. De Kalt Wasser shall sweep away all de Kranken, all de sick peoples from de face of de earth!

Uncle (to himself). Yes—so did—the Great Flood.

Doctor Ganswein had no sooner taken his leave, than my uncle called me to the bed-side. "Frank,—I've heard before —of wet-nurses—but never of—a wet Doctor. It's the old story—of the prescription that was nothing—but aqua pumpy. He musn't come again. I shall be drowned— before I'm cured. Nothing but watering, watering, watering —Egad! he takes me for a sick Hydrangea!"

Having prevented any *relapse* of Dr. Ganswein, it became necessary to find a successor; and by the advice of our Bankers, I sent for a Doctor Wolf, who was making a temporary stay in Coblenz. This selection, however, was anything but palatable to my aunt: two of the strongest of her prejudices rose up against a physician, who was not only a foreigner, but a Jew; his mere name seemed ominous: and, unfortunately, with a very unprepossessing physiognomy, his manners were abrupt and repulsive. I suspect *he* also had a hobby of his own; for one of his first questions to his patient was, whether he had ever tried a Mud Bath—a boggy remedy, of which you may read in Dr. Granville's account of the German Spas. "What's a Mud Bath?" inquired the Patient. "It is," said Dr. Wolf, "for to be in some black mud up to your middle." "If that's it," replied my uncle, "I've had it of a dirty day—in the streets of London. And I can't say—it was any benefit."

On our return to the drawing-room, the physician made his report. His patient's disorder, he said, originated in over-fatigue, the disarrangement of ordinary habits, a strange climate, unusual diet, a cold, perhaps, and a want of the necessary quantity of sleep. Knowing, by experience, that such evils are apt to beset travellers on the Rhine, I was quite satisfied; but my aunt was more inquisitive. "Hist!" said the Doctor, significantly laying his forefinger on the side of his nose; and then, with more than common mystery, he drew her aside into a corner. "Good heavens! is my dear brother in any danger?" "He is quite so bad as one can wish," answered the Doctor, with a series of solemn little nods. "Hear to me,"—and he fixed his black eyes on the changing face before him—"is your Broder rishe? Have he mosh moneys?" To my apprehension, this question merely had reference to the recommendation of some expensive baths; but it met with a darker interpretation from my aunt. "It is rather a singular question," said she, "but my brother is what is called an independent gentleman." "Dat is goot,— ferry goot," said Mr. Wolf, nodding, winking, rubbing his hands, and looking very well pleased. "Now hark to me" —and he approached his mouth to her ear—"whilst he is so bad in his bed, you shall rob him." "WHAT!" exclaimed my aunt in such a voice that the ringing monosyllable seemed to echo from every side and corner of the apartment. "You —shall—rob him"—repeated the Doctor, still more distinctly and deliberately—"You shall rob his chest." My aunt looked petrified. "Do not you understand me?" asked the dreadful Doctor, after a pause. "I am afraid I do," said my aunt, giving a sort of gulp, as if to swallow some violent speech, and then hurried into the adjoining room and locked herself in. The Doctor followed this manœuvre with his hawklike eyes, which, when the door closed, he turned upon me : but before I could attempt any explanation, he snatched up his hat, made me a low bow, and with a shrug that said as plainly as words "those unaccountable English !" he bolted out of the room and down the stairs.

When he was gone I could not resist a laugh, which was hardly suppressed by the reappearance of my aunt, who, after an anxious look round the chamber, to make sure of the absence of the detestable Doctor, cast herself down on the sofa with a fervent "Thank God !"—"Frank !—What a monster !—Wolf by name and wolf by nature ; did you hear what the wretch proposed to me ?"—and she launched off into a tale so ludicrously distorted and coloured by her own extravagant suspicions, that I could hardly preserve my gravity. "But I foretold it," she said, "from the very first glimpse of him ! There was villain stamped in his face. Did you ever before see such horrid cunning eyes, or hear such an artful insinuating voice ? Now I think of it, he is the very picture ——" She was stopped by the entrance of Martha with a bottle of medicine, which her mistress had no sooner inspected than the expression of her countenance changed from indignation and disgust to vexation and mortification. "It's really very provoking !" she exclaimed —"So very absurd !—How uncommonly annoying ! But it's all his own fault for not speaking better English," and handing to me the explanatory phial, I read as follows :—

> "Esquier Orchardt,
> For to rob him with on the chest."

Thanks, however, to Dr. Wolf and the robbing, or a sound constitution, my uncle recovered, and is now as well as ever. In the meantime, the grand Military Manœuvres commenced under the eye of the Prince Royal. Verily it was playing at soldiers on a royal scale, some 15,000 troops being collected

for the purpose, much to the inconvenience of the town and
villages where they quartered, and still more to their own
discomfort in camp, where, owing to the heavy rains, there
was a considerable mortality from a disorder which led to a
police bull of excommunication against all plums. As a
military spectacle, taking into account the number of per-
formers, the extent of the theatre, and the magnificent
scenery, it was superb. By rotation, it should be represented
at Coblenz once in eight years ; and in consequence of the
great expense of paying for the damage in a cultivated
country, it was said the piece was never to be repeated ;
nevertheless the show attracted scarcely any of the natives,
excepting the day when the Prince Royal was present : some
few travellers from our own country, a half-dozen of English
and Hanoverian officers and ourselves were the only spectators. To a novelist, who might have occasion to describe
the operations of warfare, even such an experience would
have been invaluable, enhanced as the mock battles were
by a most picturesque country. For my own part, although
a civilian, I took an extreme interest, akin to that of the
chess-player, in these Manœuvres, the purport of which I tried
to penetrate, but with little success, as might be expected not
merely from my ignorance of the science, but from the intricate and difficult nature of the country. The commander-
in-chief was the governor of the Rhenish provinces—the
veteran General Von Borstell, whó, in addition to his high
reputation as a cavalry officer, nobly proved his *moral* courage,
during the War of Liberation, by refusing to obey the order
of Marshal Blucher for the decimation of a Saxon regiment.
For such conduct there is no earthly decoration : and therefore, having received all the orders which his country, or
rather his sovereign, has to bestow, the brave, able, and
humane General Von Borstell must look forward for the

most precious and enduring of rewards, for the best and brightest act of his life, from the King of Kings.

As might be expected, several real casualties occurred during the sham warfare; and on the last day there happened an accident peculiar to these Manœuvres. As only half charges are allowed, the excited soldier, who wishes to make a little more noise, puts a load of earth or gravel into his musket. Sometimes, probably, a worse motive comes into play : however, we had just turned homewards whilst the victors of the day were firing their *feu de joie*, when on the brow of a hill we saw a poor fellow, sitting under a tree, with his jacket off, and the blood flowing down his arm. He had been shot, a minute before, with a stone, above the elbow, and was in the hands of the regimental surgeon. My aunt immediately insisted on having him into the carriage, a proposition which the doctor embraced with gratitude and avidity, as otherwise his patient must have been jolted two or three leagues in a common cart. So, supplying my aunt with some drops, in case the man should faint, the surgeon ran off to fresh claimants on his services : in fact we saw four or five of the common soldiers drop down from exhaustion, like dead men, by the side of the road. A little damped to reflect that these instances of human suffering had occurred on merely the *play-ground* of the "School of War," we returned to Coblenz, and delivered up our unlucky charge at the Military Hospital. " I do hope," said my uncle, "the King of Prussia will double that poor fellow's smart-money ; for if anything can be galling to a soldier, it must be to have all the pain and disablement of a wound without any of its glory."

You are not aware, perhaps, that *every* Prussian subject must be a soldier, consequently there can be no serving by substitute as in our militia. One morning, whilst listening

to the performance of the capital military band, I was
addressed in tolerable English by one of the privates, who
inquired how I liked their army.   He was a master baker,
he told me, in Oxford-street, and at the earnest entreaty of
his father had left his rolls for the roll-call, his basket for a
musket, and his fancy bread for brown tommy, in order to
serve his two years, and avoid the forfeiture of his civil
rights.   Instances are on record, of individuals (Stulz, the
celebrated tailor, I believe, for one) who, having realized
fortunes abroad, were seized on their return to Prussia,
treated as deserters, or sent into the awkward squad.   Even
the schoolmasters do not escape, but are compelled to join
the march of body with the march of mind.   As an *indulgence*
they have only a six weeks' drill—how different to the six
weeks at Midsummer of our schoolmasters!—but then in that
time they are expected to become proficients.   What a weary
time it must be for the poor pedagogues!   Fancy a sedentary
usher, summoned from his professional desk, round-shouldered,
stooping—shambling—suddenly called upon to unlearn all
his scholar-like habits, and learn others quite the reverse—
to hold his head very much up, to draw his back very much
in, to straighten his arms, stiffen his legs, and step out,
instead of his own shuffle, at so many strides to the minute.
Imagine him stuck up as a sentry on gusty Ehrenbreitstein,
or more likely undergoing an extra drill, in marching order,
for wool-gathering, with a problem of Euclid, and wheeling
to the wrong-about face instead of the right!   Verily it must
seem to him like a bad dream, a doleful piece of somnam-
bulism, till convinced of the hard reality by finding himself
thrust, instead of his late sober academical coat or gown, into
a Prussian blue jacket, with red collar and cuffs, and feeling
behind, instead of the flowing philosophical locks, the bald
regulation nape !

Pray comfort with this outlandish picture your neighbour
the graduate of Oxford, who used to complain so bitterly of
the irksomeness of drilling little boys in Latin and Greek.
A schoolmaster's business in Hampshire may be a sufficient
trial of Christian patience : but what is it to the complex
duties of these schoolmasters abroad? Instead of his annual
vacation, let him suppose himself, as a respite from teaching,
being taught—to drum! Let him conceive himself planted,
with his noisy parchment, and two brass-headed sticks, prac-
tising day after day, hour after hour, his monotonous rub
dub dub, rub dub dub, under the walls of Ehrenbreitstein!
Even as a listener, I have been so disgusted with this wearisome Tambour-work, that I have quite prayed for a little
Flosculous Relievo!

On the parade I met the Captain, who told me that his
regiment—an infantry one—was under orders to return to
its proper locality, Prussian Poland. Perhaps there was
some inspiration in the martial music, but the thought struck
me of joining company, at least as far as Berlin. The
Captain caught at the idea, and as my uncle makes no
objection to my absence, the whim is likely to prove more
than a freak of fancy. At least I am seriously on the look
out for a horse : so as to have no more foot exercise than
may be agreeable. As the marching order has not long to
run, my next will probably be dated from quarters, for I
shall give you a sketch of my military promenade.

This morning, as usual, I strolled about with Markham,
and, Englishman-like, I proposed, on passing the hotel, to
walk in and look at the newspapers. "Newspapers!" said
he; "you will find none here but the 'Rhein-und Mosel
Zeitung,' and I can give you a tolerable idea of the contents
beforehand. First, the king has graciously been pleased to
confer on Mr. Bridge-toll-taker Bommel, and a dozen other

officials, the 'Adler' order of the fourth class. Messrs. Kessel
and Co. have erected a steam-engine of two-horse power;
and the firm of Runkel and Rüben have established a manu-
factory of beet-root sugar. Then for foreign news, there are
half a dozen paragraphs on as many different countries—our
own amongst the rest, probably headed 'Distress in Rich
England,' and giving an account of a pauper who died in the
streets of London. As to local intelligence, the Over-Burgo-
master has ordered the substitution of a new post for an old
one, in the Clemens Platz, and a fresh handle to the pump
near the Haupt Wache. A sentimental poem, a romantic
tale, and the advertisements, fill up the dingy sheet." In
fact, on entering the saloon of the hotel, such a meagre-
looking fog-coloured journal, as he had described, was lying
on the dining-table. Markham took it up, and glanced over
it. "Yes, here they are, the list of Eagle orders and crosses,
and the foreign paragraphs. From Italy, Professor Crampini
gives his opinion on an ancient pan. From Spain nothing—
for affairs are going against Don Carlos. From Greece,
king Otho has displaced a native functionary, and put a
German in his place. From Russia—the distinguished
reception of Baron Hoggenhausen at the imperial Court.
From Austria, that Strauss has composed a new waltz.
From Saxony, the price of wool, and a proclamation of some
petty Sovereign, who, having no transmarine possessions,
ordains that all vagrants, beggars, and vagabonds in his
dominions, shall be transported beyond seas. From England
—zounds!—is it possible that Englishmen have allowed a
namesake of the immortal Shakespeare to go ragged about
the streets! To be sure the bard himself has asked 'what
is there in a name?'—and, on the principle implied, we
ought to hang the very first Patch or Thurtell that came in
our way. There is no sentimental poem in this number; but

there *is* a romantic story, and it well illustrates the oxagge-
rated notions of English wealth, which, to the natives, servo
to justify a dead set at their pockets. What do you think
of this? A lady residing in Euston-square, Now-road, loses
her only child, a little girl. The afflicted mother advertises
her in the papers, and offers as a reward—how much do you
think? Only £50,000 per annum, a mino in 'Cornwales,
and £200,000 in East India shares."

"Aro you serious?" I asked. "Perfectly; it is here,
overy word of it. Finally, there aro the advertisements, somo
of which even are characteristic—for instance, Mr. Simou, tho
notary, offers fifty dollars for the discovery of the parties who
last night broko into his gardeu and stolo and mutilatod his
statue of Napoleon :—and a lady promises a reward to the
finder of a bracelet, containing the locks and initials M. J.—
P. von F.—R. I. D.—L. A.—C. do G.—P. P.—A. von N.
—and J. St. M."

I forgot to tell you, that on a former visit to the hotel, I
found sitting at the table, with as long a faco as ho could
make of a round ono, our fellow-travoller the Cockney ; being
by his own contrivanco a détenu. Having as usual delivered
up his passport at Cologne, he persuaded himself that tho
printed Dampfschiff document ho obtained at tho packet-offico
was something equivalent to tho polico permit ; and only
discovered tho error on arriving at Coblenz. "So hero I am,"
said he, " kicking my heels, till my passport comes upward
from Cologno ;" and then added, in a genuino Bow-bell
voico, " Well, arter all, thero's no placo liko Lonnon !" He
now told me of a subsequent adventure. By ono of those
unaccountable mistakes which happon amongst "foreigners
on both sides," ho became included in a shooting-party, at a
grand battue, in the woods of Nassau. Cockney-like, ho
provided himsclf for the occasion with a great dog, of I know

not what breed; but pointer or mastiff, the animal was
equally out of place and rule. However the master was
permitted to retain the beast, on condition of keeping him at
heel, which he effected by tying Bango with a string to the
button-hole of his trousers-pocket. In this order our Cockney
was planted, at a convenient post for shooting down an
avenue, at whatever game might pass across it. For some
time nothing stirred, but at last there was a rustle of the
leaves, and a fine hare scampered along the path. Away
went Bango after the hare, and away went a huge fragment
of kerseymere after Bango, leaving the astonished sportsman
in even a worse plight than Sterne, when he treated the
starved Ass to a macaroon! "If ever I shoot again," said
he, "it shall be round Lonnon; they're up to the thing there,
pinters and all."

Apropos of sporting, the example of Markham and his
friend has brought angling into fashion with some of the
officers of the garrison. Amongst the rest we found a
captain of engineers, making his maiden essay on the banks
of the Moselle; but he complained sadly of the shyness or
inappetence of the fish, which had refused even to nibble,
although for the two last hours, as he took the trouble to
prove to us by pulling up his line: he had been fishing at
the bottom with an artificial fly! The only drawback to
the amusement is the fall of large stones, not meteoric, but
projected by the first idle Coblenzer of the lower class, who
may happen to pass by. To such a pitch was this nuisance
carried that the military piscators were obliged to post men
to intercept and punish the runaway offenders. "I can
only account for so malicious a practice," said Markham,
"by supposing that as the amusement is English, the low-
born are infected with the same petty jealousy as their
betters occasionally exhibit towards our country, from Prince

"The Pomps and Vanities of this Wicked World."

Pückler Muskau, down to Mr. Aloys Schreiber. But you have not perhaps seen the latter's sketch of the English in Baden? I have entered his description of an Englishman in my pocket-book,' for fear of meeting one without knowing it. Here it is :—

" ' If you meet a man in a great-coat that reaches down to his ankles, wide enough to enclose a whole family, and with pockets, in each of which a couple of folios might be concealed, its wearer having a careless gait, and taking notice of nothing so much as of himself, it is, without doubt, an Englishman. If he quarrel with a coachman about his fare, and with an ass-driver about his drink money—be sure it is an Englishman.'

"Now for a companion picture. If you meet a man in a frock-coat as glossy as if it had just come through a shower of rain, with pockets big enough to hold a bale of tobacco in one and a gas-pipe in the other—its wearer strutting with an indescribable swagger, so full of himself that there is no room for sauer kraut, beyond a question he is a German. If he catches up his umbrella and his precious meerschaum, leaving his wife and child to scramble after him as they may—be sure he is a German. If he has a little cross, or a snip of haberdashery at his button-hole, and a huge ring on his ungloved forefinger, you may set him down as an Aulic Counsellor into the bargain. If you see a young lady—but no, I will not imitate Mr. Schreiber in his want of gallantry to the daughters of the haughty ' Isle of Shop-keepers,' a phrase borrowed from England's bitterest enemy, and therefore sufficiently expressive of the animus of the ungrateful Guide-Book-man towards so great a majority of his Courteous Readers."

As you are a meteorologist, I must not omit to inform you, that during our walk we had an excellent sight of a

water-spout. It came down the Moselle, and at first seemed
a whirlwind of dust, in the midst of which some unlucky
jackdaws were flapping about in a very bewildered manner.
In a few seconds the dust or vapour cleared away, and the
water-spout made its appearance, extending from the water
to a vast height in the clouds, where it terminated in a
ragged funnel-shape, like the untwisting strands of a rope.
Against the black sky behind it, the general resemblance
was to a long narrow gray ribbon, bellying a little before the
wind, with several smaller curves towards the top, as if from
different currents of air. In this order it crossed the Rhine,
rather deliberately, where, surging against the bank, it caught
up a wash of linen—as it had previously carried off some
skins from a tannery—and passing to the right of the fortress,
was lost to sight behind the hills. It had scarcely disappeared, when, at an exclamation from Markham, "There's
a screw loose in the sky !" I looked up, and saw a long black
cloud slowly revolving, parallel with the earth, and pointing
with its sharp end—the other was almost flat—to the other
course taken by the other phenomenon. We have since
heard, that the water-spout dropped the linen and leather,
and expended itself, after trifling damage, not far distant
from Ems.

And now, as the convolvulus says to the setting sun, it is
time for me to close. How I wish, Gerard, you could stand
beside me, rod in hand, some fine evening, on the banks of
my favorite Lahn ! But as it cannot be, I send you a sketch
instead.

Dear love to Emily, from
Yours ever truly,
FRANK SOMERVILLE.

THE LAHN.—AN ECLOGUE.

PICTOR AND PISCATOR.

Pis. Stay! here we are, at the likeliest place on the whole water. Come put together your rod.

Pic. O my friend, what a sweet picturesque river is this you have brought me to!—But surely one of the worst for angling in the whole world!

Pis. Nay, you shall find passable sport here, I warrant you. There be good perch herein, and chub of an arm's length, and barbel; and what is better, as you are a Tyro, not shy and suspicious, like the experienced fish in your well-angled English streams, but so greedy and simple as almost to catch themselves. The Germans, however contemplative, are no followers of the gentle art.

Pic. My friend, you mistake me. My speech aimed not at the fish or the water, whereof I have had no trial, but at the beautiful scenery, which will distract me so, I shall never be able to watch my float or my fly. What feudal ruin is that which overlooks us from the top of the bushy hill?"

Pis. It is called Lahneck, and belonged aforetime to a Commandery of Teutonic Knights. But come, make ready your tackle; for here is a notable place at this rapid where the current rushes and eddies amongst the large stones.

Pic. Now I am ready. But by your good leave, being only a beginner, I will use a worm rather than a fly.

Pis. At your own pleasure. For my part, I prefer to fish at the top. Look!—I have one at the first cast!—a huge chub! A rare struggle he makes at the outset, but he hath a faint heart at bottom—anon you shall see him come into the landing-net as tame as a lamb.

Pic. How beautifully it comes out !—

Pis. Aye, doth he not ?

Pic. —Against yon dun-coloured sky. Then all those gray tints and verdant stains ! And those little feathery flying clouds !

Pis. They run very large here. You may hear them chop at the flies and chafers like a dog ! And though they be reckoned elsewhere the very worst of dishes for the table, let me tell you in this country, where they do not get fish from the great deep, a chub is a chub, as the saying is. I make bold to say, I shall obtain store of thanks from some good woman of a house for this same loggerhead.

Pic. Of course there is a tale to it !

Pis. A what ?—a tail ?—It would be a rare sort of fish without one !

Pic. I cry you mercy ! I was thinking of the old feudal castle, and some marvellous legend. There must needs be some romantic story about it, amongst the rude peasantry. How beautifully the light plays upon the crisp fragment ! Marry, 'tis quite a picture ! I should like prodigiously to take such a one.

Pis. And so you would,—provided you would bait as I do with a live chafer or a white moth. But hist ! I have him ! A still larger chub than the other !

Pic. It must be many centuries old !

Pis. How ? I did not know the chub was so long-lived. But perchance you were thinking of a carp. In the moats at Charlottenburg there be carps so venerable that their age is unknown ; and the moss has grown on their backs. But see,—you have a bite ; your float is gone half-way across the river !

Pic. Truly, I was gazing another way. Lo ! here he comes. It is a fine perch.

Sticks and Strikes.

Pis. They are caught here of four and five pounds weight, and especially nearer to Ems; for they delight in the warm springs which thereabouts bubble up in the very midst of the Lahn. But here comes an old fisherman from the village. How he stands and stares at our prey, with his mouth in a round O, as if he would take a minnow!

Pic. What is the aged man discoursing of, with such a vehement gesture and emphatic voice, in the German tongue?

Pis. He says he is gospel-sure we have some smell or some spell to our bait beyond the natural—seeing that he hath fished here the two last days all through without a fin! And little marvel, for his tackle is a German hook like a meat-hook, and a line like a clothes-line, wherewith, if he entice a fish, he throws it clean over his head. But, look again to your cork!

Pic. Pish!—'tis only a very young perch.

Pis. Nay—a Pope or Ruff. Some naturalists opine, forsooth, that on being hooked, this same fish is seized with a sort of fit or spasm, which gives him the lock-jaw. But lie bites far too boldly to be troubled with such weak nerves. But say they, when he is hooked he shuts up his mouth, which is contrary to the practice of fishes in the like case. And truly, when he hath once gotten the bait, instead of gaping like an idiot, or a chub, or a child with a hot morsel of pudding, he doth indeed shut up his mouth, as much as to say, "What I have got I mean to keep," and so locks up his jaws, and holds on like a bull-dog. But for a fit from fright—not he! Just look at his face, full front, how determined and desperate is his physiognomy! How fiercely he stares with his big black eyes—for his temper is up as well as his back-fin! Verily if he resembles a Pope at all, it is Pope Leo and not Pope Innocent.

Pic. Ay, truly, it is part and parcel of Popery : but it makes a pretty object in the landscape !

Pis. What object ?

. *Pic.* The little Popish chapel yonder, on the crest of the mountain. O, my friend, I thank thee most heartily for bringing me to angle in so fair a scene. How serene it is ! —and how much more silent for the presence of that ancient ruin, where so much riot hath been aforetime ! How largely doth an old castle, that hath made a noise in history, enhance the present peace ! Should we feel half so still or so solitary if there had never been those Knight Hospitallers, dwelling aloft, with all the shoutings of warfare and revelry, but presently dumbfounded by time ? Where now is the bold German baron, with his long line of ancestry——

Pis. He's gone—a murrain on him—line and all !

Pic. Eh ! What ?

Pis. The heaviest chuckle-headed fellow, with such a length of gut !

Pic. The bold German baron ?—

Pis. No—a chub, a chub !—but stop ! I see it—he's entangled. If haply I can but leap on to that biggest stone—

Pic. How audibly the fishes are splashing and floundering in their disport ! The sun is sinking beyond the Rhine ! Oh my friend, look at the beautiful cool tone of that gray mountain—then the dark reflection of the village and its trees in the glowing water,—the feudal castle on the other hand—half in shade—and then these rocky stones in the foreground—but—grace be with us !—what hath chanced to you ?

Pis. Chanced—why·I have fallen into the Lahn ! And the while you were poetising I have helped myself out again ! Fye, what a watery figure I am !

A Water Kelpy.

Pic. Beautiful! Nay, stop—pr'ythee do not stir—pray, pray, pray, stay as you be!

Pis. What for?

Pic. For one mere single minute. There! Just so. With the low setting sun glowing behind—and all those little jets and liquid drops, each catching the golden light—

Pis. A plague on it! Am I standing here, dripping, for a water-colour picture? Come, put up, put up, and let us back to our inn. I must beg of our civil host to befriend me with a dry suit, and to chain up the big dog.

Pic. It will be well. But wherefore dismiss the poor dog? He was very gentle and friendly to us as we came hither. Of all animals I do love a dog!

Pis. And so do I too—in my own proper plumes. But one day a poor piscatory friend of mine fell into this same river, and was so furnished with dry clothes by our host; but after snuffing awhile and growling about his legs, the big dog flew at our unlucky angler, and with much ado was hindered from stripping him of the borrowed garments.

Pic. What marvellous sagacity! How I should like to see it tried! It would be a study for a picture—The staunch Hound springing at Conrade of Montserrat!

Pis. I'faith I thank you heartily. Come, let us be stirring. A frize on it! How the fishes are rising!

Pic. What dainty colours on those changeful clouds! Well, fare thee well, feudal Lahneck! with thy visions of Teutonic Knights—

Pis. There must needs be trout here!—

Pic. With helmeted heads, and gauntlets on their hands!

Pis. In the season, haply, even salmon swim up this river, from the Rhine.

Pic. With an ancient minstrel before them, twanging melodiously on the harp! Nay, but stop—stop—stop!

Pis. What hath miscarried ?

Pic. Nothing—but an it please you to walk a little more slowly—to let us enjoy the scene. How the creeping shadows steal over the prospect, at every moment producing a new effect ! Do look at those sportive swallows dipping into the sober-tinted wave, and producing a coruscation of burning light on ring and ripple ! How soothing this still-ness ! How refreshing, after the noon-tide heat, this cool evening zephyr !

Pis. Ay, with a dry shirt, and unducked nether garments ! But here is the ferry-boat ; come, step in. Honest Charon, there is a goodly chub for thy supper, and pr'ythee thrust us speedily to the other side. Gentle, pretty country damsels, wherefore huddle so far away from me, like a flock of timid sheep ? I am but a wet man, not a wicked one. Moreover, if you crowd so to one side of the boat—ah, say I told you so !—

[*The ferry-boat heels on one side, fills, and is swamped.*
Fortunately the river is low, and nobody is drowned.]

Pic. [*Looking round him, up to his neck in water.*] What a subject for a picture ! What a singular effect !

TO PETER BAGSTER, ESQ.

MY DEAR PETER,

To prevent more funeral condolements and mis-takes, as you may have heard some rumour of my illness, this is to say, I am alive and well. But I have had a very serious attack ; so bad indeed, that I begin to think that my constitution cannot be so sapped and weak as I supposed ; or how could it have held out, not only against the disorder itself, but the German doctoring of it, which, to my mind, was the most trying and dangerous of the two! But I shall save all the medicals for Truby when I get home to Kent. At any rate, to be candid, as an honest man ought to be, even at my own expense, the notion of my going off in a moment is quite settled, for if anything could bring on sudden death, eight-and-forty hours of pain and fever were quite sufficient for a warning. Whereby you may gather that I have changed my opinion about my case; so let the doctor crack his fingers and cry out that it was all through him and his advice, to go up the river Rhine.

While I am on the subject, I ought to say that poor Kate has derived benefit as well as myself, and is a young girl for spirits compared to what she was; though mayhap she would not own to it herself, being at present in a terrible taking at what she calls a domestic misfortune, which has quite driven poor George out of her head. The same being the sudden conversion of her maid, Martha, into a papist, and such a zealous one, that she crosses her mistress as well as herself a hundred times in a day.

For my part, Peter, setting aside servants and the like, and considering only the poor and destitute orders, instead of blaming their ignorance and superstition for their being Roman Catholics, I almost wonder how they can be anything else. Having had the opportunity of studying the subject abroad by going into foreign churches and cathedrals, as well as the wretched dwellings of the lower people, it's my firm belief that their religion may be laid more to their poverty than to their ignorance. Suppose a poor old German woman in a dark dirty cold room, without fire, without candle, and without even the chirp of a cricket, by way of company. She puts on her ragged cloak, totters fifty yards, and there she is in a comfortable church, well warmed and lighted up

like a general illumination. She sees priests in magnificent
brocaded robes, great gold and silver candlesticks, and shrines
and chapels shining with jewels, mock or real is all one,
rubies, amethysts, topazes, emeralds, sapphires, and so forth ;
things which even some of her betters are apt to connect
with the treasures of Heaven and the glories of the New
Jerusalem. She hears a fine organ, finely played, and chosen
singers, with voices like angels, chanting hymns in an
unknown tongue. I mean no disrespect to the religion in
saying it's as good to her as the Italian Opera in London.
Then she enjoys the smell of frankincense, and the sight of
grand pictures, and statues, and carvings, and, above all,
there is the Virgin Mary in royal robes, with a crown, and
pearls, and velvet, and ermine, like a queen of this world,
and the poor old woman in her tatters has as free access to
her and as long audience as the greatest court lady in the
land. Is it any wonder if such a poor creature goes by
choice to a church, which, along with the bodily comfort she
wants at home, lets her share for a while in those pleasures
of sight and hearing and so forth, for which she had senses
given to her by the Almighty, as well as the rich and noble
of the earth ?

Now in England, old friend, we make the church as
unattractive, to such a poor ancient body, as we can. We
stick her in a cold aisle, on a hard bench, and take no more
pains to please her other senses. We bid her, forsooth,
admire the plain unadorned simplicity of the Protestant
religion. But the lady in the hat and feathers has been to
the Theatre, the Opera, Concerts, Exhibitions, and Balls, or
Routs, six days of the week, and instead of any denial, may
feel it a relief on the seventh to sit in a quiet church, and
listen to its simple service. Not that I wish our temples to
be turned into oratorios, or picture galleries, or stages for

"I bide my time."

showy spectacles—all I want is fair play for the lower classes. If such gratifications as the Catholic churches afford to them, are out of character with our own Protestant places of worship, the poor people ought, in justice, to be allowed to enjoy them elsewhere. But instead of that, what do we do? We shut up our tombs and monuments, set a price on St. Paul's and the Abbey; our saints shake their heads at anything like a public ball or concert in humble life; and our magistrates put down the cheap theatres, as if Tom and Jerry, at a penny a head, was twelve times more immoral than Tom and Jerry at a shilling. To my notion, such a system is more likely to produce Catholics than Protestants; and what is likelier still, to make the lower classes of no religion at all. It's just like learning, which no boy in the world would take to if you sent him to a school without a playground.

Frank, who has made acquaintance with a captain in the Prussian service, went off this morning by diligence to join the regiment on its march to Berlin. He ought to have left Coblenz in company, but was taken ill. He nearly lost his start by the coach, for when the time came, the German maid who ought to have waked him and prepared his breakfast, was snoring comfortably in her bed. But the Germans, both men and women, in such cases, are wonderfully phlegmatic. I have been told of a pig-driver who brought a porker across the Rhine, during a hard frost; the moment the porker got out of the boat, he laid himself quietly down in the snow, and instead of rousing him, the fellow coolly lugged out his flint and steel, lighted his pipe, and patiently smoked over the pig till he chose to rise of his own accord. Kätchen had no pipe; but she had some other source of philosophy, for when told that her young master had almost lost his place, she only shrugged her shoulders; and when informed that he had quite lost his breakfast, she only shrugged them again.

I have some thoughts of going up the river Rhine, as far as Schaffhausen, to see the famous waterfall; but much will depend on the weather at Frank's return. This is singing rather a different tune to my former ditties; but I know, old friend, you will be well pleased that such warnings were fancies and not facts, with

Dear Peter, your old and faithful friend,

RICHARD ORCHARD.

TO GERARD BROOKE, ESQ.

MY DEAR GERARD,

Now for some account of what Mrs. Headrigg would doubtless have called her military "experiences." The most eligible horse I could pick up was one which had carried an engineer officer at the grand manœuvres : which I purchased for about 15*l.*—trappings and all. A Prussian military cloak, with a quiet blue collar instead of a red one, happened to match the saddle-cloth, as regulation, and made me so far complete. But, as the French say, the first step is all the difficulty ; and when I ought to have stepped out of Coblenz with my friend the Captain and his 10th company, I was lying in my bed with a blister on my chest, whilst my nag went without me, like the "chief mourner" at a dragoon's funeral. The Captain left me the route, in case I should be able to join, which at last I effected. My Uncle proposed posting, but, being no disciple of Zimmerman, I preferred the Eilwagen—and, thanks to the insouciance of our German maid, who lay *dreaming* of making my breakfast. I was literally "sent empty away."

Starting on a fine fresh morning, and ascending the breezy hills in the rear of Ehrenbreitstein, it was not long before I began to feel the cravings so keenly described by the hunger-bitten heroes of Spanish romance. Scenery went for nothing. I could see no prospect but that of a déjeûner, which Schreiber's Guide promised me at the end of the stage. German travelling is proverbially "dooms slow," but, compared with my *fast*, it seemed slower than usual ; but there is no inducing a royal postilion, for the King is universal coach-owner, to go any quicker to suit his "insides." It appeared an age ere we arrived at Ems, which, like literal M's, seemed to my fancy to stand for Mocha and Muffins. At last, we stopped at the door of some hotel, ample enough to furnish a public dinner. "How long do we stay here ?" "Ten minutes, sir." "Good : a roll and a cup of coffee." And to save time, the refreshments were paid for beforehand. Good, again. But five long minutes elapsed, then six, then seven, and, at the eighth, came the roll and the cup of coffee ; boiling hot ;—with a jug of boiling-hot milk—there ought to have been a boiling hot cup and a red-hot spoon. The roll might be pocketed,—but the coffee could not well be poured in after it, à la Grimaldi. In the mean time, the post-horn kept blowing, but without making the beverage any cooler : pshaw !—the trick was palpable and provoking, and a few warm words might have fallen naturally from a scalded tongue. But the contrast between the paltriness of the fraud and the magnificent saloon in which it was perpetrated, had something in it so ludicrous that I got into the coupé again in tolerable good humour. I have since heard that such tricks upon travellers are so common, as to have been made the foundation of a German

T

farce ; and, truly, to a flying visitor they are but fly-bites which he gets rid of with a cursory d——n and a blast of the horn : but, as Markham says, when cheating and extortion come home to you as a resident, and become part of your fixtures, you have occasion to read, on week-days as well as Sundays, in the Book of Job.

Turning my back upon the inhospitable Hôtel (de Russie ?) I beheld my beloved Lahn, and could not help exclaiming, "Oh ! ye Naiads, can the scalding, parboiling springs uprising in the very middle of your native stream, be so repulsive to you, as the presence in this pretty valley— meant for silence, solitude, and sweet thoughts—of pride, pomp, vanity, the frenzy of gambling, and all the hotter passions of human nature ?"

As for Health, if there ever was such a Goddess resident at Ems, she must long since have been scared away by the infraction·of sanitary rules. For instance, you are not to eat fruit ; which,.by the practice at the Speisesaals, seems inter- preted into a gluttonous licence to eat everything else, in any possible quantity. You are to keep your mind calm and unruffled—towards which, you are supplied with public and private gaming tables ; you are not to worry yourself with business—but invited to make a business of pleasure at ever- lasting assemblies and balls. The whole thing is a profitable hoax on pretended temperance principles. The very prepara- tion for taking the waters (vide Schreiber) ought to prevent your having any occasion for them—namely, exercise, plain diet, abstinence from hot wines, or stimulative drinks—early rising and bedding, and command of your passions : in short, when you are fit to go to Ems, you need not leave Piccadilly. The rules pompously given out for your regimen at any of the great German watering-places are, in the main, quite as applicable to Norton Folgate or Bullock Smithy. If—

"there is much virtue in that if"—if a man could dismiss all thoughts of business that are bothering, all ideas of pleasure but what are innocent—if he could forget that he has a head except for pleasant thoughts, or a stomach except for wholesome things—if he would not over-walk, over-ride, over-watch, over-sleep, over-eat, over-drink, over-work, or over-play himself, to my fancy he would be a fool to leave the blessed spot, wherever he might be, for any watering place but Paradise and the River of Life.

On quitting the Lahn, the beauty of the scenery dwindles like a flower for the want of *watering*, and you enter on a lumpy-bumpy-humpy country, which is the more uninteresting as, in getting over this "ground-swell," you do it at a walk. German horses object to go up hill at any other pace ; and German postilions prevent their trotting or galloping down—by which hearse-like progress we at last looked down on the slated roofs of Langen Schwalbach or "Swallow's Brook." Whereby hangs, an't please you, a swallow tale.

THE FLOWER AND THE WEED.

A LEGEND OF SCHWALBACH.

" YES," said Mr. Samuel Brown, gently closing the book he had just been reading, and looking up cheerfully at the ceiling, "yes, I will go to Germany !"

Mr. Samuel Brown was an Englishman, middle-aged, and a bachelor; not that the last was his own fault, for he had tried as often to change his state, and had made as many offers, as any man of his years. But he was unlucky. His rejected addresses had gone through nearly as numerous editions as the pleasant work under the same title : his

heart and hand had been declined so frequently that, like the
eels under another painful operation, he had become quite
used to it.   It was even whispered amongst his friends, that
he had advertised in the *Herald* for a matrimonial partner,
but without success.   As he was well to do in the world, the
obstacle, most probably, was his person ; which, to tell the
truth, was as plain and common-place as his name.   Be that
as it may, he was beginning in despair to make up his mind
to a housekeeper and a life of celibacy, when all at once his
hopes were revived by the perusal of a certain book of
travels.

" Yes," said Mr. Samuel Brown, again opening the volume
wherein he had kept the place with his forefinger, " I will
certainly go to Germany ! " and once more he read aloud the
delightful paragraph, which seemed to him better than the
best passage in the Pleasures of Hope.   It ran thus :—

"It is this," said one of the ladies, "which makes the society of
foreigners so much too agreeable to us.   A mouth uncontaminated by a
pipe may win with words, which, if scented with tobacco, would be
listened to with very different emotions." *

" So much TOO agreeable ; " repeated Mr. Samuel Brown,
briskly rubbing his hands with satisfaction—" an uncontaminated mouth ; why I never smoked a pipe in my life,
not even a cigar !   Yes, I *will* go to Germany ! "

A single man, without encumbrance, is moved as easily
as an empty hand-barrow.   On the Saturday Mr. Samuel
Brown locked up his chambers in the Adelphi, procured a
passport from Mr. May, got it countersigned by Baron
Bülow, engaged a berth in the Batavier, sailed on Sunday,
and in thirty hours landed at Rotterdam.   The very next
morning he started up the Rhine for Nimeguen, thence to

* Mrs. Trollope's "Western Germany."

"La Belle Vue."

Cologne, and again by the first boat to Coblenz. To most persons the greater part of this water progress is somewhat wearisome; but to our hero it was very delightful, and chiefly so from a circumstance that is apt to disgust other travellers—the perpetual smoking. But Mr. Brown enjoyed it; and with expanded nostrils greedily inhaled the reeky vapour, as a hungry beggar snuffs up the fumes of roast meat. If anything vexed him, it was to see a pipe standing idle in a corner of the cabin; but he had not often that annoyance. If anything pleased him, it was to see a jolly German, with an ample tobacco-bag gaily embroidered hung at his button-hole, puffing away lustily at his meerschaum. But his ecstacy was at its height when, on entering at night the Speisesaal of the Grand Hôtel de Belle Vue, he found above a score of cloud-compelling Prussians smoking themselves and each other till they could scarcely see or be seen.

The seventh day found Mr. Samuel Brown established at Schwalbach—a selection he had prudently made to avoid any rivalship from his countrymen. In fact he was the only Englishman in the place. It was the height of the season, and the hotels and lodging-houses were full of guests, old and young, sick and well, gay and sober, gentle and simple. What was more to the point, there were shoals of single females, beautiful Fräuleins, German houris, all ready of course to listen to a foreigner so much too agreeable, and with lips never contaminated by a pipe. The only difficulty was, amongst so many, to make a choice. But our Samuel resolved not to be rash. To ask was to have, and he might as well have the best. Accordingly, he frequented the promenades and the rooms, regularly haunted the Wein-brunnen, the Stahlbrunnen and the Paulino; and dined, in succession, at all the public tables. In the meantime he could not help noticing, with inward triumph, how little

chance the natives had of gaining the hearts of their fair
countrywomen. A few, indeed, merely whiffed at a cigar,
but nine-tenths of them sucked, unweaned, at that "instrument of torture," a pipe. He saw officers, tall, handsome
men, with mustachios to drive any civilian to despair—but
they had all served at the battle of Rauchen,—and in the
Allée often verified the description by Mr. Brown's favourite
authoress :—

"The ladies throw their bonnets aside, leaving their faces no other
protection but their beautiful and abundant hair. The gentlemen, many
of them military, sit near, if a chair can be found ; or if not, stand behind
them like courteous cavaliers as they are ; excepting (oh horror of horrors !)
they turn aside from the lovely group, and smoke !"

"Yes, yes," said Mr. Samuel Brown, quoting to himself—
"*to expose these delicate sweet-looking females to the real
suffering which the vicinity of breath, infected by tobacco,
occasions, is positive cruelty !*" It was his topmost pleasure
to watch such offenders ; and when the operation was over—
when the tobacco-bag was bulging out one coat-pocket, and
the end of the tube was projecting like a tail from the other,
with what gusto used he to walk round and round the
unconscious German, sniffing the stale abomination in his
clothes, in his person, in his hair ! Better to him was that
vapid odour than all the spicy scents of Araby the Blest :
eau de Cologne, otto of roses, jasmin, millefleurs, verbena,
nothing came near it. As a baffled fox-hunter once cursed
the sweetest of Flora's gifts as "those stinking vi'lets," so
did our wife-hunter choose to consider one of the nastiest
smells in nature as the very daintiest of perfumes !

At length Mr. Samuel Brown made his election. The
Fräulein Von Nasenbeck was of good family, young and
pretty (a blonde), with a neat figure, and some twenty
thousands of dollars at her own disposal. Why, with such

advantages, she had never married, would have been a mystery, if Samuel's favourite book, which he always carried in his pocket, had not hinted a sufficient reason.

"In the same country, where the enthusiasm of sentiment is carried to the highest pitch, and cherished with the fondest reverence, the young men scruple not to approach the woman they love with sighs, which make her turn her head aside, not to hide the blush of happiness, but the loathing of involuntary disgust."

"Of course that's it," soliloquized the exulting Samuel, "but *my* lips have not been sophisticated with tobacco, and she will listen to volumes from me, when she would not hear a single syllable from one of your smoke-jacks!" The difficulty was to get introduced; but even this was accomplished by dint of perseverance; and, fortune still favouring him, one day he found himself *tête-à-tête* with his Love-Elect. Such an opportunity was not to be lost; so thrusting one hand in his pocket, as if to derive inspiration from his book, and gently laying the other on his bosom, he heaved a deep sigh, and then began, partly quoting from memory, in the following words:—"It's a pity, my dear miss, it's really a pity to witness *so glaring a defect in a people so admirable in other respects.*"

"It is how?" said the puzzled Fräulein.

"I allude," said Samuel, pointing to a group of Germans, "to your young countrymen. *To behold their youthful faces one moment beaming with the finest expression, and the next stultified by that look of ineffable stupidity produced by smoking, is really too vexatious!*"

"Ach!" ejaculated the fair Fräulein, with a slight shrug of her beautiful shoulders.

"Oh," exclaimed Samuel in a passionate tone, pressing his right hand on his heart, and looking with all the tenderness he could assume at the young lady—"Oh! that indeed is a face *whose delicacy is better fitted to receive the gales of Eden than the fumes of tobacco !*"

" Did you never smoke yourself ? " asked the Fräulein, in her pretty broken English.

" Never ! " said Samuel, with as much solemn earnestness as if he had been disclaiming a murder.

" Never!—and so help me God ! I never will ! "

The Fräulein dropped the cloth she was embroidering, and stared at the speaker till her light blue eyes seemed to dilate to twice their natural size. But she did not utter a word.

" No ! " resumed Samuel, with increasing energy ; " this mouth was never contaminated with pipe-clay, and never shall be ! Never will I fumigate the woman I love with sighs that make her turn her head right round with disgust !"

"Do you tink to smoke is so bad ? " inquired the Fräulein, with all the innocent simplicity of a child.

" Bad ! " echoed Samuel. " I think it a vile, abominable, filthy, dirty practice !—Don't you ? "

"I never tink of de matter at all, one way or anoder," replied the placid Fräulein.

" But you consider it a hateful, loathsome, nasty habit ? "

" Habit ? oh no !—For de Germans to smoke is so natural as to eat, as to drink, as to sleep ! "

" At least," said Samuel, now getting desperately alarmed, " you would not allow a smoker to approach very near your person ; for instance, to whisper to you, much less to—to— to embrace you, or offer you a salute ? "

" Why for not ? " inquired the lovely Fräulein, with un- usual vivacity. " I have been so accustomed to since I was borned. When I was one leetle child—a bibi—mine dear fader did smoke whiles he holded me on his two knees. Mine dear broder did take his pipe from out his mouth to give me one kiss. Mine cousin, Albrecht,—do you see dis

The Battle of Rauchen.

piece. of work I am making?" and she held up the embroidered cloth—"dis shall be one tobacco-bag for mine
good cousin!"

"Is it possible," exclaimed Samuel, his voice quivering
with agitation—"Born in smoke! nursed in smoke! bred in
smoke!"

"It is all so, everywhere," said the quiet Fräulein.

"Once more!" cried the trembling Samuel. "Excuse
me, but, if I may ask, would you bestow your hand—your
heart—your lovely person, on—on—on—on a fellow that
smoked?"

"I am verlobt," murmured the pretty Fräulein, blushing
and casting down her light blue eyes. "That means to say,
I am one half married to my cousin Albrecht."

"Betrothed, I suppose," muttered the disappointed Samuel.
"And—and, other German young ladies"—he asked in a
croaking voice—"are they of the same opinions?—the same
tolerant opinions as to smoking?"

"Ja wohl!—yes, certainly—so I believe."

Poor Samuel could bear no more. Taking a hurried leave
of the adorable Fräulein, he jumped up from his chair,
dashed along the Allée, climbed the hill, plunged into the
woods, and never halted till he was stopped by the stream.
Then taking a hasty glance around to make sure that he was
alone, he plucked the fatal book from his pocket, and
repeated aloud the following passage :—

"Could these young men be fully aware of the effect this habit produces
upon their charming countrywomen, I am greatly tempted to believe that
it would soon get out of fashion."

The next moment the leaf he had been reading from was
plucked out, torn into a hundred fragments and scattered to
the winds. Another, and another, and another followed,
till the whole volume was completely gutted; and then,

with an oath too dreadful to be repeated, he tossed the empty cover into the Schwalbach!

In five days afterwards Mr. Samuel Brown was back in his old chambers in the Adelphi, and in five more he had engaged a housekeeper and set in for an Old Bachelor.

At Schwalbach I dined with a solitary companion, who was carried into the room like a child, and seated at the table. By his physiognomy he was a Jew, and in spite of his helpless, crippled condition, so good-humoured and so cheerful, that I felt a blush of self-reproach and shame to think that, with good health and the use of all my limbs, I could be accessible to spleen or impatience. Ere re-entering the coach, which by rights should carry no outside passengers, I saw our merry cripple carried up a ladder and deposited in a low chair of peculiar construction, which was fastened on the roof, and not a few jokes were bandied between him and the spectators on his usual elevation. As soon as he was secured, the little fat postilion raised his horn with its huge tassels to his lips, and after blowing till his red face turned purple and the whites of his eyes to pink, there came out of the tube a squeak so thin, so poor, and so pig-like, that I involuntarily looked round for the Schwein-General, his huge whip, and its victim. Few persons would believe, on hearsay, from such an instrument, that the Germans are a musical people, or that there is a Royal prize or pool of a silver watch, or the like, for the performer who "plays the best trump." To hear a postilion taking advantage of the long Rhine bridge, where, by law, he must walk his horses, to play a solo on this impracticable instrument to the *mocking* echoes from the neighbouring mountains, you not only think that he must be a crazy Fanatico in music, but that his trumpet is *cracked* too.

Our postilion, however, whatever his merits on the horn, was a good, kind-hearted fellow, and paid great attention to his paralyzed passenger, repeatedly turning round in the saddle to point out to him what was worthy of notice on the road : at last, with a very justifiable pride in his country, he fairly pulled up on the summit of a hill called the Hohe Wurzel, which I presume to translate the Turnip Top— commanding a superb view over the Rheingau, in all the glory of its autumnal colouring, and, like other beauties, greatly enhanced by its meandering blue veins, the Rhine aud the Maine. I will only say of the view, that five minutes of it justified the whole tediousness of the journey. It was still glowing in my mind's eye when we entered Wies- baden, where we suddenly passed under an archway, like those that admit you into the yard of some of our London inns. I was struck, on turning into the gateway, by the very hilarious faces of the bystanders ; and finding, on alighting, a similar circle of grinning men, women, and boys, with their eyes cast upwards to the roof of the coach, I looked in the same direction, and saw our merry Cripple laughing, as heartily as any of them, and re-adjusting himself in his lofty chair. It appeared that his good friend the postilion, unaccustomed to outside passengers, and doubly engaged in guiding his vehicle into the town, and blowing a flourish on his horn, had totally forgotten his lame charge on the roof, who only saved himself from destruction in the archway by an extraordinary activity in prostration ! We left the *patient* Patient at Wiesbaden, most probably to make trial of the baths ; and he had so won my heart by his sweet, cheerful resignation, that I could not help wishing an angel might come down and trouble the waters, like those of Bethesda, for his sake.

The mere glimpse I had of Wiesbaden produced in me a

feeling the reverse of love at first sight. It looked to my taste too like an inland Brighton ; and I was not sorry to get away from it by even an uninteresting road, lined with fruit trees on each side. It was dusk when I arrived at Frankfort ; so, having supped, I booked myself onward, by the night coach. The Prince of Thurm and Taxis, a sort of Postmaster-general, has here his head-quarters, and nothing could be better than his travelling regulations, if they were only enforced. Thus by one article it is forbidden to smoke in the public vehicles, without the consent of the whole company, whereas, instead of regularly publishing the banns between himself and his pipe, I never yet knew a German proceed even so far as the first time of asking. Imagine, then, the discomfort of sitting all night with both windows up, and five smoking, or smoked fellow-travellers in an un-Rumfor-dized Eilwagen ! Nothing, indeed, seems so obnoxious to German lungs as the pure ether, and I can quite believe the story of a Prussian doctor, who recommended to a consumptive countryman to smoke Virginian tobacco instead of the native sort, just as an English physician in the like case would advise a change of air.

I suppose it was the effect of the narcotic, but though I certainly breakfasted bodily at Saalmünster, my mind did not properly wake up till we arrived at Fulda, an ecclesiastical city with a Bishop's palace, a cathedral, and a great many beggars. The old religious establishments, like our old Poor Laws, indubitably relieved a great number of mendicants, but made quite as many more—as witness, Fulda and Cologne. One little beggar had planted himself with his flute by the road-side, and, with a complimentary anticipation of English charity and loyalty, was blowing with all his might at " God Save the King."

· And now for a little episode. One of our wheelers chose

Birds of a Feather flock together.

U

to run restive, if such a phrase may be applied to standing as stock-still as if you had said "Burr-r-r-r-r-r !" to him; which, by the way, is a full stop to any horse in Germany. The postilion could make nothing of him, for the Germans are peculiarly and praiseworthily tender of their cattle ; so out jumped the conducteur, a little, florid, punchy man, and first taking a run backward, made a rush at the obstinate horse, at the same time roaring like a bear. That failing, he tried all the noises of which the human organs are capable ; he hooted at the obstinate beast ; he howled, growled, hissed, screamed, and grunted at him. He danced at him, anticked at him, shook his fist at his head, and made faces at him. Then he talked to him, and chirped to him. But the horse was not to be bullied or cajoled. So the little man, losing patience, made a kick at him ; but owing to the short-ness of his own legs, came a foot short. Finally he stood and looked at the brute, which unexpectedly answered ; for when he had looked long enough, the horse began to move of his own accord. But the conducteur bore the matter in mind. The next stage, having a steep ascent to face, we had six horses to our team, and several persons alighted to walk up the hill ; amongst the rest a Russian Baron and the con-ducteur. The latter, with the obstinate brute in his head, went straight up to the hedge, knife in hand, to cut a cudgel against the next stoppage,—but whether, wearing no blinkers, the six horses saw the operation, or whether, the German being a horse language, they overheard and understood his threatenings—before the little man could cut his stick the animals cut theirs, and took the heavy Eilwagen up the hill at a gallop. Luckily they stopped near the top of the ascent, and allowed the Russian to run up, "thawed and dissolved into a dew," followed by the panting, puffing conducteur, but without his unnecessary bludgeon.

On reaching the crest of the hill, we had a fine view across a woody ravine, of the castle of Wartburg; and then descending to the left, came under banks of such a ruddy soil, that I could not help exclaiming mentally, "Heaven shield us from the Vehm Gericht!" a secret tribunal, whose jurisdiction, you know, extended over the "Red Earth." Excuse the haberdashery phrases, but it was really maroon-coloured, trimmed with the richest dark-green velvet turfs. In a short time we entered Eisenach, one of the most clean-looking and quiet of towns; yet it was a poor scholar of its free school, who had begged from door to door for his maintenance, that was doomed to out-bellow the Pope's bulls, and out-preach the thunders of the Vatican! From Eisenach, passing some of the neatest, cleanest, and cosiest brick-built cottages I have ever seen out of England, we rattled into Gotha, which verily seemed the German for Gandercleugh! It was market-day, and the whole town was in a hiss and a scream with St. Michael's poultry. Everybody was buying or selling, or trying to buy or sell, a goose. Here was a living snow-white bargain being thrust into a basket;—yonder was another being carried off by the legs; a third housewife was satisfying herself and a flapping grey gander of his weight avoirdupois, by hanging him by the neck.—Saxon peasant girls were thronging in from all quarters, with baskets, like our old mail-coaches, at their backs; in which dickey one or two long-lecked anserine passengers were sitting and looking about them like other travellers in a strange place. The females were generally fair, fresh-coloured, and good-looking; and the variety of their head-gear, in caps, toques, and turbans, was as pleasant as picturesque. Some of them were quite Oriental; and even a plain straw bonnet was made characteristic, by a large black cockade on each side.

I dined at Gotha, at a table-d'hôte. Just before the soup,

a young Saxon girl came in, and modestly and silently placed a little bunch of flowers beside each plate. It seemed to me the prettiest mode of begging in the world; nevertheless, one ugly fellow churlishly threw the humble bouquet on the floor; an act the more repulsive, as great kindness to children is an amiable trait in the German character. How I wished to lay before him the chapter of Sterne and the Mendicant Monk!

A circumstance which occurred here caused me some speculation. Mine host, during the dinner, was at great pains to converse with me in my own language, but with little success. In the meantime the guests successively departed, save one, who, directly we were tête-à-tête, addressed me, to my surprise, in very good English. The same evening another gentleman who had allowed me to stammer away to him in very bad German, was no sooner seated snugly by me in the coupé of the diligence than he opened in good Lindley Murray sentences, and we discoursed for some hours on London society and literature. Perhaps the Police had on them a fit of "fly-catching," as subsequently we were detained for two hours by a very rigorous examination of passports. From some informality my own was refused the visé; but I took the matter as the German doctor treated my uncle's symptoms,—"Has he any appetite?"—None at all. "Bon!—Does he sleep?"—Not a wink. "Bon!—Has he any pain?"—A good deal. "Bon!" again. So I said Bon, too, and beg to recommend it to travellers as a very serviceable word on most occasions. Thenceforward, however, my conversable companion fought very shy of me; for he had been a refugee in England on account of his opinions, and had only just made submission, and been reconciled to the Prussian government. For my own part, I did not hear a single word on politics, from Erfurt to Halle, but a great

many on the famous hoax of Sir John Herschel's discovery of
Lunar Angels; a subject which, like any other, with plenty
of moonshine in it, took amazingly with the speculative
Germans.

On alighting at Halle, I found my friend the captain at
the coach door, who speedily introduced me at the regimental
head-quarters.· The officers welcomed me with great warmth
and friendliness; and I soon found myself seated beside a
jovial bowl of Cardinale, and for the first time in my life in
an agreeable mess. On inquiry, I was quartered, where
many a sheep and bullock had been, in Butcher street,—
where for sixpence, in a very decent bed, I had five hours of
remarkably cheap, deep sleep. At four the next morning I
rose, by trumpet-call; breakfasted, mounted, and between
the tail of the 9th and the head of the 10th company of the
19th Infantry Regiment, was crossing part of that immense
plain which surrounds Leipzig. Ere we had gone far, one of
our longest-legged Lieutenants suddenly ran out of the road
and brought captive a boy with a tinful of hot sausages. In
a few minutes, his whole stock in hand was purchased off and
paid for at his own price; and I was simple enough to be
rejoicing in the poor fellow's lucky hit, and to take the
glistening in his eyes for tears of joy, when all at once he
burst into a roar of grief and blubbering, and sobbed out that
he wished, he did, instead of a tinful of his commodity, he had
brought a cartload !—

"Man never is, but always to be, blest."

If one could suspect Nature of being so unnatural, the vast
flat we were traversing seemed intentionally laid out for
nations to fight out their quarrels in; some idea of the extent
of the plain may be formed from the fact, that at the great
Battle of Leipzig in 1813 the cannon fired on one wing could

The First of March.

not be heard at the other. As we passed through the villages, my civilian's round hat caused some curiosity and speculation amongst the natives, all practically acquainted with what was the correct costume. One man called out, "There goes the Doctor!" but from a certain gravity of countenance and the absence of moustachios, the majority set me down as the Chaplain. At all events, so much of the military character was attributed to me, that the toll-keepers forbore to make any demand, and allowed me to decide that disputed problem whether cavalry can successfully cope with the '*pike*. The foot marched on merrily, occasionally singing, some fifty or so in chorus, in excellent time and tune; and about noon, at the little town of Brenha, near Bitterfeld, the regiment halted—dismiss—and in ten minutes not a soldier was visible in the streets. They were all dining or enjoying a sleep. Not being fatigued, I amused myself with a volume presented to the Captain by a clergyman at whose house he was quartered in Nassau. The worthy pastor had, no doubt, served in his youth, and, with a lingering affection for the "sogering" (a pattern rubbed in with gunpowder is not easily rubbed out again), had made a Collection of German War Songs. The following, of which I give a literal translation, may, I believe, be attributed to his own pen. It smacks of the very spirit of Uncle Toby and Corporal Trim, and seems written with the point of a bayonet on the parchment of a drum !

LOVE LANGUAGE OF A MERRY YOUNG SOLDIER.

"*Ach, Gretchen, mein täubchen.*"

O Gretel, my Dove, my heart's Trumpet,
My Cannon, my Big Drum, and also my Musket,
O hear me, my mild little Dove,
In your still little room.

Your portrait, my Gretel, is always on guard,
Is always attentive to Love's parole and watchword;
Your picture is always going the rounds,
My Gretel, I call at every hour!

My heart's knapsack is always full of you;
My looks, they are quartered with you;
And when I bite off the top end of a cartridge,
Then I think that I give you a kiss.

You alone are my Word of Command and orders,
Yea, my Right-face, Left-face, Brown Tommy, and wine,
And at the word of command "Shoulder Arms!"
Then I think you say "Take me in your arms."

Your eyes sparkle like a Battery,
Yea, they wound like Bombs and Grenades;
As black as gunpowder is your hair,
Your hand as white as Parading breeches!

Yes, you are the Match and I am the Cannon;
Have pity, my love, and give quarter,
And give the word of command, "Wheel round
Into my heart's Barrack Yard."

In the evening I joined a party of officers, and played
Whisk, and then more cheap deep sleep—I fear it will cause
a run upon the place to quote my bill; but dinner, supper,
bed, and breakfast, seven groschen!!!

Trumpet at four. Rose and dressed in the dark; my own
fault entirely, for giving the Captain a little bottle of cayenne
pepper, wherein his servant, unacquainted with the red con-
diment, groped with his matches for half an' hour in the
vain hope of an instantaneous light. After a longish walk,
arrived at Kremnitz, a village near Grafenhainchen, where I
found my dinner waiting for me at a country inn: the
Captain quartered at Burg Kremnitz, three or four hundred
yards distant. I soon had an invitation to the château.

A She Ruffian.

The baron was absent, but his major-domo or castellan treated us with great hospitality. It was a large country-house, with a farm attached to it : the first living object I met being a pig afflicted, poor fellow, with rheumatism, which I am apt to have myself, only I do not walk about on three legs, with my head stuck on one side. There was something in the plan and aspect of the whole place that vividly reminded me of mansions familiar to me in Scotland, and the impression was confirmed by the appearance of the Castellan and Land Steward, who looked quite Scotch enough to have figured in a picture of Wilkie's. It seemed to me as if even their unintelligible language was only a broader Scotch than I was accustomed to. But the illusion was dispelled by another personage quite foreign to the picture, and I lost some of my pity for the stiff-necked pig in looking at a female who had voluntarily fixed her head in almost as irksome a position. In honour of the strange guests, she had donned a large Elizabethan ruff, which being fastened behind to the back of her cap, forbade her to look to right or left, without a corresponding wheel of the whole body. As she wore this pillory during the two days of our visit, it must have been a tolerable sacrifice of comfort to appearance. We supped on poultry, carp, and jack, and drank a very fair wine, produced on the estate. The next day being a rest, we devoted to fishing ; and having had but indifferent success at the mill, the castellan, after a shrewd inspection of our flimsy-looking tackle, gave us leave to fish in a piece of water in the garden. But his face very comically lengthened between wonder and anxiety, as he saw jack after jack hoisted out of his preserve, and was evidently relieved when we gave over the sport : indeed, he told us, half in earnest, that if we came again, he should set a guard over the ponds. He then went to fish himself, in a wooden box or lock, through which passed a small running stream; in this receptacle, having little room for exercise, the huge carp thrive and fatten like pigs in a sty. As a sample of an ill wind, the land-steward told us of a gale that blew down no less than forty thousand trees on the estate,—stopped all the roads in the vicinity, which took fourteen days in clearing; and the whole of the wreck is not yet removed! More deep cheap sleep, and a bill. What a difference between the charges of the byewaymen and the highwaymen of Germany!—amounting to "almost nothing." The villagers here very generally returned to the private soldiers the five groschen per day allowed by the king, and gave them a glass of schnaps into the bargain.

At four o'clock, blown out of bed again; breakfasted and stumbled through the dark towards a certain spot, where, by dint of flint and steel, the soldiers of the 10th company were sparkling like so many glow-worms. This early starting was generally necessary to enable us to join the main body on the high road. About noon we crossed the Elbe, by a thousand feet of wooden bridge, and entered Wittenberg. A friend of the Captain's here met us, and by his invitation, we dined with the officers of the garrison at the Casino; the same courteous gentleman kindly undertook to show me what was best worth seeing in the place. Of course my first local association was with Hamlet, whom Shakspeare most skilfully and happily sent to school at Wittenberg—for the Prince-Philosopher, musing and metaphysical, living more in thought than in action, is far more of a German than a Dane. I suspect that Hamlet is, for this very reason, a favourite in Germany. My next thoughts settled upon Luther, to whom, perhaps, Wittenberg owed the jovial size of the very article I had been drinking from, a right Lutheran beer-glass, at least a foot high, with a glass cover.

In the market-place, under a cast-iron Gothic canopy,

Mrs Schultheiss.

stands a metal statue of the Great Reformer, with a motto I heartily wish some of the reformed would adopt, instead of dandling and whining over Protestantism, as if it had been a sickly rickety bantling from its birth :—

"If it be God's work it will stand,
If it be man's it will fall."

The statue itself represents a sturdy brawny friar, with a two-storey chin, and a neck and throat like a bull's. To the reader of Rabelais there cannot be a truer effigy of his jolly fighting, toping, praying Friar John; a personage who, I have little doubt, was intended by the author for Luther. Motteux suggests as much in his preface, but abandons the idea for a more favourite theory. Rabelais and Luther, both born in the same year, were equally anti-catholic in their hearts, and attacked the abuses of Popery precisely according to their national temperaments — the witty Frenchman with banter, raillery, and persiflage, the German with all the honest dogged earnestness of his countrymen. Just turn to the memoirs of Luther compiled from his own letters, and compare the man with Friar John, the warm advocate of marriage, in his counsel to Panurge, and described as "an honest heart,—plain, resolute, good fellow; he travels, he labours, he defends the oppressed, comforts the afflicted, helps the needy, and keeps the close of the abbey."

Luther's residence in Wittenberg is now a theological college, much given, I was told, to mysticism.

In the evening, accompanied by Lieut. Von J., we drove for an hour through deep sand to our quarters, passing by the way a well, miraculously discovered by Luther when he was thirsty, by a scratch on the ground with his staff; a miracle akin to that at the marriage at Cana, in Galilee, would have been more characteristic. At Prühlitz, a very little village, the Captain found his appointed lodging in a room used as the church ; my own dormitory was the ball-room. To my infinite surprise, I found in it a four-posted bedstead ! —however, by way of making it un-English, the bed was made at an angle of about thirty degrees, so that I enjoyed all night much the same exercise and amusement in slipping down and climbing up again as are afforded by what are called Russian Mountains.

Our next day's march was across country, often through deep sand, and over such a desolate ": blasted heath," that at every ascent I expected to see some forlorn sea-coast. We halted at the general rendezvous and breakfasted à la champêtre, in the Mark of Brandenburg. No wonder the Markgraves fought so stoutly for a better territory ! To judge by the sketches produced by the officers, there had been but sorry quartering over night. One officer had such a tumbledown hut assigned to him, that his very dog put his tail between his legs and howled at it ; a second had slept in a pigeon-house, and was obliged to have the birds driven out before he could dress in the morning ; and our friend Von C., by some mistake, was billeted on the whole wide world ! Our march lasted eight hours with a grand parade, as a rehearsal, for Potzdam, by the way ; but the country being thinly peopled and the villages few and far between, the actual walk was enormously added-to by digressions on either side of the main road. Thus having arrived at a vast heath, the tenth and eleventh companies were recommended to the accommodations of a village at an hour's distance,—whilst the unlucky twelfth had to go to another as much beyond. So we started on our own steeple chase, and at last marched into Nichol, through a gazing population of married women in red toques, single women in black ones, and benedicts and bachelors in sheepskin pelisses with the wool inwards. Our

"We are Seven."

host, a sort of Dorfmeister, or village mayor, was in a robe of the same fashion. The mayoress had a round head, round forehead, round chin, two round cheeks as red as Dutch apples, a round bust that seemed inclosed in a bolster, and a round body in a superfluity of blue petticoats. The captain of the eleventh called very politely to see how I was off for quarters, before he visited his own, and in a short time after his departure I saw him walking up and down outside like a chafing lion: having been billeted by our host to sleep in the same room with a man, his wife, and their seven children. Unluckily there were no more lodgings to let in the place, and the captain was fain to occupy a shake-down on the forms in the village school-room.

I doubt if Captain Cook's first appearance amongst the Sandwiches caused more curiosity than mine did amongst the Nicholites, a party of whom kept watch in front of the house, and stared at me through the window, as if they had actually been sheep all through, instead of only in their skins. However, I contrived to give them the slip towards evening, and took a walk in the village, where I witnessed a sight akin to some so admirably described by the Blower of the Bubbles. Possibly some Schwein General had dismissed his army at the outskirts, but one long-legged pig after another came cantering or trotting into the village, and went with military regularity to his own quarters. If the door of the yard or garden was open, in he went; if not he stood and grunted and at last whined for admittance. For there is a sense of "no place like home" even in a pig. Number one, at whose gate he waited, was only a mean hovel, whereas number two was comparatively "a cottage of gentility," and the yard door stood invitingly open; but piggy stood true to the humbler tenement. Better bred swine I have certainly seen in England, but none so well taught. I almost thought

the Prussian system of universal education had been extended
to the lower animals. After the pigs came the geese, and
behaved in the same orderly way.

On leaving Nichol I had a hearty shake of the hand from
our Host and Hostess, with a hope I had been satisfied with
my entertainment and the charge for it. If I had not, I
must have been an Elwes. On the point of starting, his Worship begged to avail himself of my extended knowledge as a
traveller, to set him at rest as to a word he had read or
heard of, namely, Flanders,—"whether they were a sort of
money, like Florins?" So I briefly explained to him a
matter which, as travellers seldom visit such an out-of-the-
world village, had perhaps puzzled its worthy chief magistrate
for the last twenty years.

From the specimen I had seen, during the last march, of
the country of the Mark, it seemed rather surprising how
such a territory as the present Kingdom had accumulated
round such a nucleus. But has Prussia done growing? In
the various petty states I had previously passed through,
each had its peculiar money, its public liveries, and its striped
boundary posts of its proper colours. But at the same time
they had all embraced the Prussian commercial system ; in
some cases even enforced by Prussian doüaniers ; they were
all traversed by royal mails, bearing the arms of Frederick
William, and his coinage was current throughout. In short,
a process of amalgamation is quietly going on, founded, it is
quite possible, with ulterior views, for the Black Eagle has
never shown any disinclination to become a Roc.

Another march, with another grand rehearsal by the way,
brought us to Belitz, a garrison town, into which I had the
honour of helping to lead the regiment. The truth is, in
attempting "to go ahead" to the post-office, my horse refused
to pass the big drum, and the road narrowing over a little

Mr Schultheiss.

wooden bridge, I had no alternative but to charge through a crowd of children of all ages, or ride behind the band, cheek by jowl with the major in command, for the day. My humanity preferred the last, at the expense, I suspect, of a grand breach of military etiquette. Quarters at Schlunken-dorf, a village to the left, at a miller's, whose parlour floor, by its undulations, plainly reminded us, that it was a house built upon the sand. The moment, indeed, you stepped abroad, you were in sand up to the ankles, and some two hundred yards distant stood the mill, in an Arabian waste, as remote from corn as the traditionary mill of Buccleugh.

Here ended my marching ; for next day being a rest, and the country being so unattractive,—moreover, not having been regularly sworn to the colours, I deserted, and made the best of my way to Potzdam. I should be grossly ungrateful not to mention the uniform urbanity and friendliness of all the officers with whom I came in contact—howbeit we were seldom on speaking terms (some who had even "been to Paris" did not speak French)—nay, a large proportion being Poles, I could not always call my best friends by their names. Of the men they commanded, common justice bids me say, that not a single complaint was made against them, nor a punish-ment inflicted throughout the route. It is true that in Prussia, where every mother's son and husband must be a soldier, and every man's father or brother was, is, or will be, in the army, a kindliness and fellow-feeling will naturally prevail between the troops and those on whom they are quartered ; but independent of this consideration, the good conduct of the men seemed in a great degree to be the result of their temperament and disposition. They bore their long and fatiguing marches with exemplary patience ; none the less that every step brought them nearer to their homes in Poland and Silesia. One poor fellow, who had not been

under the domestic roof during nineteen years, was agitated
by very conceivable feelings, and quite touched me by his
recurring apprehensions that "he should not know his own
good mother from any other woman!"

The fusileer who had acted *pro tempore* as my servant,
with a manly frankness offered me his hand at parting, and
respectfully expressed his good wishes for my future health
and prosperity. Of course I gave him a solid acknowledgment of his services, but took especial care not to bid him
"drink my health," having witnessed a whimsical proof of
the force of discipline. The captain, then living at Ehrenbreitstein, one day made his servant a present of a dollar,
at the same time saying metaphorically, "There's a bottle of
wine for you." The soldier, however, took the words as a
literal command—saluted, wheeled, marched off straight to
the nearest wine-house, and in double quick time drank off a
bottle, at a dollar—which, as he was of particularly temperate
habits, took unusual effect, and sent home the obedient
soldier to his astonished master as blind and staggering as
Drunken Barnaby!

Thus ended my practical connection with the gallant
Nineteenth. But I shall often recall my chance quarters—
my provident morning foragings against a jour maigre—
when a *searching* wind might have found a roll of bread-and-
butter in one pocket, and mayhap a brace of cold pigeons in
the other—the cheerful rendezvous—the friendly greetings—
and the pic-nic by the road-side :—I shall often hear in
fancy the national "Am Rhein! Am Rhein!" chorused by
a hundred voices—the exciting charge, beaten at the steep
hill or deep ground—and the spirit-stirring bugle ringing
amidst the vast pine-woods of Germany!

Neither shall I forget the people, at whose tables I had
eaten, in whose dwellings I had lodged. Perhaps the force

of blood had something to do with the matter, howevei distant the relationship, but my liking inclined particularly to the Saxons. Yet were the others good creatures to remember. Even in the desolate country I had lately passed through, the absence of all loveliness in the scenery had been atoned for by this moral beauty. Nature, scarcely kinder than a step-mother, had allotted to them a sterile soil and a harsh climate—the pecuniary dust was as much too scarce as other sorts of dirt were over plentiful—spoons were often deficient—occasionally even knives and forks—and at times their household wants were of a very primitive character—but the people were kind, honest, hearty, humble, well-disposed, anxious to please, and easily pleased in return. Their best cheer and accommodations were offered with pleasant looks and civil words, and I cannot recall a single instance of churlishness or cupidity.

As to Potzdam—it vividly reminded me of that city in the Arabian Nights, whereof the inhabitants were all turned into marble : at least, I am sure, that on entering it I saw far more statues than living figures. On my left, in the Palace garden, was a Neptune, with his suite, without even the apology of a pond : farther off, a white figure, and a Prussian sentry, jointly mounting guard over a couple of cannon—on my right a dome, surmounted by a flying Mercury. But the grand muster was on the top of the palace, where a whole row of figures occupied the parapet, like a large family at a fire waiting for the ladders. To my taste the effect is execrable. Silence, stillness and solitude are the attributes of a statue. Except where engaged in the same action, like Laocoön and his sons, I never care to see even two together. And why should they be forced into each other's company, poor things, blind, deaf, and dumb, as they are, and incapable of the pleasures of society ?

Possibly, in the absence of living generations, the great
Frederick, like Deucalion, peopled his city with stones *ad
interim;* for you cannot walk through its handsome streets
so silent, and with so little stir of life, without feeling that it
is a city built for posterity. Of course I visited its shows ;
and first the Royal Palace, in which, next to the literary
traces of Frederick, I was most interested by a portrait over
a door of Napoleon when consul, in which methought I
traced the expression of an originally kind nature, and which
the devotion and attachment he inspired in those immediately about him seemed to justify. But power is a
frightful ossifier, and in many other instances has made a
Bony part of the human heart. Sans Souci pleased me
little, and the conceit of a statue of Justice so placed in the
garden that Frederick at his writing-table "might always
have justice in view," pleased me still less. His four-footed
favourites lie near the figure ; but whether the dogs were
brought to Justice, or Justice went to the dogs, is not upon
record. In short, Sans Souci inspired me with an appropriate
feeling ; for I left it without caring for it—and disappointed
by even the famous statue of the Queen. The spirit of the
place had infected it too. With much sweetness and some
beauty in the countenance, the face was so placid, the limbs
so round, with such a Sans-Souci-ism in the crossed legs—an
attitude a lady only adopts when most particularly at her
ease—that instead of any remembrance of the wrongs and
sufferings of the heart-broken and royal Louisa, my only
sentiment was of regret that so amiable, fair, and gentle a
being had been called so prematurely (if, indeed, she were
dead, and not merely asleep) from the enjoyment of youth,
health and happiness. The New Palace I shall like better
when it is a very old one. You will think me fastidious,
perhaps ; but I saw nothing *very* extraordinary in the Pea-

cock Island; nor yet in the Prince Royal's country-seat, except the boldness of attempting, in such a soil and such a climate, to imitate, or rather to parody—with pumpkins *pro* melons—an Italian villa.

The Garrison church is hung with sculptured helmets, flags and military trophies, appropriate enough for an arsenal, but hardly fit "visible and outward signs of an inward and spiritual grace." The interior is well furnished, too, with captured flags, and eagles, and graven lists of slain warriors; but it contains one very striking ratification of peace. Frederick the Great and his most rumbustical royal father, who could never live together in the same house, are here tranquilly sleeping side-by-side under one roof! Somehow I could not help thinking of the grasshopper of the Royal Exchange coming to lie with the dragon of Bow church!

The king reviewed the 19th on its arrival in front of the Old Palace. He stooped a little under his years; and, remembering his age, I could not help wishing that he would make a solemn gift to his people of their long overdue constitution. No monarch has been so practically taught the vicissitudes and uncertainty of human affairs; and his experience ought to urge him as far as possible to "make assurance doubly sure and take a bond of fate." The benefits he has conferred on his subjects he ought to secure to them by placing them in their own keeping: whereas, should he delay such an act of common prudence and common justice till too late, the world may reasonably infer that he was less anxious to perpetuate a system, said to be marked by profound wisdom and paternal benevolence, than to transmit his absolute authority unimpaired to his successor.

There have been so many journals, ledgers and waste-books written on Germany, that a description of the Prussian capital would relish as flat and stale as a Berlin fresh oyster.

I shall, therefore, get over the ground a little quicker than a
Droski, which is a peculiar vehicle, with a peculiar horse,
with a peculiar pace. The truth is, that, contrary to the
principle of our trotting-matches, he is backed at 20 groschen
an hour to go as few miles as possible in sixty minutes. In
consequence, with as much apparent action as the second
hand, he goes no faster than the short hand of the dial.
The other day a butcher hired a Droski to take him to a
distant part of the city, for which he was charged 20
groschen by the driver, who appealed to his watch at the
same time, owning that it perhaps went a little too fast.
" In that case, then," replied the butcher, " I'll thank you,
my friend, the next time you drive me, to put your watch in
the shafts and your horse in your pocket."

A judicious valet-de-place would first take a stranger in
Berlin to the Old Bridge, whereon stands the bronze equestrian statue of the Great Elector. Of which statue, by the
way, it is told that the Jews, with their peculiar turn for
speculation, offered to cover the court-yard of the Old
Palace with dollars in exchange for the verdigris on the
figure : but, perhaps, fearing that they would scrape down
the Great Elector into a little one, the bargain was declined.
A judicious guide, I say, would place a stranger on the
aforesaid bridge, and then ask the gentleman which of the
two Berlins he pleased to wish to see ; for, in reality, there
are two of them, the old and the new. Knowing your taste,
Gerard, I should take you across an elegant iron bridge to
show you the beautiful front of the museum : but I should
be careful of taking you within it, lest we should not come
out again, for it contains an almost matchless collection of
the early Flemish school of painting—such Van Eycks and
Hemlincks !—to say nothing of a Titian's daughter, not
merely herself but the whole picture such an eye-bewitching

Open to objection.

Y

brunette, that it still haunts me! Perhaps, in turning round
to have another look at the façade of the museum, you will
run against an immense utensil, scooped out of a rock of
granite; and, if you ask me what is its history, all I can say
is, I believe it was the wash-hand basin of the giant in the
Castle of Otranto.

That modest-looking house, too small for the great stone
helmets stuck along its front, is the private residence of the
Soldier-King, who thence sees a little to the right his Arsenal,
and to the left his Guard-house. The horse-shoe, nailed up
at one of the first-floor windows, is not, as you might suppose,
for luck, but in commemoration of being cast up through
that very window at his Majesty—not by a two-legged regi-
cide, but by an officer's charger—with what design, even
Monsieur Rochow, and all his police, could never unriddle.

I have a ticket of admission for you to the Arsenal—but
stop!—look up at those two-and-twenty hideous colossal
masks, representing the human face in all the various convulsions and agonies of a violent death! Was there ever
devised a series of decorations, remembering the place, in
such bad taste,—nay, to speak mildly, in such unchristian,
inhuman feeling? Why, Jack Ketch, out of respect to our
flesh-and-blood sympathies, draws a cap over the face of his
victims to hide their last writhings—and what is War, disguise it as we may under all its "pride, pomp, and circumstance," but a great wholesale executioner? Its horrors would
be unendurable but for the dazzling Bengal Light called Glory
that we cast on its deluge of blood and tears: but for the
gorgeous flags we wave, like veils, before its grim and
ferocious features—and the triumphant clangour of martial
music with which we drown its shrieks and groans. But here
we are disgustingly reminded of what we would willingly
forget, that a Battle is a Butchery. Faugh! the place smells

of the shambles! As yet we are only in the inner court,
but we will go no farther. Those frightful masks shockingly
illustrate that "War's a brain-spattering, windpipe-slitting
art"—and who would care to see its murderous tools,
however well-polished or tastefully arranged?

A cool walk under the fragrant Lindens is quite necessary
to sweeten such associations. We will admire the Brandenburg Gate as much as you please ; but the street, wide, and
long, and handsome as it is, does not satisfy me. The houses
want character—in short, as a picture, Prout could make
nothing of it. But look, off with your hat !—no, not to that
white-headed good old General,—but to yonder carriage. It
is not the king's, but contains a personage so in love with
Absolutism, that one cannot help wishing him such a pure
Despotism as was enjoyed by Alexander Selkirk :—

> "I am monarch of all I survey,
>   My right there is none to dispute—
>   Not a creature objects to my sway—
>   I am lord of the fowl and the brute!"

The persons of all ranks thronging up those steps are
going to the Exhibition, and if you went with them you
would see some Historical pictures, by German artists, well
worthy of your admiration. In landscape they are not so
strong : their views are deficient in what the moon wants, an
atmosphere : to be sure the painters never saw one for the
smoke ; and, between ourselves, they have as little eye for
colour as nose for smells. Finally, instead of a catalogue
raisonné, or consulting Dr. Waagen, you may go to any pipe-
shop to know which are the best, or at any rate the most
popular pictures, by the miniature copies on the bowls.
Painting is fashionable in Berlin ; and has both royal and
plebeian patrons. Look at the shutter, or flap, over that

victualling cellar (akin to our London Shades) with a loaf, a
bottle of beer, a glass, a cheese, and a dish of oysters, all
painted to the still life ! My heart leaps at it—and oh,
would that I could make my voice reach to England and ring
throughout its metropolis ! Come hither, I would cry, all ye
still-life portrait daubers—ye would-be painters and would-
not-be glaziers—ye Unfine Artists

"Come hither, come hither, come hither !"

for here are Unfine Arts for you and Unfine Patrons ! Here
you may get bread and cheese for painting them ; and
beer and wine by drawing them. You need not speak
German. Ye shall make *signs* for sausages, and they shall
be put in your plates. Come hither ! In England you are
nobodies and nothings to nobodies—but here you shall be all
Van Eycks and Hemlincks ; at least you shall paint as they
did, on shutters. Impartial hangers shall hang your works
upon hinges, and not too high up, but full in the public gaze,
in a good light, and when that is gone they shall show
you " fiery off, indeed " with lamplight and candle. Instead
of neglect and omissions, here you shall have plentiful com-
missions. You shall take off hats, brush at boots and coats,
and do perukes in oil ; and whereas in England you would
scarcely get one face to copy, you shall here take the portraits
of a score of mugs !

One sight more, and we will finish our stroll. It is the
Fish-market. Look at those great oval tubs, like the cooling-
tubs in a brewery. They contain the living fish. What
monstrous jack and carp !—and species strange to us,—and
one grown almost out of knowledge—prodigious bream! You
may look at them, but beware what you say of them, to that
old woman, who sits near them in an immense shiny black
bonnet, very like a common coal-skuttle, for if you provoke

her, no scold on the banks of Thames can be more
fluently abusive and vulgarly sarcastic! Strange it is, and
worthy of philosophical investigation; but so surely as horse-
dealing and dishonesty go together, so do fish-fagging and
vituperative eloquence. It would seem as if the powers of
speech, denied to her mute commodity, were added to the
natural gifts of the female dealer therein;—however, from
Billingsgate to Berlin, every fishmonger in petticoats is as
rough-tongued as a buffalo!

But farewell to the capital of Prussia. A letter of recall
from my uncle has just come to hand;—and I am booked
again by the Eilwagen. Considering the distance, you will
own that I have had a miraculously cheap ride hither, when
I tell you that beside paying no turnpikes, I have disposed of
my nag, at twenty shillings' loss to a timid invalid, recommended to take horse exercise. I honestly warranted the
animal sound, quiet, and free from vice; and have no
doubt it will carry the old gentleman very pleasantly, provided he is not too particular as to the way he goes; for I
shrewdly suspect, wherever soldiers may be marching, my
late horse will be sure to follow in the same direction.

I have bought some black iron Berlin-ware for Emily, and
with love to you both, am,

My dear Gerard,

Yours ever truly,

FRANK SOMERVILLE.

EXTRACTS

FROM A LETTER TO GERARD BROOKE, ESQ.

THIS is simply to announce my safe return to the banks of
the Rhine. The rest of the family party met me at Mayence,
and we returned together to Coblenz, quite enchanted with
the scenery of one of the finest portions of the renowned
river. The alleged reason for my recall was the lateness of
the season ; but I rather suspect my worthy uncle is impatient
to relate his observations and adventures to his old friends
Bagshaw and the Doctor,—as my aunt is eager to impart her
wanderings to Miss Wilmot. Like other travellers, they are
longing to publish—and no doubt will talk quartos and folios
when they return to Woodlands.

The changes I found in the family on my return, were
almost as strange as those which so astonished Rip Van
Winkle on awaking from his supernatural sleep. My Uncle
was literally a new man. His warnings had had warning,
and gone off for good : and he has now no more idea of dying
than a man of twice his age : a paradox in sound, but a
philosophical truth. My aunt, instead of perpetually remind-
ing us that she is a disconsolate widow, has almost forgotten
it herself : and it is only on a dull and very wet day that we
hear of "poor George." Even Martha is altered for the
better, for she is reconciled to her mistress, to herself, and to
her old religion. The truth is, that her zeal in the new one
was so hot, that, like a fire with the blower on, it soon
burnt itself out. Her mistress says, the re-conversion was
much hastened by a very long procession, on a very warm
day, which Martha accompanied, and returned dusty, dry,

famished, and foot-sore, and rather sorry, no doubt, that she had ever given up her seat under the Rev. Mr. Groger.

*   *   *   *   *

You will be glad to hear that poor Markham has so won my uncle's esteem, that the latter promises, between himself and Bagster, to take his affairs in hand and set them to rights. Markham, of course, is delighted; and the change in his own prospects makes him take much pleasanter views both of men and things.

*   *   *   *   *

In short, Gerard, if you, or any of your friends ever suffer from hypochondriasis, weak nerves,— melancholy — morbid sensibility—or mere ennui—let me advise you and them, as you value your lives, health and spirits—your bodies and your minds—to do as we have done, and go UP THE RHINE.

LONDON: E. MOXON, SON, AND CO, 44 DOVER STREET, W.

www.ingramcontent.com/pod-product-compliance
Lightning Source LLC
Chambersburg PA
CBHW021754110726
47902CB00006B/1523